The eye was red—and I don't just mean the iris! The whole eye looked as if it was completely filled with blood. I was petrified in both senses of the word: filled with terror and rendered immobile where I was standing, as if turned to stone. I began to sweat with fear as her red eye seemed to grow bigger and bigger.

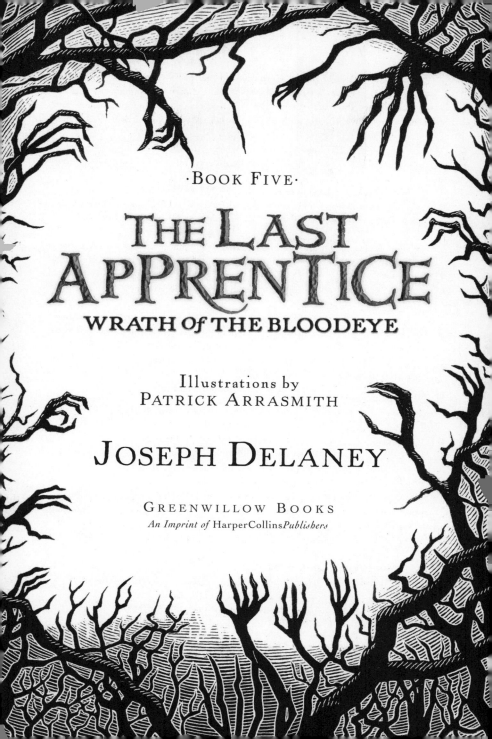

·BOOK FIVE·

# THE LAST APPRENTICE

## WRATH OF THE BLOODEYE

Illustrations by
PATRICK ARRASMITH

# JOSEPH DELANEY

GREENWILLOW BOOKS
*An Imprint of HarperCollinsPublishers*

The Last Apprentice: Wrath of the Bloodeye
Copyright © 2008 by Joseph Delaney

First published in 2008 in Great Britain by The Bodley Head, an imprint of Random House Children's Books, under the title *The Spook's Mistake*. First published in 2008 in the United States by Greenwillow Books.

The right of Joseph Delaney to be identified as the author of this work has been asserted by him in accordance with the Copyright, Designs and Patents Act, 1988.

Illustrations copyright © 2008 by Patrick Arrasmith

Library of Congress Cataloging-in-Publication Data
Delaney, Joseph, (date).
Wrath of the Bloodeye / by Joseph Delaney ;
illustrations by Patrick Arrasmith.
p. cm. — (The last apprentice ; bk. 5)
Greenwillow Books.
Summary: The continuing adventures of Tom, the seventh son of a seventh son and apprentice to the local Spook, who faces danger and death daily in his job protecting the region from evil.
ISBN 978-0-06-134461-9 (pbk. bdg.)
ISBN 978-0-06-134459-6 (trade bdg.)
ISBN 978-0-06-134460-2 (lib. bdg.)
[1. Apprentices—Fiction. 2. Supernatural—Fiction. 3. Witches—Fiction.]
I. Arrasmith, Patrick, ill. II. Title.
PZ7.D373183Wr 2008 [Fic]—dc22 2008017920
10 11 12 13 LP/RRDH First paperback edition 10 9 8 7 6 5 4

Book design by Chad W. Beckerman and Paul Zakris

# FOR MARIE

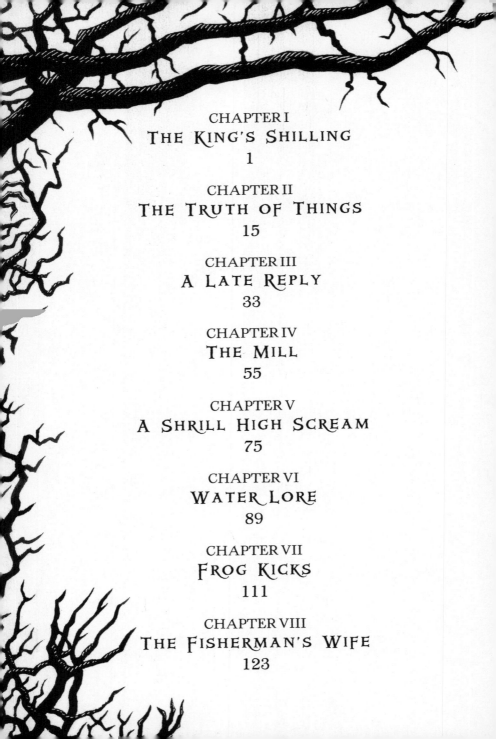

CHAPTER I
THE KING'S SHILLING
1

CHAPTER II
THE TRUTH OF THINGS
15

CHAPTER III
A LATE REPLY
33

CHAPTER IV
THE MILL
55

CHAPTER V
A SHRILL HIGH SCREAM
75

CHAPTER VI
WATER LORE
89

CHAPTER VII
FROG KICKS
111

CHAPTER VIII
THE FISHERMAN'S WIFE
123

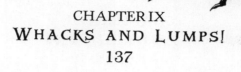

CHAPTER IX
WHACKS AND LUMPS!
137

CHAPTER X
THE SPOOK'S LETTER
153

CHAPTER XI
THE WITCH'S FINGER
171

CHAPTER XII
MORWENA
183

CHAPTER XIII
THE HERMIT OF CARTMEL
201

CHAPTER XIV
A DEAD MAN!
215

CHAPTER XV
THE DANCING FINGER
229

CHAPTER XVI
TRAIL OF BLOOD
247

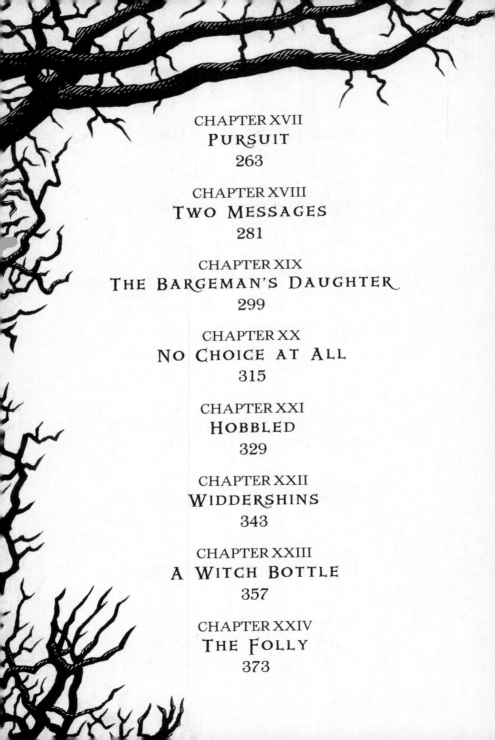

CHAPTER XVII
PURSUIT
263

CHAPTER XVIII
TWO MESSAGES
281

CHAPTER XIX
THE BARGEMAN'S DAUGHTER
299

CHAPTER XX
NO CHOICE AT ALL
315

CHAPTER XXI
HOBBLED
329

CHAPTER XXII
WIDDERSHINS
343

CHAPTER XXIII
A WITCH BOTTLE
357

CHAPTER XXIV
THE FOLLY
373

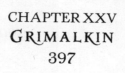

CHAPTER XXV
GRIMALKIN
397

CHAPTER XXVI
THE UNTHINKABLE
411

CHAPTER XXVII
A HARD BARGAIN
433

CHAPTER XXVIII
THE FIGHT ON THE MARSH
455

CHAPTER XXIX
WHERE I BELONG
471

CHAPTER XXX
THE BLACK BARGE
485

CHAPTER XXXI
WHOSE BLOOD?
499

THE JOURNAL OF THOMAS J. WARD
513

# WRATH of THE BLOODEYE

# CHAPTER I
## THE KING'S SHILLING

CARRYING my staff, I went into the kitchen and picked up the empty sack. It would be dark in less than an hour but I'd just enough time to walk down to the village and collect the week's provisions. All we had left were a few eggs and a small wedge of County cheese.

Two days earlier the Spook had

· 1 ·

gone south to deal with a boggart. Annoyingly, this was the second time in a month that my master had gone off on a job without me. Each time he'd said it was routine, nothing that I hadn't seen before in my apprenticeship; it would be more useful for me to stay at home practicing my Latin and catching up with my studies. I didn't argue but I wasn't best pleased. You see, I thought he'd another reason for leaving me behind: He was trying to protect me.

Toward the end of the summer, the Pendle witches had summoned the Fiend into our world. He was the dark made flesh, the Devil himself. For two days he'd been under their control, and commanded to destroy me. I'd taken refuge in a special room Mam had prepared for me, and that had saved me. The Fiend was now doing his own dark will but there was no certainty that he wouldn't come hunting for me again. It was something I tried not to think about. One thing was certain: With the Fiend in the world, the County was becoming a much more dangerous place — especially for those who fought the dark. But that didn't mean I could hide away from danger forever. I was just an apprentice now but one day I would be a spook and have to take the same risks as my master, John Gregory. I just wished he could see it that way, too.

I walked into the next room, where Alice was working hard, copying a book from the Spook's library. She came from a Pendle family and had received two years' training in dark magic from her aunt, Bony Lizzie, a malevolent witch who was now safely confined in a pit in the Spook's garden. Alice had got me into lots of trouble but eventually became my friend and was now staying with my master and me, making copies of his books to earn her keep.

Concerned that she might read something she shouldn't, the Spook never allowed her to go into his library, and only one book at a time was ever given into her keeping. Mind you, he appreciated her work as a scribe. The books were precious to him, a store of information accumulated by generations of spooks—so each carefully duplicated volume made him feel a little more secure about the survival of that knowledge.

Alice was sitting at the table, pen in hand, two books open before her. She was writing carefully into one, copying accurately from the other. She looked up at me and smiled. I'd never seen her look prettier, the candlelight illuminating her thick dark hair and high cheekbones. But when she saw I had my cloak on, her smile instantly faded and she put down the pen.

"I'm off down to the village to collect the provisions," I told her.

"Ain't no need for you to do that, Tom," she protested, concern evident in her face and voice. "I'll go while you stay and carry on studying."

She meant well but her words made me angry and I had to bite my lip to stop myself from saying something unkind. Alice was just like the Spook: overprotective.

"No, Alice," I told her firmly. "I've been cooped up in this house for weeks and I need a walk to blow the cobwebs out of my head. I'll be back before dark."

"Then at least let me come with you, Tom. Could do with a bit of a break myself, couldn't I? Sick of the sight of these dusty books, I am. Don't seem to do anything but write these days!"

I frowned. Alice wasn't being honest and it annoyed me. "You don't really want a walk down into the village, do you? It's a chilly, damp, miserable evening. You're just like the Spook. You think that I'm not safe out alone. That I can't manage —"

"Ain't that you can't manage, Tom. It's just that the Fiend's in the world now, ain't he?"

"If the Fiend comes for me, there's nothing much I can do about it. And it wouldn't make much differ-ence whether you were with me or not. Even the Spook wouldn't be able to help."

"But it's not just the Fiend, is it, Tom? County's a much more dangerous place now. Not only is the dark more powerful, but there are robbers and deserters at large. Too many people hungry. Some of 'em would cut your throat for half of what you'll be carrying in that sack!"

The whole country was at war but it was going badly for us down south, with reports of some terrible battles and defeats. So now, in addition to the tithes that farmers had to pay to the Church, half of their remaining crops had been commandeered to feed the army. That had caused shortages and driven up the cost of food; the poorest people were now on the verge of starvation. But although there was a lot of truth in what Alice said, I wasn't going to let her change my mind.

"No, Alice, I'll be all right by myself. Don't worry, I'll be back soon!"

Before she could say anything more, I turned on my heel and set off briskly. Soon I had left the garden behind and was walking along the narrow lane that led to the village. The nights were drawing in and the autumn weather had turned cold and damp, but it was still good to be away from the confines of the house and garden. Soon Chipenden's familiar gray-slated rooftops were visible and I was striding down the steep slope of the cobbled main street.

The village was much quieter than it had been in the summer, before things had deteriorated. Then it had been bustling with women struggling under the weight of loaded shopping baskets; now very few people were about, and I went into the butcher's to find myself the only customer.

"Mr. Gregory's order as usual," I told the butcher. He was a large red-faced man with a ginger beard. At one time he'd been the life and soul of his shop, telling jokes and keeping his customers entertained, but now his face was somber and much of the life seemed to have gone out of him.

"Sorry, lad, but I've not much for you today. Two chickens and a few rashers of bacon is the best I can do. And it's been hard enough keeping that under the counter for you. Might be worth your while calling in tomorrow well before noon."

I nodded, transferred the items to my sack, asking him to put them on our bill, then thanked him and set off for the greengrocer's. I did little better there. There were potatoes and carrots but nowhere near enough to last us for the week. As for fruit, the grocer could manage just three apples. His advice was the same: to try again tomorrow, when he might be lucky enough to have more in.

At the baker's I managed to buy a couple of loaves and left the shop with the sack slung over my shoulder. It was then that I saw someone watching me from across the street. It was a scrawny child, a boy of probably no more than four, with a thin body and wide, hungry eyes. I felt sorry for him so I went over, fished into the sack and held out one of the apples. He almost snatched it from my hand, and without a word of thanks, turned and ran back into the house.

I shrugged and smiled to myself. He needed it more than I did. I set off back up the hill, looking forward to the warmth and comfort of the Spook's house. But as I reached the outskirts of the village and the cobbles gave way to mud, my mood began to darken. Something didn't feel right. It wasn't the intense cold feeling that alerted me that something from the dark was approaching, but it was a definite unease. My instincts were warning me of danger.

I kept glancing back, sensing that someone was following me. Could it be the Fiend? Had Alice and the Spook been right all along? I quickened my pace until I was almost running. Dark clouds were racing overhead and there was less than half an hour before the sun went down.

"Snap out of it!" I told myself. "You're just imagining the worst."

A short stroll up the hill would bring me to the edge of the western garden and within five minutes I'd be back in the safety of my master's house. But suddenly I halted. At the end of the lane there was someone waiting in the shadows beneath the trees.

I walked a few faltering steps farther and realized it was more than just one person: Four tall burly men and a lad were staring in my direction. What did they want? I felt a sudden sense of danger. Why were strangers lurking so close to the Spook's house? Were they robbers?

As I got closer, I was reassured: They stayed under the cover of the bare trees rather than moving onto the path to intercept me. I wondered whether to turn and nod at them but then thought it better just to keep walking and not acknowledge them at all. As I passed beyond them, I gave a sigh of relief but then I heard something on the path behind me. It sounded like the chink of a coin falling onto stone.

I wondered if I'd a hole in my pocket and had dropped some of my change. But no sooner had I turned and looked down than a man stepped out of the trees and knelt on the path, picking something up. He looked up at me, a friendly smile on his face.

"This yours, boy?" he asked, holding out a coin toward me.

The truth was I wasn't sure, but it had certainly *sounded* as if I'd dropped something. So I put down my sack and staff, then reached into my breeches pocket with my left hand, intending to pull out my change and count it. But suddenly I felt a coin pressed firmly into my right hand and looked down in surprise to find a silver shilling nestling in my palm. I knew there hadn't been one in my change so I shook my head.

"It's not mine," I said with a smile.

"Well, it's yours now, boy. You've just accepted it from me. Isn't that right, lads?"

His companions stepped out of the trees and my heart sank into my boots. They were all wearing army uniforms and carried bags on their shoulders. They were armed, too—even the lad. Three of them carried stout clubs and one, with a corporal's stripe, was brandishing a knife.

Dismayed, I glanced back at the man who'd handed me the coin. He was standing up now so I could see him better. His face was weather-beaten, with narrow cruel eyes; there were scars on his forehead and right cheek—he'd evidently seen more than his fair share of trouble. He also had sergeant's stripes on his upper left arm and a cutlass at his belt. I was facing a press-gang. The war was going badly, and these men had been traveling the County, forcing men and boys into the army against their will to replace those killed in action.

"That's the king's shilling you've just accepted!" the man said, laughing in an unpleasant, mocking manner.

"But I didn't accept it," I protested. "You said it was mine and I was just checking my change—"

II

"No use making excuses, boy. We all saw what happened, didn't we, lads?"

"No doubt about it," agreed the corporal as they formed a circle around me, blocking any hope of escape.

"Why's he dressed as a priest?" asked the lad, who couldn't have been more than a year older than me.

The sergeant bellowed with laughter and picked up my staff. "He's no priest, young Toddy! Don't you know a spook's apprentice when you see one? They take your hard-earned money to keep so-called witches away. That's what they do. And there are plenty of fools daft enough to pay 'em!"

He tossed my staff to Toddy. "Hold on to that!" he ordered. "He won't be needing it anymore and it's good for firewood if nothing else!" Next he picked up the sack and peered inside. "Enough food here to fill our bellies tonight, lads!" he exclaimed, his face lighting up. "Trust your canny sergeant. Right, wasn't I, lads? Catch him on the way back *up* the hill rather than on the way down! Well worth the wait!"

At that moment, completely surrounded, I saw no hope of escape. I knew I *had* escaped from worse predicaments—sometimes from the clutches of those who practiced dark magic. I decided to bide my time and wait for an opportunity to get away. I waited patiently while the corporal took a short length of rope from his bag and bound my hands tightly behind my back. That done, he spun me to face west and pushed me roughly in the back to help me on my way. We began to march quickly, Toddy carrying the sack of provisions.

We walked for almost an hour, first west and then north. My guess was that they didn't know the more direct route over the fells and I was in no rush to point it out to them. No doubt we were heading for Sunderland Point: I'd be put on a boat to take me far south, where the armies were fighting. The longer this journey took, the more hope I had of escape.

And I had to escape, or my days as the Spook's apprentice were well and truly over.

# CHAPTER II
## THE TRUTH OF THINGS

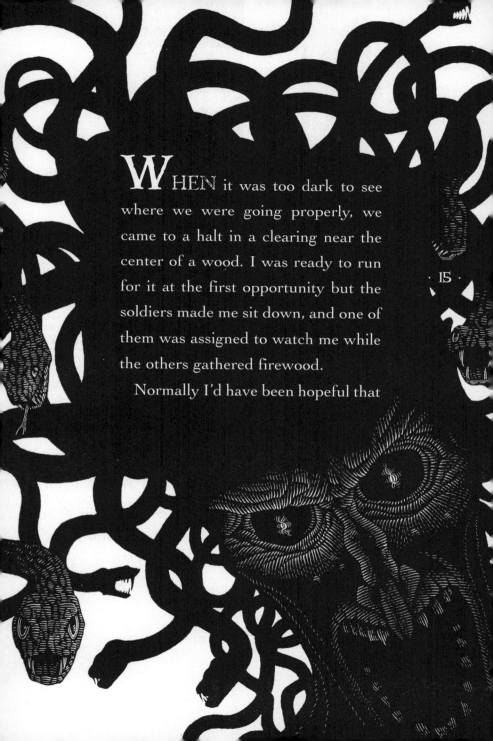

WHEN it was too dark to see where we were going properly, we came to a halt in a clearing near the center of a wood. I was ready to run for it at the first opportunity but the soldiers made me sit down, and one of them was assigned to watch me while the others gathered firewood.

Normally I'd have been hopeful that

· 15 ·

the Spook would come after me and attempt a rescue. Even in the dark he was a good tracker, more than capable of following these men. But by the time he got back from binding that boggart, I'd have been put aboard a ship and would be far beyond help. My only real hope lay in Alice. She'd expected me back and would have been alarmed once it got dark. She could find me, too; I was certain of it. But what could she do against five armed soldiers?

Soon a fire was blazing away, my staff tossed casually onto the kindling with the other wood. It was my first staff, given to me by my master, and its loss hurt me badly, as if my apprenticeship to the Spook were also going up in flames.

Helping themselves to the contents of my sack, the soldiers soon had both chickens roasting on a spit and were cutting slices of bread and toasting them over the fire. To my surprise, when the food was ready, they untied me and gave me more than I could eat. But it wasn't out of kindness.

"Eat up, boy," the sergeant commanded. "We want you fit and well when we hand you over. You're the tenth one we've taken in the past two weeks and probably the icing on the cake. A young, strong, healthy lad like you should earn us a good bonus!"

"He don't look very cheerful!" jeered the corporal. "Don't he realize this is the best thing that ever happened to him? Make a man of you, it will, lad."

"Don't look so down in the mouth, boy," the sergeant mocked, showing off to his men. "They might not take you to fight. We're short of sailors, too! Can you swim?"

I shook my head.

"Well, that's no barrier to being a jack-tar. Once overboard and in the sea, nobody lasts long. You either freeze to death or the sharks bite off your feet!"

After we'd emptied our plates they tied my hands again, and as they talked, I lay back and closed my eyes, pretending to sleep while listening to their conversation. It seemed that they were fed up with pressing for the army. They were talking about deserting.

"Last one, this is," I heard the sergeant mutter. "Collect our pay, then we'll disappear north o' the County and find ourselves some richer pickings. There's got to be better work than this!"

Just my luck, I told myself. One more and then they were finished. I was the very last one they intended to press into service.

"Not sure about that," said a plaintive voice. "Not much work anywhere. That's why my old dad signed me up to soldiering."

It was the lad, Toddy, who'd spoken, and for a moment there was an uneasy silence. I could tell that the sergeant didn't like being contradicted.

"Well, Toddy," he answered, an edge of anger to his voice, "depends who's looking for work, a boy or a man. And it depends what kind of work we're talking about. Still, I know the job for you. There's one spook who'll be looking for a new apprentice. I think that's just the job you need!"

Toddy shook his head. "Wouldn't like it much. Witches scare me."

"Just old wives' tales. There *are* no witches. Come on,

Toddy, tell me! When have you seen a witch?"

"Had an old witch in our village once," Toddy replied. "She'd a black cat and used to mutter under her breath. She had a wart on her chin, too!"

"The cat or the witch?" mocked the sergeant.

"The witch."

"A witch with a wart on her chin! Well, doesn't that just have us all shaking in our boots, lads," brayed the sergeant sarcastically. "We need to get you apprenticed to a spook and then, when you've finished your training, you'll be able to go back and deal with her!"

"No," said Toddy. "Wouldn't be able to do that. She's dead already. They tied her hands to her feet and threw her in the pond to see if she'd float."

The men roared with laughter but I couldn't see what was funny. She'd clearly been what the Spook called "falsely accused"—a poor old woman who didn't deserve to be treated like that. Those who sank were presumed innocent but often died of shock or pneumonia if they hadn't already drowned.

"Well, Toddy? Did she float?" the sergeant demanded.

"She did, but facedown in the water. They fished her out to burn her but she was already dead. So they burned her cat instead."

There was another burst of cruel laughter even louder than the first, but the conversation soon became desultory before ceasing altogether. I think I must have dozed off because I suddenly became aware that it had grown extremely cold. Only an hour previously, a chill damp autumn wind had been gusting through the trees, bending the saplings and causing older branches to creak and groan; now everything was perfectly still and the ground was coated with hoar frost that sparkled in the moonlight.

The fire had died right down until there were just a few glowing embers. There was plenty of wood lying in a heap at the side, but despite the bitterly cold air, nobody had made a move to fuel the fire. All five soldiers were simply staring at the cooling embers as if in a trance.

Suddenly I sensed something approaching the clearing. The soldiers did, too. They came to their feet as one and peered out into the darkness. A shadowy figure emerged from among the trees, moving toward us so silently that it appeared to be floating rather than walking. As it drew nearer, I felt fear rising in my throat like bile and stood up nervously.

My body was already cold, but there's more than one kind of cold. I'm the seventh son of a seventh son and I can sometimes see, hear, or sense things that ordinary people can't. I see ghosts and ghasts, hear the dead talk, feel a special kind of cold when something from the dark approaches. I had that feeling now, stronger than I'd ever felt it before, and I was scared. So scared that I began to tremble from head to foot. Could it be the Fiend, come for me at last?

There was something about the head of the approaching figure that disturbed me deeply. There was no wind yet its hair seemed to be moving, writhing in an impossible way. Could this be the Fiend approaching now?

The figure moved closer; suddenly it entered the clearing so that moonlight fell on it properly for the first time. . . .

But it wasn't the Fiend. I was looking at a powerful malevolent witch. Her eyes were like fiery coals and her face was contorted with hatred and malice. Yet it was her head that terrified me most of all. Instead of hair she had a nest of black snakes that writhed and coiled, forked tongues flickering, fangs ready to inject their venom.

Suddenly there was a moan of animal terror from my right. It was the sergeant. For all his brave words, his face was now deformed by fear, his eyes bulging in his head, mouth open as if to scream. But instead he gave another moan, deep from within his belly, and set off into the trees, heading north at full pelt. His men followed, with Toddy bringing up the rear, and I could hear them in the distance, their frantic footsteps receding until they'd faded away altogether.

In the silence I was left alone to face the witch. I had no salt, no iron, no staff, and my hands were still bound behind my back, but I took a deep breath and tried to control my fear. That was the first step when dealing with the dark.

But I needn't have worried. Suddenly the witch smiled and her eyes ceased to glow. The coldness within me ebbed. The snakes stopped writhing and became a head of black hair. The contortions of the face relaxed into the features of an exceptionally pretty girl and I looked down at the pointy shoes that I knew so well. It was Alice, and she was smiling at me.

I didn't return her smile. All I could do was stare at her, horrified.

"Cheer up, Tom," Alice said. "Scared 'em so much they ain't going to follow us. You're safe enough now. Ain't nothing to worry about."

"What have you done, Alice?" I said, shaking my head. "I sensed evil. You looked like a malevolent witch. You must have used dark magic to do that!"

"Ain't done nothing wrong, Tom," she said, reaching out to untie me. "The others were scared and it spread to you, that's all. Just a trick of the light really . . ."

Appalled, I pulled away from her. "Moonlight shows the truth of things, you know that, Alice. It's one of the things you told me when we first met. So is that what *I've* just seen? What you really are? Have I seen the truth?"

"No, Tom. Don't be silly. It's just me, Alice. We're friends, ain't we? Don't you know me better than that? Saved your life more than once. Saved you from the dark, I have. Ain't fair, you accusing me like that. Not when I've just rescued you again. Where would you be now without me? I'll tell you: on your way to war. You might never have come back."

"If the Spook had seen that . . ." I shook my head. It would have been the end of Alice for sure. The end of her time living with us. My master might even have put her in a pit for the rest of her days. After all, that's what he did with witches who used dark magic.

"Come on, Tom. Let's be away from here and back to Chipenden. The cold's starting to get into my bones."

With those words, she cut my bonds and we headed straight back toward the Spook's house. I carried the sack with what was left of the provisions and we walked in silence. I still wasn't happy at what I'd seen.

❍ ❍ ❍

The next morning, as we tucked into our breakfast, I was still worrying about what Alice had done.

The Spook's pet boggart made our meals; it was mostly invisible but occasionally took the form of a ginger cat. This morning it had cooked my favorites—bacon and eggs—but this breakfast was probably one of the worst it had ever put on the table. The bacon was burned to a crisp and the eggs were swimming in grease. Sometimes the boggart cooked badly when something had upset it. It seemed to know things without being told. I wondered if it was concerned about the same thing I was: Alice.

"Last night when you walked into the clearing, you scared me, Alice. Scared me badly. I thought I was facing a malevolent witch — one of a type I'd never met before. That's exactly what you looked like. You had a head of snakes rather than hair and your face was twisted with hatred."

"Stop nagging me, Tom. It ain't fair. Just let me eat my breakfast in peace!"

"Nagging? You *need* nagging! What did you do? Come on, tell me!"

"Nothing. I did nothing! Leave me alone. Please, Tom. It hurts me when you go on at me like that."

"It hurts me to be lied to, Alice. You did something and I want to know exactly what." I paused, blazing with anger, and the words slipped out of my mouth before I could stop them. "If you don't tell me the truth, Alice— then I'll never trust you again!"

"All right, I'll tell you the truth," Alice cried, tears glistening in her eyes. "What else could I do, Tom? Where would you be now if I hadn't come along and got you away? Ain't my fault that I scared you. Aimed at them, it was, not you."

"What did you use, Alice? Was it dark magic? Something Bony Lizzie taught you?"

"Nothing special. Similar to glamour, that's all. It's called dread. Terrifies people, it does, and makes 'em run away in fear for their lives. Most witches know how to do it. It worked, Tom. What could be wrong with that?

You're free and nobody got hurt, did they?"

Glamour was something a witch used to make herself appear younger and more beautiful than she really was, creating an aura that enabled her to bind a man to her will. It was dark magic and had been used by the witch Wurmalde when she'd tried to unite the Pendle clans in the summer. She was dead now, but dead too were men who'd been in thrall to the power of glamour and had only realized too late the threat she represented. If dread were another version of that same dark magic, it worried me that Alice had used such power. It worried me deeply.

"If the Spook knew, he'd send you away, Alice," I warned her. "He'd never understand. For him nothing ever justifies using the power of the dark."

"Then don't tell him, Tom. You don't want me to be sent away, do you?"

"Of course not. But I don't like lying either."

"Then just say that I caused a distraction. That you got away in the confusion. Not far from the truth, is it?"

I nodded but I was still far from happy.

○ ○ ○

The Spook returned that evening, and despite feeling guilty at withholding the truth, I repeated what Alice had said.

"Just made a lot of noise from a safe distance," Alice added. "They chased me but I soon lost 'em in the dark."

"Didn't they leave somebody guarding the lad?" my master asked.

"Tied Tom's arms and legs so he couldn't run away. I circled back and cut him free."

"And where did they go afterward?" he asked, scratching at his beard worriedly. "Are you sure you weren't followed?"

"They talked about going north," I told him. "They seemed fed up with press-gang work and wanted to desert."

The Spook sighed. "That could well be true, lad. But we can't afford to take a chance on those men coming looking for you again. Why did you go down into the village alone in the first place? Haven't you the sense you were born with?"

My face flushed with anger. "I was sick of being molly-coddled. I can look after myself!"

"Can you now? Didn't put up much of a fight against those soldiers, did you?" my master retorted scathingly. "No, I think it's time I packed you off to work with Bill Arkwright for six months or so. Besides, my old bones ache too much now to give you the combat training you need. Harsh though he is, Bill's licked more than one of my apprentices into shape. And that's exactly what you need! And just in case that press-gang come back looking for you, you're better off away."

"But they wouldn't be able to get past the boggart, would they?" I protested.

In addition to kitchen duties, the boggart kept the gardens safe from the dark and any sort of intruder.

"Yes, but you're not always going to be protected here, are you, lad?" the Spook said firmly. "No, it's best if we get you away."

I groaned inside but said nothing. My master had been muttering for weeks about seconding me to Arkwright, the spook who worked the part of the County north of Caster. It was something my master usually arranged for his apprentices. He believed that a concentrated period of training with another spook was beneficial—that it was good to get different insights into our trade. The danger from the press-gang had simply hastened his decision.

Within the hour he had written the letter while Alice sulked by the fire. She didn't want us to be separated, but there was nothing either of us could do about it.

What was worse, my master sent Alice to post the letter rather than me. I began to wonder if I'd be better off up north after all. At least Bill Arkwright might trust me to do something by myself.

# CHAPTER III
## A LATE REPLY

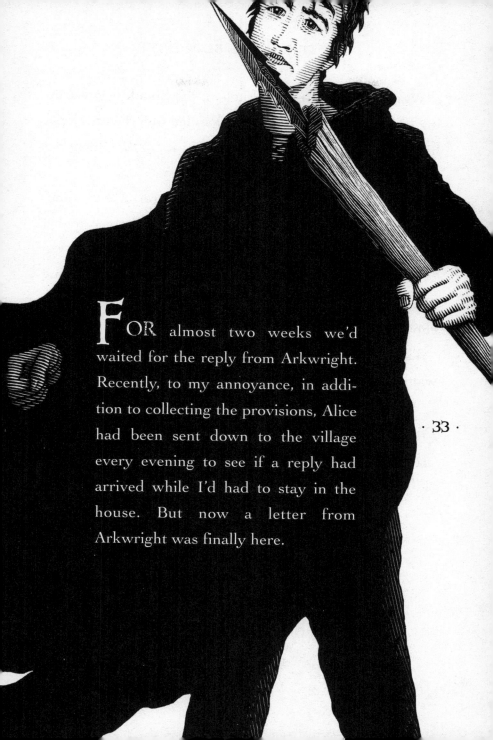

FOR almost two weeks we'd waited for the reply from Arkwright. Recently, to my annoyance, in addition to collecting the provisions, Alice had been sent down to the village every evening to see if a reply had arrived while I'd had to stay in the house. But now a letter from Arkwright was finally here.

· 33 ·

When Alice entered the kitchen, the Spook was warming his hands at the fire. As she handed him the envelope, he glanced at the words scrawled on it. *To Mr. Gregory of Chipenden.*

"I'd know that handwriting anywhere. About time, too!" my master commented, annoyance strong in his voice. "Well, girl, thanks for that. Now run along!"

With a downward turn of her mouth, Alice obeyed. She knew she'd find out what Arkwright had written soon enough.

The Spook opened the letter and began to read while I waited impatiently.

When he'd finished, he handed it to me with a weary sigh. "You might as well look, too, lad. It concerns you. . . ."

I began to read, my heart slowly sinking into my boots as I did so.

*Dear Mr. Gregory,*
*My health has been poor of late and my*
*duties heavy. But although it's not a good*

*time for me to be burdened by an apprentice, I cannot refuse your request, for you were always a good master to me and gave me a sound training that has served me well.*

*At ten o'clock on the morning of the eighteenth day of October, bring the boy to the first bridge over the canal north of Caster. I will be waiting there.*

*Your obedient servant,*
*Bill Arkwright*

"You don't need to read between the lines to tell that he's none too keen to take me on," I commented.

The Spook nodded. "Aye, that's plain enough. But Arkwright always was a bit down in the mouth and overly concerned with the state of his health. Things probably won't be half as bad as he makes out. He was something of a plodder, mind, but he did complete his time, and that's more than can be said for most of the lads it's been my misfortune to train!"

That was true enough. I was the Spook's thirtieth apprentice. Many apprentices had failed to complete their training; some had fled in fear, while others had died. Arkwright had survived and had plied our trade successfully for many years. So, despite his seeming reluctance, he probably had a lot to teach me.

"Mind you, he's come on a lot since he's been working by himself. Ever heard of the Coniston Ripper, lad?"

Rippers were a dangerous type of boggart. The Spook's last apprentice, Billy Bradley, had been killed by a ripper: It had bitten off some of his fingers and he'd died of shock and loss of blood.

"There's an entry in the Bestiary in your library about it," I told him.

"So there is, lad. Well, it killed over thirty people. Arkwright was the one who dealt with it. Ask him about it when you get the chance. No doubt he's proud of what he did, and so he should be. Don't let on what you know—let him tell you the story himself. Should help to get your working relationship off to a good start! Anyway," the Spook said, shaking his head, "that letter's barely arrived in time. It's best if we get to bed early tonight and set off soon after dawn."

My master was right: The meeting with Arkwright was scheduled for the day after tomorrow and it was about a day's journey to Caster over the fells. But I wasn't feeling too happy at having to set off so suddenly. He must have noticed my glum face because he said, "Cheer up, lad, Arkwright's not that bad. . . ."

And then his expression changed as he suddenly understood what I was feeling. "*Now* I see what's the matter. It's the girl, isn't it?"

I nodded. There would be no place for Alice at Arkwright's house, so we'd be parted for about six months. Despite all the mollycoddling I'd suffered recently, I was going to miss her. Miss her badly.

"Couldn't Alice just travel with us to the bridge?" I asked.

I expected the Spook to refuse. After all, despite the fact

that Alice had saved our lives on more than one occasion, she was still half Deane and half Malkin and came from witch-clan stock. My master didn't fully trust her and rarely involved her in our business. He still believed that one day she might fall under the influence of the dark. I was glad he didn't know how convincingly she'd appeared as a malevolent witch the other day.

But to my astonishment, he nodded his agreement. "I don't see why not," he said. "Off you go and tell her now."

Fearing that he might change his mind, I left the kitchen immediately and went to look for Alice. I expected to find her in the next room, copying one of the books from the Spook's library. But she wasn't there. To my surprise, she was outside sitting on the back step, staring out at the garden with a gloomy expression on her face.

"It's chilly out here, Alice," I said, smiling down at her. "Why don't you come back inside? I've got something to tell you. . . ."

"Ain't good news, is it? Arkwright's agreed to take you, hasn't he?" she asked.

I nodded. We'd both been hoping that Arkwright's delayed reply meant he would refuse the Spook's request. "We're setting off early tomorrow," I told her, "but the good news is that you're coming with us to see me off at Caster—"

"To me that's a lot of bad news with hardly a pinch of good. Don't know what Old Gregory's fretting about. That press-gang ain't coming back, are they?"

"Maybe not," I agreed. "But he wants to get me off to Caster at some point and now seems as good a time as any. I can hardly refuse. . . ."

Although I hadn't mentioned it to Alice, I also reckoned that one reason the Spook was sending me to Arkwright's was to get me away from her for a while. Once or twice recently I'd noticed him watching when we were laughing or talking together, and he kept warning me about getting too close to her.

"Suppose not," Alice said sadly. "But you will write to me, Tom, won't you? Write every week. That way it'll make time pass more quickly. Won't be much fun for me alone in the house with Old Gregory, will it?"

I nodded but I didn't know how often I'd be able to manage it. The post wagon was expensive and letters cost money to send. The Spook didn't usually give me money unless it was for a specific need, so I'd have to ask him and I didn't know how he'd react. I decided to wait and see what sort of a mood he was in at breakfast.

"That was one of the best breakfasts I've ever tasted," I said, mopping up the last of my runny egg yolk with a large piece of bread. The bacon had been fried to perfection.

The Spook smiled and nodded in agreement. "That it was," he said. "Our compliments to the cook!"

In response a faint purring could be heard from somewhere under the large wooden table, showing that the pet boggart appreciated our praise.

"Could I borrow some money for my stay with Mr. Arkwright?" I asked. "I wouldn't need very much. . . ."

"*Borrow?*" asked the Spook, raising his eyebrows.

"*Borrow* suggests that you intend to pay it back. That's not a word you've used before when I've given you money for your needs."

"There's money in Mam's trunks," I told him. "I could pay you back next time we visit Pendle."

My mam had returned to her homeland, Greece, to fight the rising power of the dark there. But she'd left me three trunks. As well as potions and books, one of them had contained three large bags of money, which were now safely stored in Malkin Tower, guarded by Mam's two feral lamia sisters. In their domestic form lamias had the appearance of human females but for a line of yellow and green scales on their spines. However, these two sisters were in their wild state, with insectlike wings and sharp talons. They were strong and dangerous and could keep the Pendle witches at bay. I wasn't sure when we'd be going back to Pendle, but I knew it would happen one day.

"So you could," replied the Spook in answer to my suggestion. "Is there anything special that you want money for?"

"It's just that I'd like to write to Alice each week—"

"Letters are expensive, lad, and I'm sure your mam wouldn't want you to fritter away the money she left you. Once a month will be more than adequate. And if you're writing to the girl, you can send me a letter as well. Keep me informed about everything that's going on and put both letters in the same envelope to keep the costs down."

Out of the corner of my eye I saw Alice's mouth tighten as she listened to what he said. We both knew that it wasn't really the money that concerned him. He'd be able to read what I'd written to Alice and do the same with her letter once she'd replied. But what could I say? A letter a month was better than nothing so I'd just have to make the best of it.

After breakfast the Spook took me to the small room where he kept his boots, cloaks, and staffs. "It's about time I replaced that staff of yours that got burned, lad," he told me. "Here, try this one for size."

He handed me one made from rowan wood, which would be very effective against witches. I lifted it and checked the balance. It was perfect. Then I noticed something else. There was a small recess near the top—

the right size to accommodate my forefinger.

"I think you know what that's for!" exclaimed the Spook. "You'd best try it. See if it's still in good working order."

I eased my finger into the recess and pressed. With a loud click a sharp blade sprang out of the other end. My previous staff hadn't had a retractable blade—though I'd once borrowed the Spook's, which did. But now I'd have my own.

"Thanks," I told him with a smile. "I'll take good care of it!"

"Aye, and better care than you took with the last one! Let's hope you don't have to use it, lad, but it's better to be safe than sorry."

I nodded, then rested the point of the blade against the floor, exerted pressure and eased it back into its recess.

Within the hour, the Spook had locked up the house and we were on our way. My master and I were each carrying our staffs but, as usual, I was carrying both bags. We were well wrapped up against the cold: he and I in our cloaks, Alice in her black woolen winter coat, its hood up to keep her ears warm. I even wore my sheepskin jacket—though in truth it wasn't a bad morning at all. The air was crisp, but the sun was shining and it was good to be walking toward the fells heading north toward Caster.

As we began to climb, Alice and I drew a little way ahead so that we could talk out of earshot. "It could be worse," I told her. "If Mr. Gregory were planning to go to his winter house, you'd have to go with him and we'd be at opposite ends of the County."

Usually the Spook wintered at Anglezarke, far to the south, but he'd already told me that this year he'd remain in his more comfortable house in Chipenden. I'd just nodded and made no comment. I supposed it was because Meg Skelton, the love of his life, was no longer in Anglezarke and the house held too many painful memories. She and her sister, Marcia, were lamia witches and the Spook had been forced to send them back to Greece, even though it had broken his heart.

"Ain't telling me anything I don't know already," Alice

said bitterly. "Still too far apart to visit each other, aren't we, so what difference does it make? Anglezarke or Chipenden—still adds up to the same thing in the end!"

"It's no better for me, Alice. Do you think I *want* to spend the next six months with Arkwright? You should have read the letter he sent. He says he's ill and doesn't even want me there. He's only taking me grudgingly as a favor to the Spook."

"And do you really think I want to be left at Chipenden with Old Gregory? He still doesn't trust me and probably never will. Won't ever let me forget what's been an' gone, will he?"

"That's not fair, Alice. He's given you a home. And if he found out what you did that night, you'd lose that home forever and probably end up in a pit."

"I'm sick of telling you *why* I did it! Don't be so ungrateful. Not in league with the dark and never will be—you can be sure of that. Once in a while I use what Lizzie taught me because I have no choice. I do it for you, Tom, to keep you safe. Nice if you could appreciate that," she snapped, glancing behind to see that my master was still at a safe distance.

We both lapsed into silence after that, and even the brightness of the morning couldn't lift our mood. The day wore on as we trudged north. It was nearly a month beyond the autumn equinox and the daylight hours were shortening, with the long cold winter approaching. We were still descending the lower slopes east of Caster when the light began to fail, so we found ourselves a sheltered hollow to bed down in for the night. The Spook and I gathered wood and got a fire going while Alice caught and skinned a couple of rabbits. Soon they were spitting and hissing in the flames while my mouth began to water.

"What's it like to the far north of Caster?" I asked the Spook.

We were sitting cross-legged before the fire while Alice turned the spit. I'd offered to help but she'd have none of it. She was hungry and wanted the rabbits cooked to perfection.

"Well," my master replied, "some say it's got the best

scenery in the whole County and I wouldn't argue with that. There are mountains and lakes, with the sea to the south. To the very extreme north of the County there's Coniston Lake and the Big Mere east of it—"

"Is that where Mr. Arkwright lives?" I interrupted.

"Nay, lad, not so far north as that. There's a long canal that runs in a northerly direction, from Priestown through Caster and into Kendal. His house is on the west bank. It's an old water mill fallen into disuse but it serves him well enough."

"What about the dark?" I asked. "Anything in that part of the County that I haven't met before?"

"You're still green behind the ears, lad!" snapped the Spook. "There are plenty of things you've still to face and you don't need to go north of Caster to find 'em! But what with the lakes and the canal, danger mostly comes from the water in those parts. Arkwright's the expert on water witches and other creatures that make their homes in bog and slime. But I'll let him tell you himself. It'll be his job to train you for a while."

Alice continued to turn the spit while we sat staring into the flames. She was the one to break the silence and there was concern in her voice.

"Ain't happy that Tom's going to be up here alone," she said. "The Fiend's in the world permanent now. What if he comes looking for Tom and we're not around to help him?"

"We must look on the bright side, girl," the Spook replied. "Let's not forget that the Fiend has visited this world many times before. It's not the first time he's been here."

"That's true enough," agreed Alice. "But apart from the first time, usually they were short visits. Some coven or witch would call him up. Lots of stories about that, there are, but most agree that Old Nick never stuck around for more than a few minutes at most. Just time enough to make a bargain or grant a wish in exchange for a soul. But this is different. He's here to stay, with plenty of time to do exactly what he wants."

"Aye, girl, but no doubt the Fiend'll be busy finding mischief of his own to carry out. Do you think he *wanted* to be bound to the will of the covens? Now that he's free he'll do what he pleases—not what they told him to do. He'll be dividing families, turning husband against wife and son against father; placing greed and treachery in human hearts; emptying churches of their congregations; making food rot in the granary and cattle waste away and die. He'll swell the savagery of war into a blood-tide and make soldiers forget their humanity. In short, he'll be increasing the burden of human misery and making love and friendship wither like crops struck by the blight. Aye, it's bad for everyone, but for now Tom's probably as safe as anyone who follows our trade and fights the dark."

"What powers does he have?" I asked, feeling nervous with all this talk of the Devil. "Is there anything more you can tell me? What should I be most worried about if he does come looking for me?"

The Spook stared at me hard, and for a moment I thought he wasn't going to answer. But then he sighed and began to summarize the powers of the Fiend.

"As you know, it's said that he can take on any shape or

size he likes. He may resort to trickery to get what he wants, appearing out of thin air and looking over your shoulder without you knowing it. At other times he leaves a calling card—the Devil's mark, a series of cloven hoof-prints burned into the ground. Why he does that is anyone's guess, but it's probably just to scare people. Some believe that his true shape is so appalling that one glance would kill you from sheer terror. But that might just be a story to scare children into saying their prayers."

"Well, the idea of it certainly scares me!" I said, glancing over my shoulder into the darkness of the hollow.

"The Fiend's greatest power, though," continued my master, "is his ability to tamper with time. He can speed it up so that, to anyone in his vicinity, a week passes by in less than an hour. He can do the reverse, too: make a minute seem to last an eternity. Some say he can stop time altogether, but there are very few accounts of that happening. . . ."

The Spook must have noticed my worried expression. He glanced sideways at Alice, who was staring at him wide-eyed.

"Look, it's no use worrying ourselves unnecessarily," he said. "We're all at risk now. And Bill Arkwright will be able to guard Tom just as well as I can."

Alice looked far from satisfied by the Spook's words, but soon she shared out the rabbits and I was too busy eating to worry any more about it.

"It's a fine night," said the Spook, looking upward.

I nodded in agreement, still stuffing pieces of juicy rabbit into my mouth. The sky was bright with stars and the Milky Way was a gleaming silver curtain strung across the heavens.

But by morning the weather had changed and a mist cloaked the hillside. It wasn't a bad thing because we still had to skirt Caster. Within its ancient castle they tried witches before hanging them on a hill just outside the city. Some priests considered a spook and his apprentice to be enemies of the Church, so it wasn't a place for us to linger.

We passed the town to the east and strode onto the first northerly bridge over the canal just before ten. The mist hung heavily over the water and everything was silent. The canal was wider than I'd expected. Were it possible to walk on water, twenty strides would have been needed to cross from one bank to the other. The water, though, was still and murky, suggestive of depth. There wasn't a breath of wind and the surface reflected back the arch of the bridge to form an oval, and when I looked down, I could see my own sad face staring back up at me.

A cinder towpath ran parallel to each bank of the canal, bordered by a straggly hawthorn hedge on either side. A few forlorn, leafless trees draped their stark branches over the paths, and beyond them the fields rapidly disappeared into the mist.

There was no sign of Arkwright. We waited patiently for almost an hour, the chill starting to eat into our bones, but still he didn't turn up.

"Something's wrong," the Spook said at last. "Arkwright has his faults, but tardiness was never one of them. I don't like it! If he's not here, then something has prevented him. Something beyond his control."

# CHAPTER IV
# THE MILL

THE Spook had just decided that we should press on north toward Kendal when we heard muffled sounds approaching. They were the steady beat of hooves and the swish of water. Then, looming out of the mist, we saw two huge shire horses harnessed one behind the other. They were being led down the towpath by a

man in a leather tunic and were pulling a long narrow barge behind them.

As the barge passed underneath the bridge, I saw the man glance back up toward us. Then he brought the horses to a gradual halt, tethered them on the towpath, and walked up onto the wooden bridge with a steady, unhurried stride and a confident roll of his shoulders. He wasn't a tall man but he was thick-set, with large hands, and despite the chill, underneath the leather jerkin the top two buttons of his shirt were open, revealing a thatch of brown hair.

Most men would cross the road to avoid passing too close to a spook, but he smiled broadly, and to my astonishment, walked right up to my master and held out his hand. "I expect you're Mr. Gregory." The stranger beamed. "I'm Matthew Gilbert. Bill Arkwright asked me to collect the boy."

They shook hands, my master returning his smile. "I'm pleased to meet you too, Mr. Gilbert," the Spook replied, "but isn't he well enough to come himself?"

"No, it's not that, although he has been poorly," Mr. Gilbert explained. "It's just that they've found a body in the water—it had been drained of blood like the others. It's the third in two months, and Bill's gone north to investigate. Of late the dark seems to be rearing its ugly head more often and he's been kept really busy."

The Spook nodded thoughtfully but didn't comment. Instead he put his hand on my shoulder. "Well, this is Tom Ward. He expected to walk; no doubt he'll be pleased to get himself a ride. . . ."

Mr. Gilbert smiled and then shook my hand. "I'm very pleased to meet you, young Tom. But now I'll let you say your good-byes in peace. So I'll see you down there," he said, nodding toward the barge and then making his way down.

"Well, lad, don't forget to write. You can send us a letter after the first week to let us know how you've settled in," the Spook said, handing me a couple of small silver coins. "And here's something for Bill Arkwright to help toward your keep." And he placed a guinea in my hand.

"I can't see you having any problems. Just work as hard for Arkwright as you have for me and all should be well. For a while you're going to have a different master with his own way of working and it'll be your task to adapt to him—not the other way round. Keep your notebook up to date and write down everything he teaches you—even if it's not quite the same as I've taught. It's always good to have another perspective, and by now Arkwright is an expert on things that come out of the water. So listen well and be on your guard. The County's a dangerous place at present. We all need to keep our wits about us!"

With that the Spook gave me a nod and turned on his heel. Only when he'd left the bridge did Alice approach. She put her arms right round me and hugged me close.

"Oh, Tom! Tom! I'll miss you," she said.

"And I'll miss you," I replied, a lump coming to my throat.

She pulled away and held me at arm's length. "Take care of yourself, please. I couldn't bear it if anything were to happen to you. . . ."

"Nothing's going to happen," I said, trying to reassure her. "And I can look after myself. You should know that by now."

"Listen," she said, looking quickly over her shoulder, "if you're in trouble or you need to tell me something urgently, use a mirror!"

Her words shocked me and I took a step backward. Witches employed mirrors to communicate, and I'd seen Alice use one once. The Spook would be horrified by what she was saying. Such practices belonged to the dark, and he would never approve of us communicating in that way.

"Ain't no cause to look at me like that, Tom," Alice insisted. "All you have to do is place both hands against a mirror and think about me just as hard as you can. If it don't work the first time, then keep trying."

"No, Alice, I'm not doing anything like that," I told her angrily. "It's something from the dark, and I'm here to fight it, not be part of it —"

"Not that simple, Tom. Sometimes we need to fight the

dark *with* the dark. Remember that, despite what Old Gregory might say. And be careful. Ain't a good part of the County to be. I was up there once with Bony Lizzie and lived on the edge of the marsh not too far from Arkwright's mill. So take care, please!'"

I nodded, then impulsively leaned forward and kissed her on the left cheek. She drew back and I saw tears welling in her eyes. The parting was hard for both of us. Then she turned and ran from the bridge. Moments later she'd disappeared into the mist.

I walked sadly down onto the towpath. Matthew Gilbert was waiting for me, and he simply pointed to a wooden seat at the front of the barge. I sat myself down and looked about. Behind me were two huge wooden hatches, their padlocks hanging loose. This was a working barge and no doubt a cargo of some sort was stowed down there.

Moments later we were heading north. I kept glancing back toward the bridge, hoping against hope that Alice would appear so I could see her one last time. She didn't, and it gave me a pain in my chest to leave her behind like that.

Every so often we passed a barge traveling in the opposite direction. Each time Mr. Gilbert exchanged a cheery wave with the other bargeman. These craft varied in size but all were long and narrow with one or more hatches. But whereas some were well kept, with bright, colorful paintwork, others were black and grimy, with fragments of coal on their decks, suggesting what lay in the hold.

At about one o'clock Mr. Gilbert brought the horses to a stop, freed them from their harness, and tethered them on the edge of some rough grassland at the side of the canal. While they grazed, he quickly made a fire and proceeded to cook us some lunch. I asked if I could help in any way but he shook his head.

"Guests don't work," he said. "I'd rest while you can. Bill Arkwright works his apprentices hard. Don't get me wrong, though; he's a good man, good at his job, and he's done a lot for the County. And he's tenacious, too. Once he's got the whiff of his quarry he never gives up."

He peeled some potatoes and carrots and boiled them in a pan over the fire. We sat at the rear of the barge, our feet dangling over the water, eating with our fingers from two wooden plates. The food hadn't been cooked long enough, and both the carrots and the potatoes were still hard. But I was hungry enough to eat both the bargeman's horses, so I just chewed thoroughly and swallowed. We ate in silence, but after a while, out of politeness, I tried to engage the bargeman in conversation.

"Have you known Mr. Arkwright long?" I asked.

"Ten years or more," Mr. Gilbert replied. "Bill used to live at the mill with his parents, but they died years ago. Since becoming the local spook, he's become a very good customer of mine. Takes a big delivery of salt every month. I fill five large barrels for him. I also bring him other provisions: candles, food—you name it. Especially wine. Likes a tipple, Bill does. Not your common elderberry or dandelion wine for him. Prefers his wine red. It comes by ship to Sunderland Point then overland to

Kendal, where I take it aboard once a month. He pays me well."

I was intrigued by the quantity of salt. In combination with iron, spooks used salt to coat the inside of pits when binding boggarts. It could also be used as a weapon against creatures of the dark. But we used relatively small amounts and bought small bags from the village grocer. Why would he need five barrels of salt every month?

"Is that your cargo now — salt and wine?" I asked.

"At the moment the hold is empty," he replied, shaking his head. "I've just delivered a load of slate to a builder in Caster, and I'm heading back up to the quarry to collect some more. We carry all sorts of stuff around in this job. I'll carry anything but coal — it's so plentiful and cheap that it's not even worth bothering to lock the hatches in case of theft. And that black stuff gets everywhere so I leave that to the specialist carriers."

"So, Mr. Arkwright's mill — is it right on the canal?"

"Close enough," Mr. Gilbert replied. "You won't be able to see it from the barge — it's hidden by trees and bushes—but from the canal bank you could throw a small stone into the edge of the garden without straining too hard. It's a lonely place, but no doubt you'll be well accustomed to that."

We lapsed into silence again, but then I thought of something that had struck me on the journey. "There are a lot of bridges over the canal. Why does it need so many?"

"I wouldn't quarrel with that observation," Mr. Gilbert said, nodding. "When they dug the canal, it cut a lot of farms in two. They'd paid the farmers for taking their land but also had to provide them with access to fields that lay on the other side of the canal. But there's another reason. Horses and barges travel keeping to the left. So when you want to change direction, your horses can switch banks. Anyway, we'd best get on now. You would do well to reach the mill before dark."

Mr. Gilbert hitched the horses to the barge, and we were soon moving slowly north again. It had been misty at dawn, but rather than being burned off by the sun, the mist soon became a dense fog that closed the visibility to a few paces. I could see the backside of the nearest horse, but its companion and Matthew Gilbert were hidden from view. Even the rhythmical *clip-clop* of hooves was muffled. Every so often we passed under a bridge, but apart from that there was nothing to see and I grew weary just sitting there.

About an hour before dark Mr. Gilbert brought the horses to a halt and walked back to where I was sitting. "Here we are!" he called out cheerily, pointing out into the mist. "Bill Arkwright's house is straight over there."

Collecting my bag and staff, I clambered out onto the towpath. There was a large post on the canal bank, to which Mr. Gilbert tethered the leading horse. The upper section of the post resembled a hangman's scaffold, and from this hung a large bell.

"I ring the bell when I bring supplies," he said, nodding toward the post. "Five clear rings to tell him it's me with a delivery and not somebody needing a spook — it's customary to ring three times in that case. Bill comes out and collects what I've brought. If there's a lot, I sometimes help him carry it back to the boundary of the garden. He's none too keen on anyone going closer than that!"

I understood. He was just like my master in that respect. People needing help rang a bell at the crossroads, and I was usually sent to find out what they wanted.

All I could see beyond the post was a gray wall of fog, but I heard the gurgling of a stream somewhere below. At this point the canal was elevated above the surrounding fields. From the towpath a steep grassy bank sloped into the fog.

"It's only about ninety paces or so to the edge of his garden," Mr. Gilbert said. "At the foot of this bank there's a stream. Just follow it. It flows right under the house and used to drive the waterwheel when it was a working mill. Anyway, good luck. I'll probably see you again next time I'm passing by with salt — or cases of wine," he added, giving me a wink.

With that he untied the horses and walked off into the fog. Once more there came the muffled sound of hooves and the barge glided away northward. I remained standing there until the sound of hooves faded away altogether. Then, apart from the babble of water below me, I was enveloped in a blanket of silence. I shivered. I'd hardly ever felt so alone.

I scrambled down the steep bank and found myself on the edge of a fast-flowing stream. The water surged toward me before rushing into a dark tunnel under the canal, no doubt to reappear on the other side. The visibility had improved somewhat but was still no better than a dozen paces in any direction. I began to walk upstream, following a muddy track in the direction of the house, expecting it to loom out of the fog at any moment.

But all I could see were trees—drooping willows on both banks, their branches trailing into the water. They immediately impeded my progress, and I kept having to duck. At last I reached the perimeter of Arkwright's garden, a seemingly impenetrable thicket of leafless trees, shrubs, and saplings. First, however, there was another barrier to cross.

The garden was bounded by a rusty iron fence: sharp-pointed, six-foot palings linked by three rows of horizontal bars. How could I get into the garden? The fence would be difficult to climb, and I didn't want to risk being impaled on the top. So I followed the curve of the railings to the left, hoping to find another entrance. By now I was beginning to get annoyed with Matthew Gilbert. He'd told me to follow the stream but hadn't bothered to explain what I'd find or how actually to reach the house.

I'd been following the railings for a few minutes when the going began to get very soggy underfoot. There were tussocks of marsh grass and pools of water, and in order to find slightly firmer ground I was forced to walk with my right shoulder almost touching the railings. But at last I came to a narrow gap.

I stepped through into the garden, to be confronted by a trench filled with water. The water was murky and it was impossible to say just how deep it might be. It was also at least nine paces across—impossible to jump even with a running start. I looked right and left but there was no way around it. So I tested it with my staff and, to my surprise, found the water came no higher than my knees. It looked like a defensive moat but was surely too shallow. So what was it for?

Puzzled, I waded across, quickly soaking the bottoms of my breeches in the process. Thickets were waiting for me on the other side, but a narrow path led through them, and after a few moments it opened out onto a wide area of rough grass, from which grew some of the largest willow trees I'd ever seen. They emerged from the fog like giants, with long, thin wet fingers that trailed against my clothes and tangled in my hair.

At last I heard the babbling of the stream again—before catching my first glimpse of Arkwright's mill. It was bigger than the Spook's Chipenden house, but size was the only impressive thing about it. Constructed of wood, it was dilapidated and sat oddly on the ground, the roof and walls meeting at strange angles; the former was green with slime, and grass and small seedlings sprouted from the gutters. Parts of the building looked rotten and unsound, as if the whole structure were just biding its time, waiting for its inevitable demise in the first storm of the winter.

In front of the house the stream hurled itself at the huge wooden waterwheel, which remained idle, immobile despite the furious efforts of the torrent. The water rushed on into a dark tunnel beneath the building. Looking at the wheel more closely, I could see that it was rotten and broken and probably hadn't moved for many a long year.

The first door I came to was boarded up, as were the three windows closest to it. So I walked on toward the stream until I reached a narrow porch enclosing a large, sturdy door. This looked like the main entrance so I knocked three times. Perhaps Arkwright was back by now? When nobody came in response, I rapped again, harder this time. Finally I tried the handle but found the door locked.

What was I supposed to do now? Sit on the step in the cold and damp? It was bad enough in daylight but soon it would be dark. There was no guarantee that Arkwright would be back before then. Investigating the body in the water might take him days.

There was a way to solve my problem. I had a special key, made by Andrew, the Spook's locksmith brother. Although it would open most doors and I expected the one before me to present little difficulty, I was reluctant to use it. It just didn't seem right to go into someone's house without their permission, so I decided to wait a little longer to see if Arkwright turned up after all. But soon the cold and damp began to seep into my bones and changed my mind for me. After all, I was going to live there for six months, and he was expecting me.

The key turned easily in the lock, but the door groaned on its hinges as it slowly opened. The mill was gloomy within, the air damp and musty and tainted with the strong odor of stale wine. I took just one step inside, allowing my eyes to adjust, then looking about me. There was a large table at the far end of the room, at the center of which was a single candle set within a small brass candlestick. I put down my staff and used my bag to wedge open the door and allow some light into the room. Pulling my tinderbox from my pocket, I had the candle lit within moments. That done, I noticed a sheet of paper on the table held in position by the candlestick. One glance and I could see that it was a note for me so I picked it up and began to read.

Dear Master Ward,

It seems that you have used your initiative; otherwise you would have spent the night outside in the dark, an experience that would be less than pleasant. Here you will find things very different from Chipenden.

Although I follow the same trade as Mr. Gregory, we work in different ways. Your master's house is a refuge, cleansed from within; but here, the unquiet dead walk and it is my wish that they do so. They will not harm you, so leave them be. Do nothing.

There is food in the larder and wood for the stove by the door, so eat your fill and sleep well. It would be wise to spend the night in the kitchen and await my return. Do not venture into the lowest part of the house nor attempt to enter the topmost room, which is locked.

Respect my wishes both for your good and for mine.

Bill Arkwright

# CHAPTER V
## A SHRILL HIGH SCREAM

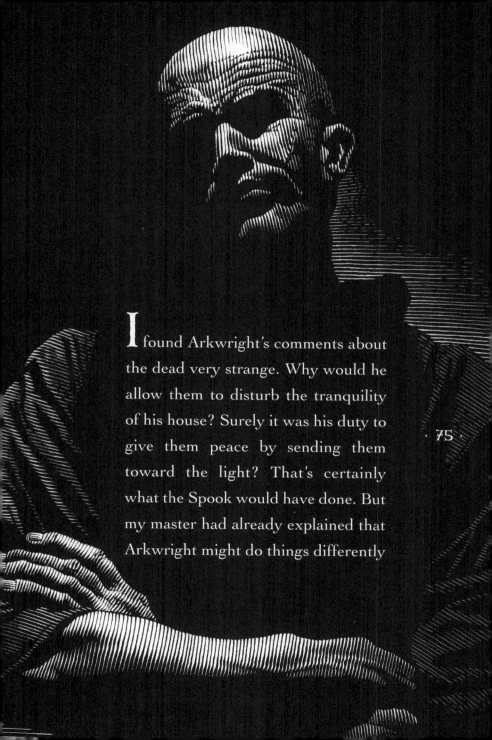

I found Arkwright's comments about the dead very strange. Why would he allow them to disturb the tranquility of his house? Surely it was his duty to give them peace by sending them toward the light? That's certainly what the Spook would have done. But my master had already explained that Arkwright might do things differently and it would be my duty to adapt to his ways.

I looked about, now able to see the room properly for the first time. It was not in the least inviting; it wasn't really a living room at all. The windows were boarded up, so no wonder it was gloomy. No doubt it had been used for storage when the building was a working mill. There was no fireplace, and apart from the table the only items of furniture were two hard-backed wooden chairs, standing in opposite corners of the room. But there were several crates of wine stacked against the wall and a long row of empty bottles. Dust and cobwebs festooned the walls and ceiling, and although the front door opened directly into the room, Arkwright clearly used the room only as a means to reach the other parts of the house.

I moved my bag away from the door before closing and locking it. Next I took the candle from the table and went through to the kitchen. The window over the sink wasn't boarded up, but it was still very foggy outside and the light was starting to fail. On the window ledge lay one of the biggest knives I'd ever seen. It certainly wasn't for the preparation of food! However, the kitchen was tidier than I'd expected, free of dust, with plates, cups, and pans neatly stacked in wall cupboards and a small dining table and three wooden chairs. I found the larder filled with cheese, ham, bacon, and half a loaf.

Rather than a fireplace, there was a large stove, wider than it was tall, with two doors and an iron chimney that twisted over it to enter the ceiling above. The left-hand door opened to reveal a frying pan; the right was filled with wood and straw, ready for lighting. No doubt this was the only way to heat and cook in a wooden building like this.

Wasting no time, I used my tinderbox to light the stove. The kitchen soon filled with warmth, and then I began frying three generous rashers of bacon. The bread was dry and past its best but still good enough to toast. There was no butter, but the food went down very well and I was soon feeling much better.

I began to feel sleepy so I decided to go upstairs and look at the bedrooms, hoping to work out which one was intended for me. I carried the candle with me and it proved to be a wise decision. The stairs could hardly have been darker. On the first floor there were four doors. The first led to a lumber room full of empty boxes, dirty sheets, blankets, and miscellaneous rubbish that gave off an unpleasant smell of mold and decay. The walls had damp patches, and some of the heaped sheets were heavily mildewed. The next two doors each led to single bedrooms. In the first the crumpled sheets showed that the bed had been slept in; the second contained a bed with a bare mattress. Was that meant to be mine? If so, I longed to be back in Chipenden. There was no other furniture in the bleak, uninviting room, and the air was chilly and damp.

The fourth room had a large double bed in it. The blankets lay in an untidy heap at its foot, and again the sheets were rumpled. Something didn't feel right in this room, and the hairs on the back of my neck began to rise. I shivered, lifted the candle higher, and approached the bed. It actually looked wet, and when I touched it lightly with my

fingers, I found it saturated. It couldn't have been wetter
if someone had emptied half a dozen bucketfuls of water
over it. I looked at the ceiling but could see no hole there
nor any signs of staining due to leaks. How had it got so
wet? I quickly backed away through the door, closing it
firmly behind me.

The more I thought about it, the less I liked this floor.
There was another level above, but Arkwright had
warned me, so I decided to take his advice and sleep on
the kitchen floor. At least it didn't feel damp and the heat
from the stove would keep me warm until morning.

Just after midnight something woke me. The kitchen was
in almost total darkness, with just the faintest of glows
from the stove.

What had disturbed me? Had Arkwright returned
home? But the hairs on the back of my neck were rising
again and I shivered. Arkwright had said that the unquiet
dead were present in the house. If so, more than likely I'd
soon know about it.

Just then there was a deep rumbling sound from somewhere below that vibrated right through the walls of the
mill. What was it? It seemed to be getting louder and
louder.

I was intrigued but I decided not to get up. Arkwright
had told me to do nothing. It was none of my business.
Even so, the noise was scary and disturbing, and I couldn't
get back to sleep, no matter how hard I tried. Eventually
I worked out what the sound was. The waterwheel. The
waterwheel was turning! Or at least it sounded like it.

Then there was a shrill scream, and the rumbling
stopped as quickly as it had started. It was a scream so
terrible and filled with such extreme anguish that I covered my ears. Of course that didn't help. The sound was
inside my head—the remnants of something that had
taken place many years earlier in this mill. I was listening
to someone in terrible pain.

At last the scream faded away and everything became
peaceful and quiet again. What I'd heard would have
been enough to drive most people from the building. I was

a spook's apprentice and such things were part of the job, but I still felt scared—my whole body was trembling. Arkwright had said that nothing here would harm me but there was something strange going on. Something more than just a routine haunting.

Even so, gradually I became calmer, and soon I was fast asleep again.

I slept well, too well. It was long past sunrise when I awoke to find that someone else was with me in the kitchen.

"Well, boy!" a deep voice boomed. "You're easily taken unawares. It doesn't pay to sleep too deeply in these parts. Nowhere is safe!"

I sat up quickly, then stumbled clumsily to my feet. Facing me was a spook, holding his staff in his left hand and a bag in his right. And what a bag! It could have easily contained both my master's and my own within it. Then I noticed the tip of the staff. My master's staff and mine both had retractable blades but this staff had a clearly visible, wicked-looking knife at least twelve inches long, with six backward-facing barbs, three on each side.

"Mr. Arkwright?" I asked. "I'm Tom Ward. . . ."

"Aye, I'm Bill Arkwright, and I guessed who you must be. I'm pleased to meet you, Master Ward. Your master speaks highly of you."

I stared at him, trying to rub the sleep from my eyes. He wasn't quite as tall as my master, but he was sturdier in a sort of wiry way that suggested strength. His face was gaunt and he had large green eyes and a strikingly bald head, from which not even a solitary hair sprouted; it was shaved as closely as that of a monk. On his left cheek was a vivid scar, which looked to be from a wound recently inflicted.

I also saw that his lips were stained purple. The Spook didn't drink, but once, when he'd been ill, raving with the fever, he'd drunk a whole bottle of red wine. Afterward his lips had been that same purple color.

Arkwright leaned his staff against the wall next to the inner door, then put down his bag. There was a chink of glass as it made contact with the kitchen floor. He held out his hand toward me and I shook it. "Mr. Gregory thinks well of you, too," I told him, reaching into my pocket and pulling out the guinea. "He sent you this to help toward my keep. . . ."

Arkwright took it from me, put it to his mouth, and bit into it hard. He inspected it closely, then smiled and nodded his thanks. He'd checked to make sure it was a real guinea made out of gold rather than some counterfeit. That annoyed me. Did he think my master would try to cheat him? Or was it me he suspected?

"Let's trust each other for a while, Master Ward," he said, "and see how we get on. Let's allow time enough to give us a chance to judge each other."

"My master said you'd have lots to teach me about the area north of Caster," I continued, trying not to show my irritation about the guinea. "About things that come out of the water . . ."

"Aye, I'll be teaching you about that all right, but mostly I'll be toughening you up. Are you strong, Master Ward?"

"Quite strong for my age," I said uncertainly.

"Sure about that, are you?" Arkwright said, looking me up and down. "I think you'll need a bit more muscle on you to survive in this job! Any good at arm wrestling?"

"Never tried it before."

"Well, you can try it now. It'll give me an idea of what needs to be done. Come over here and sit yourself down!" he commanded, leading the way to the table.

I'd been the youngest by three years and had missed those family games, but I remembered my brothers Jack and James arm wrestling at the kitchen table back at the farm. In those days Jack always won because he was older, taller, and stronger. I would be at the same disadvantage against Arkwright.

I sat down facing him, and we placed our left arms together and locked hands. With my elbow on the table, my arm was shorter than his. I did my best, but he exerted a strong, steady pressure, and despite my best attempts to resist he bent my arm back until it was flat against the table.

"That the best you can do?" he asked. "What about if we give you a little help?"

So saying, he went over to his bag and returned carrying his notebook. "Here, put this under your elbow. . . ."

With the notebook raising my elbow from the tabletop, my arm was almost as long as his. So when I felt the first steady pressure from his arm, I brought all my strength to bear just as suddenly as I could. To my satisfaction I managed to force his arm a little way back, and I saw the surprise in his eyes. But then he countered with a strength that forced my arm to the surface of the table in seconds. With a grunt he released my hand and stood up while I rubbed my sore muscles.

"That was better," he said, "but you need to harden those muscles if you're going to survive. Hungry, Master Ward?"

I nodded.

"Right then, I'll cook us some breakfast and after that we'd better start getting to know each other."

He opened his bag to reveal two empty wine bottles

along with other provisions: cheese, eggs, ham, pork, and two large fish. "Caught this morning, these!" he exclaimed. "Don't come much fresher. We'll have one between us now and the other for breakfast tomorrow. Ever cooked fish?"

I shook my head.

"No, *you've* got the luxury of that boggart doing all your chores for you," said Arkwright, shaking his own head in disapproval. "Well, here we have to do things for ourselves. So you'd better watch me while I cook this fish because you'll be doing the other one tomorrow. You don't mind doing your share of the cooking, do you?"

"Of course not," I replied. I just hoped I'd be able to manage. The Spook didn't think much of my cooking.

"That's all right, then. When we've finished breakfast, I'll show you around the mill. We'll see if you're as brave as your master makes out."

# CHAPTER VI
## WATER LORE

THE fish tasted good, and Arkwright seemed keen to chat as we ate.

"The first thing to remember about the territory I protect," he said, "is that there's a lot of water about. Water is very wet and that can be a problem. . . ."

I thought he was trying to make

another joke so I smiled, but he glared at me fiercely. "That's not meant to be funny, Master Ward. In fact it's not funny at all. By wet I mean that it saturates everything, soaks into the ground, into the body, and into the very soul. It permeates this whole area and is the key to all the difficulties we face. It's an environment within which denizens of the dark thrive. We are of the land, not of water. So it is very difficult to deal with such creatures."

I nodded. "Does permeate mean the same thing as saturate?"

"That it does, Master Ward. Water gets everywhere and into everything. And there's a lot of it about. There's Morecambe Bay for a start, which is like a big bite taken out of the County by the sea. Dangerous channels like deep rivers cross the shifting sands of the bay. People cross over when the tides permit, but tides come in fast and sometimes a thick mist comes down. Every year the sea claims coaches, horses, and passengers there. They vanish without a trace.

"Then there are the lakes to the north. Deceptively calm some days but very deep. And there are dangerous things that come out of the lakes."

"Mr. Gregory told me that you bound the Coniston Ripper. And that it had killed over thirty people before you made the shores of the lake safe."

Arkwright positively glowed when I said that. "Aye, Master Ward. At first it was a mystery that baffled the locals," he explained. "It seized lone fishermen and pulled them overboard. People assumed the missing men had drowned, but if so, why weren't their bodies washed ashore? At last there were too many victims and I was called in. It wasn't an easy task. I suspected a ripper, but where was its lair? And once drained of blood, what had happened to the bodies? Well, Master Ward, you need both patience and perseverance in this job, and finally I tracked it down.

"Its lair was a cave right under the lakeshore. It dragged its victims up onto a rock shelf and fed at leisure. So I dug into the cave from the bank above. Its lair was a sight straight out of a nightmare. It was full of bones and corpses—rotting flesh heaving with maggots, together with other more recent bodies emptied of blood. I'll never forget that stench. I waited for that ripper for three days and nights until it finally arrived with a fresh victim. It was too late to save the fisherman, but I finished the ripper off with salt and iron."

"When Mr. Gilbert met us at the canal, he said you'd gone north to deal with a body found in the water that had been drained of blood like two others before it. Was that the victim of a ripper? Is there another one at large?"

Arkwright stared through the window as if deep in thought, and there was quite a delay before he answered. "No, it was a water witch. Their numbers have been increasing lately. But she was well away by the time I arrived. She'll strike again no doubt, and we'll just have to hope that she takes her next victim a little closer to home so that I'll have time to hunt her down. But it's not just rippers and water witches we have to watch out for. There are skelts to beware of. . . ."

"Ever heard of a *skelt*?" he asked me.

I shook my head.

"It's very rare and lives in crevices, either submerged or close to water. Instead of a flexible tongue, a long hollow, bony tube protrudes from its snout. The tube's sharp and pointed at the end so the creature can suck up the blood of its victims."

"That sounds awful," I said.

"Oh, it is," replied Arkwright. "But that foul creature's sometimes a victim, too. It's occasionally used in water-witch rituals. After it's taken the blood of its victim—one chosen for it by the witches—draining him slowly over a period of days until he breathes his last, the witches dismember the skelt and eat it alive. The blood magic gained is thrice that obtained by the witch draining the victim directly."

Arkwright suddenly stood up and reached across the sink to seize the big knife on the window ledge. He brought it back to the table.

"I killed a skelt once using this!" he said, placing it

before me. "That blade's got a lot of silver in the alloy, just like the blade on my staff. I took the skelt by surprise and cut its limbs off! A very useful weapon, that. I also caught a young one near this canal less than five years ago. Two in five years suggests that they're increasing in number."

By now we'd finished our breakfast so Arkwright eased his chair away from the table and patted his belly. "Did you enjoy the fish, Master Ward?"

I nodded. "Yes, thanks, it was really good."

"The leg of a water witch would be even better," he said. "You might get to try it before your six months is up."

My jaw dropped and I stared at him in astonishment. He ate witches?

But then he burst out laughing. "Just my sense of humor, Master Ward. I wouldn't touch a witch's leg with a barge pole, even roasted to perfection. Mind you, my dogs wouldn't be so fussy — as you might find out one day!"

I wondered where he kept his dogs. I'd neither seen nor heard them.

"But it's water witches that are the worst problem in these parts," Arkwright went on. "Unlike other witches they *can* cross water—especially stagnant water. They can stay under the surface for hours at a time without breathing; they bury themselves in the mud or marsh, waiting for an unsuspecting victim to walk by. Would you like to see one, Master Ward?"

In the summer the Spook and I had been to Pendle and fought the three main witch-clans there. It had been hard and we'd been lucky to survive, so I'd had my fill of witches for a while. It must have shown on my face, because when I nodded, Arkwright gave a little smile.

"You don't look very enthusiastic, Master Ward. Don't you worry. She won't bite. I've got her safe and sound, as you'll soon see! I'll give you a tour of the mill and show you the witch, but first let's sort out your sleeping arrangements. Follow me!"

He left the kitchen and I followed him up the stairs and into the single bedroom with the bare mattress. I thought he was going to confirm that this would be my room, but instead he dragged the mattress from the bed.

"Let's get this downstairs!" he said briskly, and together we carried it down to the kitchen. That done, he went back up, returning immediately with a bundle of sheets and blankets.

"They're a bit on the damp side," he said, "but they'll soon dry out in this kitchen, and then we'll get them back to your room again. Well now, I've got a few things to do upstairs, but I'll be back within the hour. In the meantime, why don't you write up your first lesson on water witches and skelts? You have brought your notebook with you?"

I nodded.

"Well, go and get it, then!" he ordered.

Sensing his impatience, I rummaged in my bag and brought the notebook back to the table, along with my pen and a small bottle of ink, while Arkwright went upstairs.

I wrote up everything I could remember about my first lesson and wondered what Arkwright was doing for so long upstairs. At one point I thought I heard him talking to someone. But after less than an hour he came down, and as he passed by, I smelled wine on his breath. Then, holding a lantern aloft and gripping his staff in his left hand, he led the way into the room I'd first entered.

Apart from the absence of the candlestick, which I'd taken into the kitchen, it was just as before: a chair in each corner, crates and empty wine bottles, the solitary table, and three boarded-up windows. But the brighter light from the lantern revealed something I hadn't noticed previously.

To the right of the outer door was a trapdoor. Arkwright handed his staff to me, bent, and with his free hand grasped the iron ring and pulled it open. Wooden steps led down into the darkness, and there was the sound of the stream rushing over its bed of pebbles.

"Well, Master Ward," Arkwright said, "usually it's safe enough but I've been away from home for six days so anything could have happened in the meantime. Stay close — just in case."

With that he started to descend, and I followed him into a deeper gloom, carrying his staff, which was far heavier than the ones I was used to. A stink of damp and rotten wood assailed my nostrils, and I found myself standing not in a flagged cellar, but in mud on the bank of the stream. To our left stood the huge arc of the static water-wheel.

"I thought I heard that wheel turning last night," I murmured. I was sure it hadn't really turned and was all part of the strange haunting; something that had happened in the past. But I was curious and half hoped that Arkwright might tell me what was going on.

Instead he glared at me and I could see the anger rising red in his face. "Does it look like it's capable of moving?" he shouted.

I shook my head and took a step backward. Arkwright cursed under his breath, turned his back on me, and led us under the mill, bowing his head as he walked.

Soon we came to a square pit, and Arkwright halted with the toes of his big boots actually hanging over its edge. He beckoned me forward and I stood at his side but kept my own toes well clear. It was a witch pit with thirteen iron bars so there was no danger of falling in. That didn't mean you were entirely safe, though. A witch could reach up through the bars and grasp your ankle. Some were very fast and strong and could move faster than you could blink your eye. I wasn't taking any chances.

"A water witch can burrow, Master Ward, so we have to thwart that. Although you can see only the top row of bars, this is effectively a cage in the shape of a cube with the other five surfaces buried in the earth."

That was something I was already familiar with. The Spook used that type of cage to confine lamia witches, which were also adept at burrowing.

Arkwright held the lantern out over the pit. "Look down and tell me what you see."

I could see water reflecting the light, but at the side of the pit was a narrow muddy shelf. There was something on it but I couldn't quite make it out. It seemed to be half buried in the mud.

"I can't see it properly," I admitted.

He sighed impatiently and held out his hand for his staff. "Well, it takes a trained eye. In bad light you could step on a creature like this without realizing it. It would fasten its teeth into you and drag you down to a watery grave within seconds. Maybe this'll help. . . ."

He took the staff from me and slowly lowered it, blade first, between the two bars directly above the shelf before jabbing suddenly downward. There was a shriek of pain, and I caught a glimpse of long tangled hair and hate-filled eyes as something flung itself off the ledge into the water, making a tremendous splash.

"She'll stay at the bottom for an hour or more now. But that certainly woke her up, didn't it?" he said with a cruel smile.

I didn't like the way he'd hurt the witch just so that I could see her better. It seemed unnecessary—not something my own master would have done.

"Mind you, she's not always that sluggish. Knowing I'd be away for quite a few days, I gave her an extra shot of salt. Put too much into the water and it'd finish her off, so you have to get your calculations right. That's how we keep her docile. Works the same way with skelts—with anything that comes out of fresh water. That's why I have a moat running around the garden. It may be shallow but it's got a very high concentration of salt. It's to stop anything getting in or out. This witch here would be dead in seconds if she managed to escape from this pit and tried to cross that moat. And it stops things from the marsh getting into the garden.

"Anyway, Master Ward, I'm not as soft-hearted as Mr. Gregory. He keeps live witches in pits because he can't bring himself to finish them off, whereas I do it just to punish them. They serve one year in a pit for every life they've taken—two years for the life of a child. Then I fish them out and kill them. Now, let's see if we can catch a glimpse of that skelt I told you I'd captured near the canal. . . ."

He led the way to another pit almost twice the size of the first. It was similarly covered with iron bars, but there were many more of them and they were far closer together. Here there was no mud shelf, just an expanse of dirty water. I had a feeling that it was very deep.

Arkwright stared down at the water and shook his head. "Looks like it's lurking near the bottom. Still docile after the big dose of salt I tipped into the water. It's best to let sleeping skelts lie. There'll be plenty of opportunity to see it before your six months are up. Right. We'll take a walk around the garden now. . . ."

"Does she have a name?" I asked, nodding at the witch pit as we passed.

Arkwright came to a halt, looked at me, and shook his head. There were several expressions flickering across his face, none of them good. Clearly he thought I'd said something really stupid.

"She's just a common water witch," he said, his voice scathing. "Whatever she calls herself, I neither know nor care! Don't ask foolish questions!"

I was suddenly angry and felt my face redden. "It can be useful to know a witch's name!" I snapped. "Mr.

Gregory keeps a record of all the witches that he's either heard of or encountered personally."

Arkwright pushed his face very close to mine so that I could smell his sour breath. "You're not at Chipenden now, boy. For the present I'm your master and you'll do things my way. And if you ever speak to me in that tone of voice again, I'll beat you to within an inch of your life! Do I make myself clear?"

I bit my lip to stop myself answering back, then nodded and looked at my boots. Why had I spoken out of turn like that? Well, one reason was that I thought he was wrong. Another was that I didn't like the tone of voice *he'd* used to speak to *me*. But I shouldn't have let my anger show. After all, my master had told me that Arkwright did things differently and that I would have to adapt to his ways.

"Follow me, Master Ward," Arkwright said, his voice softer, "and I'll show you the garden."

Rather than leading the way back up the steps to the front room, Arkwright walked back toward the waterwheel.

At first I thought he was going to squeeze past it, but then I noticed a narrow door to the left, which he unlocked. We strode out into the garden. I saw that the mist had lifted but still lingered in the distance beyond the trees. We made a complete inner circuit of the moat; from time to time Arkwright halted to point things out.

"That's Monastery Marsh," he said, jabbing his finger toward the southwest. "And beyond it is Monks' Hill. Never try to cross that marsh alone—or at least not until you know your way around or have studied a map. Beyond the marsh, more directly to the west, is a high earthen bank that holds back the tide from the bay." I looked around, taking in everything he said. "Now," he continued, "I want you to meet somebody else. . . ."

That said, he put two fingers in his mouth and let out a long, piercing whistle. He repeated it, and almost immediately from the direction of the marsh, I heard something running toward us. Two large wolfhounds bounded into view, both leaping the moat with ease. I was used to farm dogs, but these animals had a savage air about them and seemed to be heading directly toward me. They had more wolf in them than dog, and had I been alone, I'm sure they'd have pulled me to the ground in seconds. One was a dirty-looking gray with streaks of black; its companion was as black as coal but for a dash of gray at the tip of its tail. Their jaws gaped wide, teeth ready to bite.

But at Arkwright's command, "Down!" they halted immediately, sat back upon their haunches, and gazed up at their master, tongues lolling from their open mouths.

"The black one's the bitch," Arkwright said. "Her name is Claw. Don't turn your back on her; she's dangerous. And this is Tooth," he added, pointing to the gray. "Better temperament, but they're both working dogs, not pets. They obey me because I feed 'em well, and they know not to cross me. The only affection they get is from each other. They're a pair, all right. Inseparable."

"I lived on a farm. We had working dogs," I told him.

"Did you now? Well, you'll have an inkling of what I mean. No room for sentiment with a working dog. Treat them fairly, feed them well, but they have to earn their keep in return. I'm afraid there's little in common between farm dogs and these two, though. At night they're usually kept chained up close to the house and trained to bark if anything approaches. During the day they hunt rabbits and hares out on the edge of the marsh and keep watch for anything that might threaten the house.

"But when I go out on a job, they come with me. Once they get a scent they never let it go. They hunt down whatever I set 'em on. And if it proves necessary, on my command they kill, too. As I said, they work hard and feed well. When I kill a witch, they get something extra in their diet. I cut out her heart and throw it to them. That, as your master will already have told you, stops her from coming back to this world in another body and also from using her dead one to scratch her way to the surface. That's why I don't keep dead witches. It saves time and space."

There was a ruthless edge to Arkwright—he certainly wasn't a man to cross. As we turned to walk back to the house, the dogs following at our heels, I happened to

glance up and saw something that surprised me. Two separate columns of smoke were curling upward from the
roof of the mill. One must be from the stove in the
kitchen. But where was the second fire? I wondered if it
was coming from the locked room I'd been warned about.
Was there something or someone up there Arkwright didn't
want me to see? Then I remembered about the unquiet
dead that he allowed the run of his house. I knew he was
a man who was quick to anger, and I was pretty sure
that he wouldn't want me prying, but I was feeling very
curious.

"Mr. Arkwright," I began politely, "could I ask you a
question?"

"That's why you're here, Master Ward."

"It's about what you put in the note you left me. Why do
you allow the dead to walk in your house?"

Again an angry expression flickered across his face.
"The dead here are family. *My* family, Master Ward. And
it's not something I wish to discuss with you or anyone
else, so you'll have to contain your curiosity. When you

get back to Mr. Gregory, ask him. He knows something about it, and no doubt he'll tell you. But I don't want to hear another word on the matter. Do you understand? It's something I just don't talk about."

I nodded and followed him back to the house. I might be there to ask questions, but getting them answered was another matter!

# CHAPTER VII
# FROG KICKS

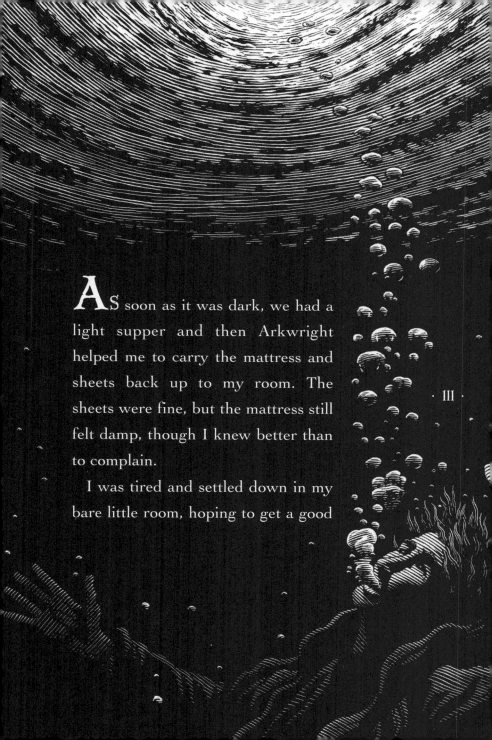

As soon as it was dark, we had a light supper and then Arkwright helped me to carry the mattress and sheets back up to my room. The sheets were fine, but the mattress still felt damp, though I knew better than to complain.

I was tired and settled down in my bare little room, hoping to get a good

· III

night's sleep, but within the hour I was awoken by the same disturbing noises I'd heard the night before: the deep rumble of the waterwheel and that terrible scream that made the hairs on the back of my neck stand on end. But this time, as the sound finally faded away, I heard two sets of footsteps climbing the stairs from the kitchen.

I was sure that Arkwright was still in bed, so I knew it had to be the ghosts that haunted the mill. The sounds reached the landing and passed my bedroom door. I heard the door of the next room open and then close, and something sat down on the large double bed—the one with the saturated sheets. The springs creaked as if something was turning over, trying to get comfortable, and then there was utter silence.

For a long while the peace continued, and I was just starting to relax and drift off to sleep when a voice spoke from the other side of my bedroom wall.

*"I can't get myself comfy,"* complained a man's voice. *"Oh, I wish I could sleep in a dry bed just once more!"*

*"Oh, I'm sorry, Abe. So sorry. I don't mean to cause you such*

*discomfort. It's the water from the millstream. The water I drowned in. Can't ever get away from it, no matter how hard I try. My broken bones ache but the wet plagues me most of all. Why don't you go and leave me be? Nothing good can ever come of our staying together like this."*

*"Leave you? How can I ever leave you, my love? What's a bit of discomfort when we've got each other?"*

At that the woman began to cry, filling the whole house with misery and pain. Moments later there were heavy boots descending the stairs from the room above. But these footsteps weren't ghostly. I'd thought Arkwright had gone to bed, but he must have been upstairs in that topmost room.

He came along the landing and I heard him halt at the door beyond mine and open it before calling out: "Please come upstairs. Why don't you climb the stairs to my room, where you'll both be warm and comfortable? Let's talk. Tell me tales from the days when we were all happy together."

There was a long pause and then I heard him climb the

stairs once more. I didn't hear the ghosts following him, but after a while there was the murmur of his voice from above, as if he were engaging somebody in conversation.

I couldn't make out what was being said, but at one point Arkwright laughed with what sounded like forced joviality. After a while I drifted off to sleep again, and when I awoke, gray light filled the room.

I was up before my new master and managed to cook the fish to his satisfaction. We ate in silence. I just didn't feel comfortable with him and really missed living with the Spook and Alice. John Gregory could be a bit stern at times, but I liked him. When I occasionally spoke out of turn, he put me firmly in my place, but he certainly didn't threaten to beat me.

I wasn't looking forward to my lessons much, but I would have felt even worse if I'd known what was going to happen next.

"Can you swim, Master Ward?" Arkwright asked as he rose from the table.

I shook my head. There'd never been much need to learn. The only water near our farm had been a few shallow streams and ponds while the nearest river had a good solid bridge over it. And as for my master, John Gregory, he'd never even mentioned swimming. For all I knew he couldn't swim himself.

"Well, we need to sort that out as soon as possible. Follow me! And don't bother to bring your staff. Mine's the only one we'll be needing. You won't be needing your jacket or cloak either!"

I followed Arkwright through the garden and downstream toward the canal. Once up on the canal bank, he came to a halt and pointed down at the water.

"Looks cold, doesn't it?"

I nodded. It made me shiver just to look at it.

"Well, it's only October now and it'll be a lot colder before the winter's out, but sometimes we've no choice but to plunge in. Being able to swim could save your life in this part of the County. And what chance would you have against a water witch if you couldn't swim? So jump in, Master Ward, and let's make a start. The first part's the hardest and the sooner you get it over with the better!"

I just stared at the murky canal water. I couldn't believe I was supposed to jump into that. When I hesitated and turned back to face him, about to protest, Arkwright sighed and reversed his staff so that he was gripping the end with the murderous spear and barbs. Next, to my utter astonishment, he leaned forward and pushed me hard in the chest. I overbalanced, fell back, and hit the canal with a tremendous splash. The shock of the cold water made me gasp, but by then my head was already under the water and I began to choke as it surged up my nose and into my open mouth.

For a moment I didn't know which way up I was. Only too aware that I was out of my depth, I thrashed around. Mercifully, my head soon bobbed above the surface and I could see the sky. I heard Arkwright shout something, but then, before I could even suck in a breath, I went under again. I was floundering, panicking, drowning, moving my arms and legs in all directions, trying to grab hold of something, anything, that would pull me to safety.

Why didn't Arkwright help? Couldn't he see that I was drowning? But then something prodded me in the chest and I reached out and gripped it tightly. Holding on like grim death, I felt myself being pulled through the water. The next moment someone wrapped their fingers tightly in my hair and dragged me to the surface.

I was against the bank, looking up into Arkwright's grinning face. I tried to speak, tried to give him a piece of my mind. How stupid was that? He'd tried to drown me! But I was still choking and gasping for breath, water not words being expelled from my mouth.

"Listen, Master Ward, when a diver wants to go deep, the easiest way is for him to hold a big stone so the weight takes him down quickly. You won't sink to the bottom because it's easier to float than sink. Your body does it naturally. All you need to do is keep your head up so you can breathe and learn a few strokes. Have you seen a frog kick its legs?" he asked me.

I looked at him in puzzlement. Only now was I able to

suck in the first proper lungfuls of air. It was so good just to be able to breathe.

"I'll pull you along with my staff, Master Ward. Practice frog kicks. We'll work on your arms tomorrow. . . ."

I wanted to let go of his staff and pull myself onto the bank, but before I could move or protest, Arkwright began walking south along the canal bank, his left hand pulling the staff so that I had to follow.

"Kick!" he commanded.

I did as he ordered. The chill was starting to get into my bones so I needed to move in order to keep warm. After a few hundred yards he changed direction.

"Kick! Kick! Kick! Come on, Master Ward, you can do better than that. Kick harder! Imagine a water witch is after you!"

After about fifteen minutes he pulled me out of the water. I was cold and saturated and my boots were full of dirty water. Arkwright looked down at them and shook his head.

"Of course, swimming is a lot easier without your heavy

boots, but you might not get the chance to take them off. Anyway, let's get you back to the mill so you can dry off."

I spent the rest of the morning wrapped in a blanket before the stove, getting the warmth back into my body. Arkwright left me alone and spent a lot of the time upstairs. I was far from happy at the methods he'd used to try and teach me to swim and certainly wasn't looking forward to my next lesson.

Late in the afternoon he led me out into the garden, this time telling me to bring my staff. He stopped in a clearing and turned to face me.

I looked at him in astonishment. He was holding his staff raised at forty-five degrees, as if he intended to hit me with it or defend himself. But he'd reversed it again so that the blade was at the bottom, the thicker end at the top.

"Turn your staff as I've done!" he commanded. "No doubt your blade would stay retracted but we wouldn't want any accidents, would we? Now, try and hit me! Let's see what you're made of!"

I swung at him halfheartedly a few times, and he parried each blow easily.

"That the best you can do?" he asked. "I'm trying to see what you're capable of so I know how to help you improve. Try harder. Don't worry, you won't hurt me. Mr. Gregory said you were good at jabbing. Let's see what you can do. . . ."

So I tried. I really tried. I swung fast until I was breathing hard, and then finally I tried a jab—the special trick my master had taught me. You feinted with one hand before flicking the staff to the other. It was a trick that had saved my life when I'd faced the witch assassin Grimalkin. I felt sure I'd get through Arkwright's guard, but when I tried it, he knocked aside my staff with ease.

But he seemed satisfied that I'd finally tried my best and started showing me how to position my feet better as I made each lunge. We carried on until it was almost dark and then he called a halt.

"Well, Master Ward, this is only the beginning. Get a good night's sleep because it'll be an even harder day tomorrow. I'll start by getting you to work with the dogs. Then it'll be back to the canal for your second swimming lesson, followed by more combat training. Next time I'll be trying to hit *you*! Let's hope you can defend yourself or you'll have a bruise to show for each defensive skill you lack."

We went in to a well-deserved supper. It had been a difficult day, to say the least, but there was one thing I did have to admit. Arkwright's methods might be harsh but he was a good teacher. I felt that I'd learned a lot already.

# CHAPTER VIII
## THE FISHERMAN'S WIFE

As it happened, I didn't get any training the next day. We'd no sooner finished our breakfast than there was the sound of a distant bell. It rang three times.

"Sounds like trouble," Arkwright observed. "Bring your staff, Master Ward. Let's go and see what the matter is."

That said, he led the way into the garden, across the salt moat, and toward the canal. A tall elderly man was waiting beneath the bell. He was clutching a piece of paper to his chest.

"So you've decided . . . ," Arkwright said when we drew near.

The man nodded. He was thin as well as tall, with gray, wispy hair around his temples. It looked as though a strong gust of wind would blow him over. He held the paper out so that Arkwright could see. There were nineteen names on one side, three on the other. "We had a vote yesterday," he said, a plaintive whine to his voice. "It was decided by a large majority. We don't want her living nearby. It's not right. Not right at all . . ."

"I told you last time," Arkwright said, sounding irritated. "We don't even know for sure that she *is* one. Have they any children?"

The thin man shook his head. "No children, but if she *is* one, your dogs will know, won't they? They'll be able to tell?"

"Perhaps, but it's not always as simple as that. Anyway, I'll come and sort it out—one way or the other."

The man nodded and hastened away northward along the canal.

When he'd gone, Arkwright sighed. "Not one of my favorite jobs, this. A bunch of *good* folks farther north think a local fisherman's living with a selkie," he said, the word *good* heavy with sarcasm. "They've been dithering for almost a year, trying to make up their minds. Now they want me to deal with it."

"A selkie? What's that?" I asked.

"A selkie is a shape-shifter and what's commonly known as a seal-woman, Master Ward. Mostly they spend their lives in the sea but occasionally they take a fancy to a man—perhaps spying him when he's out in his boat or mending his nets. The more attached to him they become, the more human they appear. The change takes a day or so at the most—they shift into a perfect female form, into the semblance of an extremely attractive woman. The fisherman usually falls head over heels in love at the very first meeting and marries the selkie.

"They can't have children, but apart from that it's a perfectly happy marriage. I don't see the harm in it, but if there's a complaint, we have to act. It's part of the job. We have to make people feel safe. That means using the dogs. Selkies sometimes live among people for years before there's even the faintest whiff of suspicion. Mostly it's the women who stir up their menfolk to complain. They get jealous. You see, as well as having more than her fair share of beauty, a selkie hardly ages at all."

"That fisherman—if his wife is a selkie," I asked, "is he likely to know?"

"After a while some work it out. But they don't complain. . . ."

With that Arkwright shrugged his shoulders and let out a long piercing whistle. Almost immediately it was answered by the distant barking of the dogs, and they bounded up, jaws agape, teeth threatening. Soon he was leading us north, striding along the canal bank with Tooth and Claw panting at his heels and me following a few paces behind. Before long we passed the man from the village; Arkwright didn't even nod in his direction.

I didn't like the sound of this job at all, and hard though he seemed, Arkwright clearly wasn't happy about it either. In one respect a selkie reminded me of a lamia: They could also shape-shift slowly into human form. I thought of Meg, the lamia witch my master once loved. How would he have felt if someone had gone after her with dogs? No better than the fisherman would feel when we went after his wife. My mam was probably a lamia, too, just like her sisters, and I knew how my dad would feel if she was hunted down like this. The whole situation made me feel bad. If the fisherman's wife did no harm, why did she have to be hunted?

We left the canal, heading west toward the coast, and soon a level expanse of flat, light brown sand came into view. The day was chilly—there was no warmth in the sun, although it was sparkling on the distant sea. Giving the wolfhounds a wide berth, I moved up to walk at Arkwright's side. I was curious and had questions to ask.

"Do selkies have any powers?" I asked. "Do they use dark magic?"

He shook his head without looking at me. "Their only real power is to shift their shape," he replied morosely. "Once in human shape, they can revert back in minutes if threatened."

"Does a selkie belong to the dark?" I asked.

"Not directly," he answered. "They're like humans in that respect: They can go either way."

Soon we passed through a small hamlet of seven or so houses where the faint stink of rotten fish tainted the air. There were fishing nets and a couple of small boats in view but no sign of any people. Not even a twitch of lace curtains. They must have seen Arkwright coming and knew to stay indoors.

Once clear of the hamlet, I saw a solitary cottage in the distance and saw a man mending his nets on a small hillock behind it. In front on the edge of the sands, a washing line stretched from a metal hook in the wall by the front door to a wooden post. Clothes flapped on only half of the line. A woman came out of the cottage carrying an armful of wet clothes and a handful of pegs and started to hang out her washing.

"Well, let's see what's what," Arkwright growled, giving a low whistle. Immediately both dogs bounded forward. "Don't worry, Master Ward," he continued. "They're well-trained. If she's human, they won't so much as lick her!"

He suddenly began to sprint toward the house, and at that moment the fisherman looked up from his mending and came to his feet. His hair was white and he looked quite old. I saw then that my master wasn't running toward the woman; his target was the fisherman. But the dogs were. The woman looked up, dropped her washing, pulled her skirts above her knees, and began to run toward the distant sea.

Without thinking I began to run, too, following the dogs toward their prey. Was she a selkie? If not, why had she run away? Perhaps her neighbors were vindictive and she'd been expecting trouble. Or maybe she was simply afraid of dogs; some people were. And Tooth and Claw would scare anybody. But something about the way she made directly for the sea unnerved me.

She looked young—far younger than the fisherman, young enough to be his daughter. We were closing on her now, despite the fact that she was running fast, long hair streaming behind her, legs pumping. She seemed to have no chance of outrunning Tooth and Claw. The sea was still a long way out. But then I noticed the channel directly ahead. It was like a river running through the sands, and the tide was racing in from the west. The choppy water already looked deep. Claw was at the woman's heels now, jaws open wide, but suddenly she put on an extra spurt, almost leaving the dog standing.

Then she began to throw off her clothes as she ran and dived straight into the water. I reached the edge of the channel, looking down into the gulley. There was no sign of her. Had she drowned? Chosen to die that way rather than be ripped apart by the dogs?

The dogs were howling, running along the banks but

not following. Then a face and shoulders appeared briefly above the water. The woman glanced back toward me and I knew. . . .

It was no longer a human face. The eyes were bulbous, the skin sleek. She was a selkie, all right. And now she was safe in her watery home. But I was surprised by the dogs. Why hadn't they pursued her into the sea?

She was swimming powerfully up the channel against the surge of the tide, heading for the open sea. I watched her bobbing head for a few moments until she disappeared from sight. Then I turned and walked slowly back toward the cottage, the dogs following forlornly at my heels. In the distance I could see Arkwright, his arms wrapped around the fisherman, holding him fast. He'd prevented him from going to the aid of his wife.

As I drew closer, Arkwright released the man, who began to wave his arms frantically. Up close he looked older than ever.

"What harm were we doing? What harm?" wailed the fisherman, tears streaming down his face. "My life's over now. She was all I lived for. Nearly twenty years we've been together, and you end it like that. And for what? The word of a few jealous so-called neighbors. What kind of man are you? She was gentle and kind and wouldn't harm a soul!"

Arkwright shook his head but didn't answer. He turned his back on the fisherman, and we strode away toward the hamlet, beyond which dark, heavy rain clouds were gathering. As we approached, doors started opening and curtains twitched. Only one person came out into the street, however: the thin man who'd rung the bell and summoned us to this unhappy task. He approached and held out a handful of coins. It looked like they'd taken a collection to pay my master's bill. It was a surprisingly prompt payment. John Gregory rarely got paid immediately after a job. He often had to wait months—sometimes until after the next harvest.

I thought for a moment that Arkwright wasn't going to accept the money. Even when it was in his hand, he looked more likely to throw it back in the man's face than put it in his pocket. But pocket it he did and without a word moved on up the street.

"Won't she come back when we've gone?" I asked as we began to walk back toward the canal.

"They never come back, Master Ward," Arkwright answered, his face grim. "Nobody knows why but she'll spend years out at sea now. Maybe the rest of her long life. Unless she spies another man she takes a fancy to. Perhaps she'll get lonely out there. . . ."

"Why didn't the dogs follow her into the water?" I asked.

Arkwright shrugged. "Had they caught her first she'd have been dead by now; make no mistake. But she's very strong in her own element and well able to defend herself. Left alone she's harmless, so I don't ever put the dogs at risk unnecessarily. With a water witch it's different and I expect the animals to put their lives on the line. But for a seal-woman, why bother? She's no real threat to anybody. She's away now and the villagers will feel safer in their beds tonight. So our job's done."

It seemed cruel to me, and I was far from happy at having taken part in what seemed an unnecessary act. Nearly twenty years they'd been together, and now the fisherman would face a lonely and bitter old age. I vowed to myself, there and then, that when I became a spook, there were some jobs I wouldn't touch.

# CHAPTER IX

## WHACKS AND LUMPS!

WE were back at the mill by early afternoon just as it started to rain. I'd hoped that we were going to eat, but Arkwright told me to get my notebook and sit at the kitchen table. It seemed that he was going to give me a lesson.

I sat waiting for quite a while, and finally he came out of the front room

clutching a lit lantern and a bottle of red wine, which was already half empty. Had he drunk all that just now? He wore a scowl darker than a thundercloud and didn't look in any mood for teaching.

"Write up what I taught you this morning," he said, placing the lantern in the center of the table. I looked at it in surprise: It was a bit gloomy in the kitchen but still light enough to work by. Then he took a big gulp from the wine bottle and stared through the grimy kitchen window at the torrential rain cascading from the roof.

While I wrote, working within the large circle of yellow light, Arkwright just continued to stare, taking the occasional swig from the bottle. By the time I'd written up all I'd learned about kelpies, it was almost empty.

"Finished, Master Ward?" he asked as I put down my pen.

I nodded and gave him a smile, which he didn't return. Instead he drained the last of the wine and came swiftly to his feet.

"I think it's time for some whacks and lumps! Get your staff and follow me!"

My mouth opened and I looked at him in astonishment. I was nervous, too. I didn't like the hard, cruel gleam in his eye. He snatched up his own staff and the lantern and strode off, his shoulders rolling aggressively. So I picked up my staff and rushed to follow at his heels.

He led me through the kitchen and along the corridor to the door at the end. It had two heavy bars but both of them were drawn back.

"Ever been inside here, Master Ward?"

I shook my head, and Arkwright opened the door and stamped down a couple of steps into the gloom. I followed him, and he hung the lantern from a hook in the middle of the ceiling. The first thing I noticed was that the room had no windows. It was perhaps ten feet by ten feet and set lower than the rest of the house, with stone flags rather than a wooden floor.

"What are whacks and lumps?" I asked nervously.

"It's the phrase I sometimes use for practicals. You'll have practiced throwing your chain in Mr. Gregory's garden and using your staff against that dead tree stump.

Yesterday we took it a step further when you tried to hit me and failed. But now it's time to move on to something a little more painful. I'm going to do my best to whack you with my staff. No doubt you'll suffer a few lumps and bruises, but you'll gain useful combat skills as well. Come on, Master Ward. Let's see what you're made of!"

That said, he swung his staff at me, aiming for my head. Just in time I stepped backward, the heavy wooden end missing my nose by inches. He came at me again and I was forced to back away.

The Spook often made me practice the physical skills we used in fighting the dark. Trained and watched by my master, I'd worked at them until I was weary. But it had paid off in the end. In dangerous situations they'd saved my life. But I'd never fought against *him*, staff against staff. And Arkwright had been drinking again, which seemed to make him more hot-tempered.

He came in fast with his second blow, swinging his staff hard. Just in time I managed to block it with my own, the contact jarring up my arms and into my shoulders. I was moving widdershins, retreating warily, wondering if he really did intend to hurt me or was simply forcing me to practice my defense.

The answer came quickly. He feinted to the right, then swung his staff in a sharp arc to strike high on my left shoulder. The shock of that contact was tremendous and I immediately dropped my staff.

"Pick up your staff, Master Ward. As yet we've hardly begun. . . ."

My left hand was shaking as I grasped the staff. My shoulder was throbbing, the whole arm tingling.

"Well, you're in trouble already, Master Ward. Had you practiced and readied yourself for this eventuality, you'd have been able to fight right-handed!"

I lifted my staff in defense now, gripping it with both hands to steady it. Three blows rained in hard, three tremendous thwacks against the wood. Each time I barely managed to block; had I failed, the blows would have struck my head or body. Arkwright was breathing faster now and his face was red with anger, his eyes bulging from their sockets, the veins standing out on his temples. He looked like he wanted to kill me: Time after time he swung at me ferociously until I lost count of the blows that I'd parried. As yet, I hadn't struck a blow of my own, and my own anger was building inside me. What sort of man was this? Was this any way for a spook to train his apprentice?

He had the superior strength. He was a man and I was still a boy. But maybe I did have one thing to my advantage: speed. . . .

All I had to do was take my chance. No sooner had that thought entered my head than my chance came. He swung. I ducked. He overbalanced slightly—probably because of the wine he'd drunk—extended himself, and I struck him hard on the left shoulder, a precise retaliation for the hurt he'd inflicted on me.

But Arkwright didn't drop his staff. He just came back harder than ever. One blow caught me on the right shoulder, another on the same arm, and it was *my* staff that fell onto the flags. The next thing I knew he'd swung his staff toward my head. I tried to step back, but it caught me a glancing blow on my forehead and I stumbled to my knees.

"Get up," he said, looking down at me. "I didn't hit you that hard. Just a little tap to show you what could have happened in a real fight. That final blow *could* have meant you'd never see daylight again. Life is tough, Master Ward, and there are lots of foes out there who'd just love to see you six feet under. It's my job to train you well. My job to make sure you have the skills to stop 'em! And if it costs you a few lumps, then so be it. It'll be a price well worth paying!"

I was relieved when, at last, he declared the lesson over. The rain had stopped and he was going to check the canal to the south, taking the dogs with him. He told me to review my Latin nouns and verbs while he was away. It seemed to me that he didn't want me with him and would be happier if I went back to the Spook.

Obediently I worked on my verbs for a while but found it hard to concentrate. It was then that I heard a noise from somewhere above. Was it the first floor or the one above that?

I listened carefully at the foot of the stairs. After a few moments it started up again. It wasn't footsteps or bumps and bangs — I couldn't quite place the noise. It was a sort of crunching. Was there somebody up there? Or was it one of the ghosts I'd heard the previous night? The ghost of one of Arkwright's family?

I knew it wasn't wise to go upstairs; my new master certainly wouldn't like it. But I was bored and curious and angry with him for that blow to my head. He'd called it a "little tap" but it had been more than that. I was also just about fed up with him and his secrets.

He was out and what he didn't know wouldn't hurt him. So I set off up the stairs, one step at a time, trying to make as little noise as possible. On the first-floor landing, directly outside the double room, I paused and listened intently. I thought I could hear a faint rustling from inside. I eased open the door and entered the room, but it proved to be deserted. On the double bed, the covers were still pulled back. Once more I touched the sheet lightly with my finger. The mattress felt the same. Saturated with water. But there was something slightly different. The covers appeared to be pulled down slightly farther today.

I shivered, left the room quickly, and checked inside the other three. There, nothing seemed to have changed. I was standing in my own room when I heard the sound again. It came from the floor above.

So, very curious by now, I continued up the stairs. On the next landing there was only one door. I tried the handle and found it locked. I should have turned and gone back down the stairs then. After all, Arkwright had specifically warned me to keep away from this room. But I wasn't happy with the way he'd treated me—that and the way he often refused to answer my questions. So on impulse and a little annoyed, I pulled my special key from my pocket and opened the door.

Once inside I was struck by the size of the room. I saw by the light of two large candles that it was big. Very big.

Its floor space was the whole area of the house. The second thing I noticed was the temperature. It was warm and dry. There was another stove, twice the size of the one in the kitchen, and it was radiating heat. Next to it was a large coal scuttle, from which protruded a poker and a pair of tongs.

Bookshelves covered two whole walls—so Arkwright *did* have a library of his own. The floor was a very dark polished wood, and there was a lamb's-wool rug placed before three chairs that stood facing the stove. It was then that I noticed something in the far, rear corner. . . .

At first glance I'd thought that the candles were resting on two low oblong tables. But I was wrong. They were actually two coffins, side by side, each supported by trestles. I walked toward them, feeling the hairs begin to rise on the back of my neck. The room was gradually growing colder. Or so it seemed. It was a warning that the unquiet dead were approaching.

I looked at the coffins and read the brass plaques. The first one was shiny and said: ABRAHAM ARKWRIGHT.

But unlike this first coffin, which was clean and polished and looked almost new, the wood of the second casket appeared rotten and was covered in mildew; to my astonishment, I could actually see steam rising from it into the warm air. The brass plate was tarnished and it was only with great difficulty that I managed to read what was etched there: AMELIA ARKWRIGHT.

Then I saw, just below the brass plate, a thin golden ring resting on the wood. It looked like a wedding ring. It must have been Amelia's.

I heard two sounds behind me: the clink of metal upon metal, then the door of the stove being opened. I spun around to see the stove door open and a poker being thrust into the burning coals. As I watched, it began to move. That was the noise I'd heard from below. The crunching, stirring sound of the fire being poked!

Afraid, I turned to leave the room immediately and ran down the stairs. What kind of ghost was this? Boggarts could manipulate matter, throwing rocks and boulders, breaking dishes and throwing pans about a kitchen. But not ghosts. Certainly not ghosts. Their power was usually confined to scaring people, very rarely driving the weak-minded to the edge of insanity. Ghosts didn't usually have the power to do you much physical harm. Sometimes they tugged at your hair; strangler ghosts put their hands about your throat and squeezed. But this was a spirit beyond anything I'd been taught about or encountered. It had lifted the heavy metal poker from the coal scuttle, opened the door of the stove, and started to poke the fire.

That was all bad enough, but there was worse to come. At the foot of the stairs, waiting in the hall, Arkwright stood clutching another half-empty bottle of wine, his face like thunder.

"I've been listening here for a few moments and couldn't believe I was hearing right. Haven't just been in your own room, have you, Master Ward? You've been med-dling. Been pushing your nose in where it doesn't belong!"

"I heard a noise upstairs," I said, halting on the bottom step. He was blocking my way.

"There are lots of noises upstairs, and as you well know, they're caused by the unquiet dead. By my family. And that's *my* business," he said, his voice now dangerously quiet, "and nothing to do with you at all. Wait here!"

Still carrying the bottle, he pushed past me roughly and ran up the stairs two at a time. I heard him walk along the landing on the first floor and go into three of the rooms. Then he went up the next flight of stairs, and I heard a bellow of rage. I'd forgotten to lock the door behind me. I knew he'd be furious that I'd gone into his private room. He wouldn't want me to see the coffins. . . .

Arkwright came bounding down the stairs and ran right at me. For a moment I thought he was going to hit me with the bottle, but he used his right hand to clout me across my left ear. Trying to dodge the blow, I over-balanced, lost my footing, and crashed onto the hall floor. I looked up, my head ringing, gasping for breath. I felt stunned and nauseous: The fall had driven all the breath from my body. Arkwright lifted his boot and I thought he was going to kick me, but instead he crouched close to my head, his furious eyes glaring into mine.

"Well," he said, his sour breath right in my face. "Let that be a lesson to you. I'm off again with the dogs to check the marsh. In the meantime get on with your studies. If this ever happens again, you won't know what's hit you!"

After he'd gone I paced backward and forward across the kitchen floor, seething with anger and hurt. No apprentice should have to endure what I'd suffered.

It didn't take me long to decide what to do. My stay with Arkwright was over. I would head back to Chipenden. No doubt the Spook would be far from pleased to see me returning so early. I'd just have to hope that he would believe everything that had happened to me and take my side.

Without further thought I picked up my bag and staff, crossed the front room to the porch door, and stepped out into the garden. I hesitated. What if the dogs were close and caught my scent?

I listened carefully but all I could hear was the whine of the wind across the marsh grass. Moments later, I was wading across the salt moat, glad to see the back of Arkwright and that dank old mill. Soon I'd be back with Alice and the Spook.

# CHAPTER X
## THE SPOOK'S LETTER

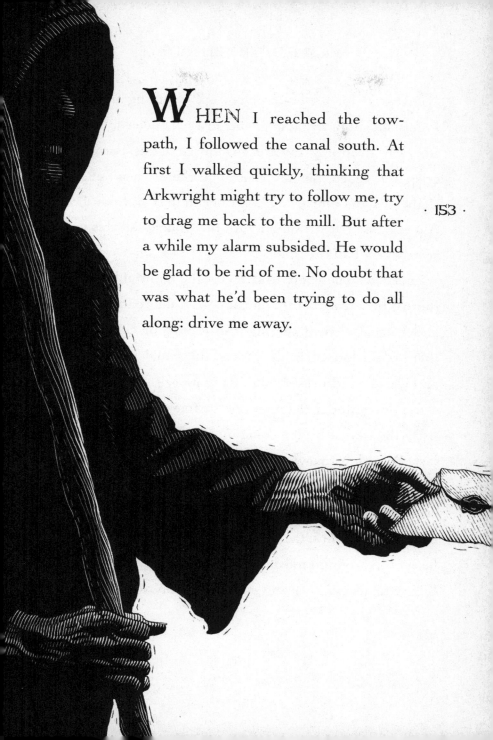

WHEN I reached the towpath, I followed the canal south. At first I walked quickly, thinking that Arkwright might try to follow me, try to drag me back to the mill. But after a while my alarm subsided. He would be glad to be rid of me. No doubt that was what he'd been trying to do all along: drive me away.

· 153 ·

I walked for an hour or so, still seething inside, but eventually both my anger and my headache faded. The sun was dropping toward the horizon but the air was crisp and sharp, the sky clear, and there wasn't even the slightest sign of mist. My heart began to soar. Soon I'd see Alice; I'd be back training with the Spook. All this would seem like a bad dream.

I needed somewhere to sleep for the night; it looked like there'd be a frost before morning. On the road the Spook and I usually spent the night in a barn or cowshed, but there were lots of bridges over the canal between here and Caster, and I resolved to wrap myself in my cloak and settle down under the next one I came to.

By the time a bridge came in sight the light was fading fast. But a low growl to my right brought me to a sudden halt. Under the hawthorn hedge that bordered the towpath crouched a large black dog. One glance told me that it was one of Arkwright's: the ferocious bitch he called Claw. Had he sent her to hunt me down? What should I do? Retreat? Or try to get past her and continue on my way?

I took a careful step forward. She remained still but was watching me intently. One more step brought me level with her and resulted in another warning growl. Watching her carefully over my right shoulder, I took another step, then another. Moments later I was striding away, but I heard her bound out onto the towpath and begin to pad along behind me. I remembered what Arkwright had said. *"Don't turn your back on her; she's dangerous."*

And now Claw was walking behind me! I glanced back and saw that she was keeping her distance. Why was she following me? I decided that I wouldn't sleep under this bridge. I'd keep walking until I reached the next one. By then the dog might have got fed up and gone home. As I reached the arch, to my dismay another wolfhound emerged and moved toward me with a low, threatening growl. It was Tooth.

Now I was scared. One big dog was in front of me, the other behind. Slowly and very deliberately, I placed my bag on the ground and readied my staff. Any sudden move and they might attack. I didn't think I could deal with both. But what choice did I have? I pressed the recess in my staff and there was a click as the blade emerged.

It was then that someone spoke from the darkness under the arch of the bridge: "I wouldn't try that if I were you, Master Ward! They'd rip your throat out before you could move!"

Arkwright stepped out to confront me. Even in the poor light I could see the sneer on his face.

"Heading back to Chipenden, are you, boy? You've barely lasted three days! That's the fastest *any* lad has run away. I thought you'd more guts than that. You're certainly not the apprentice Mr. Gregory made you out to be. . . ."

I didn't speak because anything I said was likely to provoke him to anger. I'd probably get another battering; he might even set the dogs on me. So I just pushed the blade shut and waited to see what he would do. Did he intend to drag me back to the mill?

He whistled, and both dogs took up position at his heel. Shaking his head, he walked toward me, then thrust his hand inside his cloak and pulled out an envelope.

"This letter's from your master to me," he said. "Read it and make up your mind. You can either go back to Chipenden or continue your training here."

That said, he handed me the letter and set off north along the towpath. I watched until both he and the dogs were out of sight. Then I took the letter from the envelope. It was the Spook's writing all right. It was difficult to read because by now the light was dim. Even so, I read it twice.

To Bill Arkwright

I ask you to train my apprentice, Tom Ward, beginning as soon as you possibly can. The need is urgent. As you will know from my previous letter, the Fiend has been released into the world, and the danger from the dark has increased for us all. But although I have mostly kept it from him, my fear is that soon, once again, the Fiend will attempt to destroy the boy.

I must be blunt. After the harsh way you treated my previous apprentice, I'd thought never to entrust another lad to your care. But it must be done. The threat to Tom Ward grows daily. Even if the Fiend does not come against him directly, I fear that he will send some other denizen of the dark. Either way, the boy must be toughened up and taught the hunting and combat skills he urgently needs. If the lad survives, I believe he will prove to be a powerful weapon against the dark, perhaps the most potent born into our world for many decades.

So, in the hope that I'm not making a big mistake, I reluctantly place him in your hands for a period of six months. Do what must be done. And as for you, Bill Arkwright, I offer you the same counsel as I did when you were my apprentice. To fight the dark is your duty. But is that fight worth it if, as a consequence, your own soul withers and dies? You have much to teach the boy. Teach him well as I taught you. But my hope is that, in teaching, you may also be taught. Set aside the bottle once and for all. Put your bitterness behind you and become the man you are meant to be.

John Gregory

I thrust the letter back into the envelope and pushed it into my breeches pocket. That done, I went into the darkness under the bridge and, wrapping myself in my cloak, lay on the cold, hard ground. It was a long time before I fell asleep. I'd a lot to think about.

The Spook had tried to keep his fears from me — but not very successfully. He really did think that the Fiend would come back to destroy me. That's why he'd been mollycoddling me. He'd sent me to Arkwright to be trained and toughened up. But did that mean I had to be battered black and blue by a drunkard? The Spook seemed to have had reservations. Arkwright treated another of the Spook's apprentices badly. Yet, despite that, he'd *still* sent me to this cruel new master. That meant he thought it was important. It was then that I remembered something Alice had once said to me after we'd confronted Mother Malkin and I'd stopped her burning the witch.

*"Get harder or you won't survive! Just doing what Old Gregory says won't be enough. You'll die like the others!"*

Many of my master's apprentices had been killed while learning their trade. It was a dangerous job, all right, especially now that the Devil had entered our world. But did getting harder mean that I had to be cruel like Arkwright? Let my own soul wither and die?

The arguments went round and round in my head for a long time, but at last I fell into a deep, dream-less sleep and despite the cold slept soundly until the first gray light of dawn. It was another misty morn-ing, but now my mind was clear and sharp. On wak-ing I found that I'd arrived at a decision. I would go back to Arkwright and continue my training.

Firstly, I trusted my master. Despite his reluctance he thought going to Arkwright was the right thing to do. Secondly, my own instincts agreed. I sensed something important here. If I went back to Chipenden, I would miss the training that was supposed to take place here. And if I missed it, I would be the poorer for it. Still, it would be hard, and I certainly didn't relish the thought of spending six months with Arkwright.

When I got back to the mill, the front door was unlocked and I could smell cooking even before I reached the kitchen. Arkwright was frying eggs and bacon on the top of the blazing stove.

"Hungry, Master Ward?" he asked without bothering to turn around.

"Yes, I'm starving!" I replied.

"No doubt you're cold and damp, too. But that's what you get spending a night under a dark, dank canal bridge when you could've been sleeping in relative warmth. But we'll speak no more about it. You're back and that's what counts."

Five minutes later we were sitting at the table, tucking in to what proved to be an excellent breakfast. Arkwright seemed a lot more talkative than the day before.

"You sleep deeply," he said. "Too deeply. And that worries me. . . ."

I stared at him in puzzlement. What did he mean?

"Last night I sent the bitch back to guard you. Just in case anything came out of the water. You've read your master's letter. The Fiend might send something after you at any moment, so I couldn't take any chances. When I returned, just before dawn, you were still in a very deep sleep. You didn't even know I was there. That's just not good enough, Master Ward. Even asleep you must be alert to danger. We need to do something about that."

As soon as we'd finished breakfast, Arkwright stood up. "As for your curiosity, it's what killed the cat. So to save you from pushing your nose in again where it doesn't belong, I'm going to show you what's what and explain the situation in this house. After that, I never want you to mention it again. Do I make myself clear?"

"Yes," I said, pushing back my chair and standing, too.

"Right, Master Ward, then follow me. . . ."

Arkwright led the way directly up to the room with the double bed—the one saturated with water. "There are two ghosts that haunt this mill," he said sadly. "The spirits of my own dad and mam. Abe and Amelia. Most nights they sleep together in this bed. She died in the water. That's why it's so wet.

"You see, they were a loving couple and now, even in death, they refuse to be separated. Dad was repairing the roof when he had a terrible accident. He fell to his death. My mam was so distraught at losing him that she killed herself. She just couldn't live without him so she threw herself under the waterwheel. It was a painful, horrific death. The wheel dragged her under and broke every bone in her body. Because she took her own life, she can't cross to the other side, and my poor dad stays with her. She's strong despite her suffering. Stronger than any ghost I've encountered. She keeps the blaze going, trying to warm her cold, wet bones. But she feels better when I'm close by. They both do."

I opened my mouth to speak but no words came. It was a terrible tale. Was this why Arkwright was so hard and cruel?

"Right, Master Ward, there's more to see. Follow me. . . ."

"I've seen enough, thanks," I told him. "I'm really sorry about your mam and dad. You're right, it's none of my business—"

"We've started so we'll go on to the end. You're going to see it all!"

He led the way up the next flight of stairs and into his private room. There were only embers in the bottom of the stove but the air was warm. The poker and tongs were in the coal scuttle. We passed by the three chairs and went directly to the two coffins in the corner.

"My parents are both bound to their bones," he told me, "so they're not able to move much beyond the confines of the mill. I dug 'em up and brought 'em here where they'd be more comfortable. Better than haunting that windswept graveyard on the edge of the marsh. They don't mean anyone any harm. Sometimes the three of us sit in here together and talk. That's when they're happiest. . . ."

"Can't anything be done?" I asked.

Arkwright turned on me, his face livid with anger. "Don't you think I haven't *tried*? That's why I *became* a spook in the first place! I thought my training would give me the knowledge to set them free. But it all came to nothing. Mr. Gregory came here eventually to see if he could help. He did his best but it was useless. So now you know, don't you?"

I nodded and lowered my eyes, unable to meet his gaze.

"Look," he said, his voice much softer, "I'm struggling against a private demon of my own—the Demon Drink, to give it its full title. It makes me harder and crueler than I would be otherwise, but at the moment I just can't manage without it. It takes away the pain—allows me to forget what I've lost. No doubt I've let things go a bit, but I still have a lot to teach you, Master Ward. You've read that letter: It's my duty to toughen you up and ready you for the increasing threat from the Fiend. And there's evidence here that the dark is rising faster than ever before. Ever since I heard you were coming, my task has grown harder. I've never seen so much water-witch activity. It may well be directed at you. So you've got to be ready. Do I make myself clear?"

I nodded again.

"We've got off to a bad start. I've trained three apprentices for Mr. Gregory but not one of them had the barefaced cheek to come up here. Now you know the situation, I expect you to stay out of this room. Have I got your word on that, Master Ward?"

"Yes, of course. I'm really sorry," I told him.

"Good. Well, that's sorted out, then. So now we can start again. For the rest of the day it'll be lessons indoors to make up for the waste of yesterday afternoon. But tomorrow we'll be spending time on practical work again."

Arkwright must have seen the look of dismay on my

face. I certainly didn't relish fighting with staffs again. He shook his head and almost smiled. "Don't worry, Master Ward. We'll give your bruises a few days to fade before we fight again."

The following week was hard, but thankfully we didn't fight again, and my bruises did slowly begin to fade.

A lot of the time was spent working with the dogs. Being close to them made me nervous, but they were well-trained and obedient so I felt safe enough while Arkwright was there. There were boggy woodlands to the east and we practiced using the dogs to flush out witches. The scariest part was when I had to play the part of the witch by hiding in the undergrowth. Arkwright called it "Hunt the Apprentice!" The dogs would circle round behind and drive me straight toward the place where he waited with his barbed staff. It reminded me of rounding up sheep. When it was finally my turn to hunt him, I started to enjoy it.

Less enjoyable were the swimming lessons. Before I

went into the water again I was made to practice the strokes by balancing facedown across a chair with my arms and legs sticking out on either side. Arkwright taught me to breathe in while pulling my arms wide and back with my hands cupped in a scooping motion. Then I would breathe out, thrusting my arms forward, while simultaneously giving the strongest frog kick I could manage. I soon became proficient, but it was a lot harder to do the same thing in the canal.

The first day I swallowed a lot of dirty water and was sick. But subsequently Arkwright joined me in the canal, and with him by my side in case I got into trouble, my confidence steadily grew and I soon managed my first strokes unaided. On the whole things were a lot better, and Arkwright seemed to be making an effort with his drinking. He only reached for the bottle after supper, and that was my cue to get myself off to bed.

By the end of the week I could manage five widths of the canal, turning quickly each time by kicking against the bank with my feet. I could also do the "dog paddle"; it didn't seem as effective as the other stroke but it enabled me to float in the same spot without sinking—something really useful for someone who'd been as nervous about swimming as me!

"Well, Master Ward," Arkwright told me, "you're starting to make progress. But tomorrow it's back to hunting with the dogs, and this time we'll try something different. It's about time you learned to cope with the marsh."

# CHAPTER XI
## THE WITCH'S FINGER

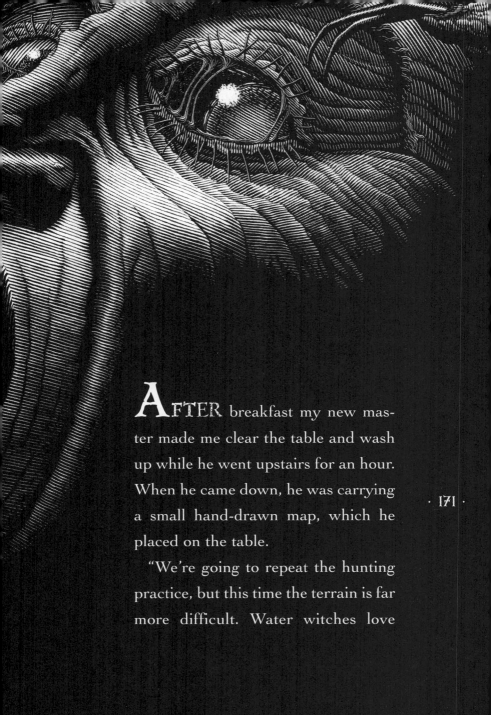

AFTER breakfast my new master made me clear the table and wash up while he went upstairs for an hour. When he came down, he was carrying a small hand-drawn map, which he placed on the table.

"We're going to repeat the hunting practice, but this time the terrain is far more difficult. Water witches love

· 171 ·

marshland and sometimes we have to go in there and flush 'em out!

"Here are the canal and the mill," he said, pointing with his finger, "and here's the marsh to the southwest. The most treacherous area, which could swallow you up in the blink of an eye, is the mere, so keep away. Little Mere, they call it. It's not a big lake, but a dangerous bog extends for some way around it — particularly to the south and east. The rest might prove difficult going but you'd probably survive.

"Now, there are lots of paths through the marsh, three of them marked on this map. It's up to you to work out the best routes. One of 'em might even allow you to outrun the dogs. . . ."

When my jaw dropped, Arkwright smiled, showing a lot of teeth. "This is where you're heading for," he said, pointing to the map again. "It's the ruin of a small monastery on Monks' Hill. Not much left of it now but a couple of walls and some foundations. Reach there before the dogs get you and you've won. That means you won't have to do it again tomorrow! And remember, this is for your own good. Familiarizing yourself with tracts of bog like this is an important part of your training. Right. You've got a couple of minutes to study that map and then we'll get started."

I spent a nervous few moments peering at Arkwright's map. The most northerly path was the most direct and would allow the least time for the dogs to run me down. It passed close to the Little Mere, with its treacherous, dangerous bogland, but I thought it was worth taking a chance. So, my route chosen, I went out into the garden, ready to get it over with.

Arkwright was sitting on the porch step, the two dogs at his feet. "Well, Master Ward, know what you're doing?"

I smiled and nodded.

"We could leave it until tomorrow if you like," he offered. "The mist's starting to close in again."

I looked beyond the garden. The mist was creeping in from the west, drifting across the marsh in tendrils to form a gray curtain. But I still felt confident about the path I'd chosen. Might as well get it over with.

"No, I'll do it now. How much start do I get?" I asked with a smile. The hunting and swimming had made me a lot fitter, I thought. It would be nice to win and I wondered if I could.

"Five minutes!" Arkwright growled. "And I've already started counting . . ."

I spun away and started to sprint toward the salt moat.

"Oi!" Arkwright shouted. "You won't be needing your staff!"

Without even looking back, I threw it from me and splashed through the moat. I'd show him! Those dogs were fast and fierce, but with a five-minute start they'd never catch me.

Moments later I was sprinting along my chosen path, the mist closing in on either side. I'd been running for only a couple of minutes when I heard the dogs barking. Arkwright hadn't kept his word! He'd released them already! He was doing his best to give me the training I needed, but despite that he always liked to win. Annoyed, I drove myself even harder, my feet fairly flying along the path.

But the visibility quickly shrank to a few feet and I was forced to slow right down. Relying on scent, the dogs wouldn't have the same handicap, and it slowly began to dawn on me that I wouldn't outrun them after all. Why hadn't I accepted his offer to wait until tomorrow? As I ran, my feet started splashing, and I realized that I'd reached the more dangerous part of my journey: the point closest to the mere.

I could still hear the muffled barks of the dogs behind me. The mist distorted the sound and made it difficult to tell how close they were. By now I was reduced to a steady jog—far too slow.

It was then that I heard a strange, plaintive cry from somewhere above. What was it? Some sort of bird? If so, it was one I'd not heard before. A few moments later it was repeated, and for some reason that eerie sound unnerved me. There was something quite unnatural about it. But I carried on, aware that the dogs must be gaining on me.

After another three or four minutes I saw a shape on the path ahead. Slowly I came to a halt, the dogs momentarily forgotten.

What was it? I peered into the mist and saw a woman walking ahead of me, shiny dark hair down to her shoulders. She was dressed in a green shawl and a long brown skirt that brushed the ground. I strode on quickly. Once beyond her, I could start running again. Even better, her presence might put the dogs off my trail.

I didn't want to scare the poor woman by coming up behind her and taking her unawares, so when I was about ten paces away, I called out in a friendly voice, "Hello! Would you mind if I came past? I know the path's really narrow but if you keep still, I'll be able to squeeze by — "

I expected the woman to step to one side or look round to see who'd spoken. But she just stopped on the path with her back to me. The dogs sounded really close now. I just *had* to get past her or they'd be upon me and Arkwright would have won.

At that moment I felt a sudden chill, a warning that

something from the dark was near. But it came far too late. . . .

When I was just a couple of paces behind her, the woman suddenly spun round to look at me, and my heart lurched up into my mouth at the nightmare that confronted me. Her mouth opened to reveal two rows of yellow-green teeth, but instead of normal canines she had four immense fangs. I retched as her foul breath washed over me. Her left eye was closed, the right one open—a vertical slit like the cold eye of a snake or lizard—and her nose was a beak of sharp bone without any covering of flesh or even skin. Her hands looked human but for her fingernails, which were sharp, curved talons.

Her hair shone because it was saturated with water, and what I'd taken for a shawl was a smock covered in green scum, while on the lower half of her body she wore a ragged skirt caked with brown marsh slime. Her feet, which now protruded from beneath her hem, were bare and streaked with mud but they weren't human: The toes were webbed, each ending in a sharp talon.

I was about to turn, ready to flee back the way I'd come, when suddenly she touched two fingers to the upper lid of her left eye and it opened very wide.

The eye was red—and I don't just mean the iris! The whole eye looked as if it was completely filled with blood. I was petrified in both senses of the word: filled with terror and rendered immobile where I was standing, as if turned to stone. I began to sweat with fear as her red eye seemed to grow bigger and brighter.

I didn't even seem to be breathing; a constricting, choking sensation gripped my throat and upper chest. Neither could I tear my eyes away from the witch. If only I could look away, perhaps her power over me would be broken? I strained every muscle in my body but to no avail. I just couldn't move.

Like a serpent, her left hand struck out toward my face. Her taloned forefinger went straight into my left ear, and I felt a stab of pain as it curved and pierced it right through.

She stepped off the path into the marsh, dragging me

after her. Two more paces and my feet began to sink into the bog. I flailed my arms at her, but I was in agony from the talon that impaled my ear and could do nothing but follow in her wake as we sank deeper and deeper into the marsh.

How I wished I'd brought my staff. But even that couldn't have helped because I was under the spell of the blood-filled eye, unable to move. What was she, some sort of water witch? I tried to shout for help, but all that escaped my lips was an animal moan of terror and pain.

The next moment there was a growl from the path behind and something black launched itself at my captor. I had a glimpse of Claw's bared fangs, then the witch's talon was ripped from my ear and I fell backward. For a moment the marsh closed over my head. Instinctively I closed my mouth and held my breath, but even so the slime oozed up my nose, and I felt myself sinking. Being able to swim was of little help. I was floundering, trying to get my head clear, when I felt hands grip me by the shoulders and start to drag me backward.

Within moments I was lying on my back on the path and Arkwright was kneeling beside me, staring down with something approaching concern on his face. Then he put his fingers in his mouth and let out a piercing whistle, and the dogs came back, stinking of the marsh, steam rising from their bodies. Claw was whimpering with pain but she had something in her mouth.

"Give it here!" Arkwright commanded. "Drop it! Drop it now!"

With a growl, Claw allowed something to drop from her jaws into his open hand.

"Good dog! Good dog! What a wonderful girl you are! Finally, after all these years!" Arkwright shouted, his voice filled with triumph. "We'll find her now! She won't get away this time."

I looked at what he was holding in his hand, hardly able to believe what I was seeing.

It was a finger. A long forefinger with a green hue to the skin. And instead of a fingernail, it had a curved talon. Claw had bitten off the witch's finger.

# CHAPTER XII
## Morwena

$A$FTER we returned to the mill, Arkwright rushed out for the local doctor to attend to my ear. Despite his reluctance to allow a stranger into his home, he must have thought the injury serious enough to make an exception. The truth was, I didn't think it was that bad. It certainly wasn't hurting much. If anything worried me, it was the possibility of it becoming infected.

Arkwright watched critically as the doctor dressed my wound. He was a tall man with an athletic build and a healthy outdoor complexion, but he was as nervous as most people are in the presence of a spook and asked no questions about how I'd got the wound.

"I've cleaned it as well as I can but there's still some risk of infection," he warned, looking anxiously down at the dogs, which growled threateningly at him. "Still, you're young and youth has resilience. It'll leave a bit of a scar, though."

Once I'd been attended to, the doctor set to work on the wounded dog, who whined with pain while Arkwright held her down. Her injuries weren't life-threatening, but there were deep gouges in her chest and back where they had been raked by talons. The doctor cleaned these, then smeared them liberally with ointment.

As he picked up his bag to leave, he nodded at Arkwright. "I'll call back the day after tomorrow to see how both my patients are doing."

"I wouldn't waste your time, Doctor," Arkwright growled, handing him a coin for his trouble. "The boy's strong and I'm sure he'll be fine. As for the bitch, she'll be right as rain in a couple of days. But if it does prove necessary, I'll contact you."

With those words, the doctor was dismissed and Arkwright escorted him across the moat.

"Claw saved your life," he said on his return. "But it wasn't for love of you. You're going to have to work hard with these dogs. We'll see if they'll let you feed them, but now we need to talk. How did it happen? How did the witch manage to get so close to you?"

"She was walking on the path ahead. I was running hard, trying to stay ahead of the dogs, and just wanted to pass her. When she turned round, it was too late. She hooked her talon through my ear before I could move."

"Not many have survived being hooked, Master Ward, so you can count yourself lucky. Very lucky indeed. That method of seizing prey is practiced by all water witches. Sometimes they thrust their finger into the mouth and spear the inside of the cheek," he said, and pointed to the scar on his own left cheek.

"Aye, that's her mark on me. I was lucky to get away. The same witch did it! It happened about seven weeks ago. Afterward poison set in and I took to my bed for three weeks and almost died. Occasionally she stabs her victim through the hand, usually the left. Sometimes she even hooks upward into the lower jaw and wraps her finger around the teeth. Had she done that, she'd have had a much better grip. As it was, she couldn't pull too hard or your ear might have ripped. But with a grip on your jaw, she'd have dragged you away into the marsh long before the bitch bit off her finger."

"Who is she?" I asked. It seemed to me that Arkwright knew a lot about her.

"She's an old enemy of mine, Master Ward. One that I've hunted for a long time—the oldest and most dangerous of all the water witches."

"Where has she come from?" I asked.

"She's very old," he began. "Some say a thousand years

or more. I wouldn't necessarily agree with that myself, but she's roamed this land for a very long time, in other counties as well as this. Stories about her go back for centuries. Marshes and fens are her favorite haunts but she likes lakes and canals, too. I don't dignify common water witches with a name because they aren't like land-based witches. Most have lost the power of speech and are little better than animals. But this one's special: She's got two names. Morwena is her true name, but Bloodeye is the name some folk call her in the County. She's crafty. Very crafty. She often goes for easy prey such as young children but can easily pull a grown man into the water, draining him of blood while she slowly drowns him. However, as you know to your cost, her left eye is her most potent weapon. A single glance from that bloodeye can paralyze her prey."

"How can we manage to get close to her?" I asked. "One glance and we'll be rooted to the spot."

Arkwright shook his head. "It's not quite as bad as it seems, Master Ward. Some, like you, have been close and still survived to tell the tale. You see, she must conserve her power for when it's most needed. That left eye is often closed, the lids bound together with a sharp piece of bone, and it has a further limitation: It can bind only one person at a time."

"You seem to know a good deal about her," I said.

"I've been hunting her for ten years, but never has she come here, so close to my home. Never before has she ventured onto the paths of Monastery Marsh. So what brings her here? That's the question we must ask. It was you she waited for on the marsh path, so I think that Mr. Gregory's warning might prove correct."

"You mean . . ."

"Aye, lad, it might well be that the Fiend has sent her against you. And that's going to cost her dear. Because now I have her finger and we'll be able to use that to track her back to her lair. After all those fruitless years, now at last I'll have her!"

"Can the dogs follow a trail across water?" I asked in amazement.

Arkwright shook his head and gave me a rare grin.

"They're good but not *that* skilled, Master Ward! If something comes out of the water and goes overland, even across a deep bog, they can track it. But not through water. No, we'll find Morwena's lair by another method. But only when we're at full strength. We'll leave it a few days until Claw's and your own wounds have healed."

I nodded in agreement because my ear was beginning to throb.

"In the meantime," said Arkwright, "I've got a book about her. I suggest you sit by the stove and read it so you know exactly what we're up against."

So saying, he went up the stairs and came down a few moments later carrying a leather-bound book, which he handed to me. The title on the spine was *Morwena*.

He left me alone and went out with the dogs. Immediately I noticed that the book was written in Arkwright's own hand. He was the author! I began to read.

*There are many legends and accounts describing the genesis of Morwena. Some consider her to be the offspring of another witch. Others believe that she was somehow born of the soft earth, spawned from bog and slime, gestated within the very depths of Mother Earth, the deepest chasms her womb. The first seems more likely, but if so, who was the mother? Neither in legends, folktales, nor the many dubious histories I have researched is she named.*

*However, all agree on one thing: the identity of Morwena's father. Her progenitor was the Fiend, also known as "the Devil," "Old Nick," "the Father of Lies" or "the Lord of Darkness".*

I paused there, shocked by those words. The Fiend had sent his own daughter to kill me! I realized how lucky I'd been to survive that encounter with her on the marsh. But for Claw, I'd be dead. I read on, now starting to skip passages that were difficult or unclear in any way. Soon it was apparent that although Arkwright had taught me some things about Morwena, there was much more to learn.

*Morwena is by far the most notorious of all water witches, her killings too numerous to document. She feeds upon blood, and that is the source of her dark, magical power.*

*Historically, human sacrifices were usually made to her as the moon waxed toward fullness, when blood was most able to augment her strength. Newborn babes best fed her cruel needs, but when children could not be found, adults of all ages were welcome. The young were cast into the Blood Pool; older offerings were chained in a subterranean chamber until the propitious moment.*

*When particularly thirsty, Morwena*

*sometimes drinks the blood of large animals, such as cattle and horses. If desperate, small animals will suffice: ducks, chickens, rats, and even mice are drained.*

*Morwena rarely leaves the water and it is said that she cannot survive much more than an hour or so on dry land, where she is also at her weakest.*

So that was something else to remember. But how to lure her out of her habitat? If two of us attacked her simultaneously, one would be free of the spell cast by her bloodeye. That could be the key to defeating her.

The next morning my ear was less painful, and while I made the breakfast, Arkwright took both dogs out onto the marsh paths. He was away for well over an hour.

"There's neither hide nor hair of the witch out there!" he said on his return. "Well, after breakfast we'll carry on with your lessons, but this afternoon you can get yourself down to the canal. I'm expecting a delivery of salt. Five barrels. They're not that big but they're heavy and you'll have to carry each one and keep it clear of the damp. We use some of it for cooking and preserving so I don't want it spoiled."

So it was that, about an hour after noon, I strolled down to the canal bank to wait for Mr. Gilbert. I wasn't alone. Arkwright had sent Claw with me just in case Morwena was lurking within the still waters.

I'd been at the mill for over a week and this was my chance to let Alice and the Spook know how I was getting on. So I took pen, ink, envelope, and paper, and while I waited for the bargeman, I wrote two short letters. The first was to Alice.

Dear Alice,

I am missing you and our life at Chipenden very much.

Being Arkwright's apprentice isn't easy. He is a

hard, sometimes cruel man, but despite that, he knows his job very well and has much to teach me about things that come out of the water. Recently we've had an encounter with a water witch that he calls Morwena. Soon we are going to find her lair and hunt her down once and for all.

I hope to see you soon.

Love,

Tom

Next I wrote my letter to the Spook.

Dear Mr. Gregory,

I hope you are well. I must confess that I did not get off to a good start with Mr. Arkwright, but the situation has settled down now. He has a good knowledge of things that come out of the water, and I hope to learn a lot.

Recently, on a marsh path close to the water mill, I was attacked by a water witch called Morwena. It seems that she is an old enemy of Arkwright's who has never, until now, ventured so close to his house. Perhaps you've heard of her. Arkwright says she is the Fiend's own daughter and he thinks that she has been sent against me by her father.

Soon we are going to hunt her down. I look forward to working with you again in the spring.

Your apprentice,

Tom Ward

Both letters written, I sealed them into an envelope which I addressed: *To Mr. Gregory of Chipenden.*

As I sat on the bank of the canal to wait for Matthew Gilbert, Claw sat to my left, her eyes constantly flicking between me and the water. It was a crisp, bright day and the canal looked anything but threatening, yet it was reassuring to have her there to guard me.

About an hour later, the barge came into sight from the south. After mooring the barge Mr. Gilbert unhitched the horses and tethered them to graze.

"Well, that saves me ringing the bell!" he called out merrily when he saw me. I helped lift the barrels of salt from the hold and onto the bank. Although relatively small, they were heavy.

"I'll have a five-minute break before I set off again," he said, settling himself down on the stern of the barge, his feet resting on the towpath. "How've you found it working for Bill Arkwright? It looks like you've got yourself an injury already." He gestured toward my ear.

I grinned and sat down beside him. "Yes, it's been a hard start, as you predicted," I told him. "So bad that I nearly went back to Mr. Gregory. But we're getting along better now. I'm starting to grow used to the dogs as well," I said, nodding toward Claw.

"Dogs like this take a bit of getting used to, no doubt," Mr. Gilbert said. "As does their master. More than one lad has gone back to Chipenden with his tail between his legs, so you wouldn't be the first. If you ever decide to leave, I pass here on my way south every Wednesday. It's a salt run that eventually takes me to the end of the canal at

196

Priestown. As far as speed goes, it's no faster than walking but it would save your legs and get you through Caster by the most direct route. Might be a bit of company for you, too. I've a son and a daughter about your age. They take turns to help me on the barge from time to time."

I thanked him for the offer, then handed him the envelope with a coin to pay the post wagon. He promised to drop it off at Priestown. As he harnessed the horses, I lifted one of the barrels. I tried positioning it under my arm.

"On your shoulder! That's the best way!" Mr. Gilbert called out cheerfully.

His advice proved sound. Once in position, the barrel was easy to carry. So, with Claw at my heels, I made the five trips to the house in just under half an hour.

After that, Arkwright gave me another theory lesson.

"Open your notebook, Master Ward. . . ."

I opened it immediately and looked up, waiting to hear what he would say.

"Your heading is Morwena," he told me. "I want you to write down everything I've told you and you've read so far. Such knowledge will come in useful. It'll soon be time to go a-hunting. We've got her finger and we'll be putting it to very good use."

"How *are* we going to use it?" I asked.

"You'll find out soon enough, so curb your impatience. The dog's wounds don't seem to have become infected, and so far your ear hasn't dropped off. Assuming there's no change tomorrow, we'll set off across the sands to Cartmel. If we find out what we need to know—well then, we might not be back here for quite some time. Not until we've dealt with Morwena once and for all!"

# CHAPTER XIII
## THE HERMIT OF CARTMEL

SOON after dawn the following day, with the dogs at our heels,
we made our way toward Cartmel;
the quickest way was across the
sands of Morecambe Bay. It was

another bright day, and I was
happy to get away from the mill for
a while. I was looking forward to
seeing the County north of the bay,

with its picturesque mountains and lakes.

Had I been with the Spook, I'd have been carrying both bags, but it seemed that Arkwright always carried his own. We didn't have very far to walk before we reached Hest Bank, the starting point for our journey across the sands. Here we found two coaches and three horsemen, as well as a number of people on foot. The bare sands seemed to be inviting us to cross, and the sea was a long way out; I wondered what they were all waiting for and asked Arkwright.

"It may look safe now, but the sands of the bay can be treacherous," he replied. "A sand guide will walk ahead of the front coach—a man who knows the tides and terrain like the back of his own hand. We have to cross two river channels; the second one in particular, the Kent, can be dangerous after heavy rains. It can turn to quicksand. We're waiting now for the ebb tide to reach the point that'll give those carriages time to cross safely.

"Never try to walk across the bay without a guide, Master Ward. I've lived here most of my life and even I wouldn't try it. You might have just learned to swim but even a grown man with years of experience wouldn't survive. The water comes in down the channels so fast you can soon get cut off and drown!"

A tall man wearing a wide-brimmed hat approached; he walked barefoot and carried a staff. "This is Mr. Jennings, the sand guide," Arkwright told me. "He's watched over these sands for almost twenty years."

"It's a grand day!" Mr. Jennings called out. "Who's this you've got with you, Bill?"

"A good day to you, Sam. This is Tom Ward, my apprentice for the next six months."

The sand guide's suntanned, weather-beaten face cracked into a smile as he shook my hand. He had the air of a man who enjoyed his work. "No doubt, Bill, you'll have warned him of the dangers of these sands?"

"I've told him, all right. Let's just hope he listens."

"Aye, let's hope so. Not everybody does. We should be setting off in about half an hour."

That said, he moved away to chat with the others.

Eventually we set off, Sam Jennings striding ahead of the coaches, with those on foot bringing up the rear. The flat sands were still wet and marked with an intricate pattern of ridges made by the tides. There had been hardly any wind before, but now a stiff breeze was blowing into our faces from the northwest while in the far distance the sun was dazzling off the sea.

The coaches traveled slowly and we caught up with them when we reached the first riverbed. Sam went into the channel to inspect it, wading in as far as his knees. He paddled about two hundred paces east before whistling and waving his stick to indicate the point where we should cross. Then he walked back toward the first coach.

"This is where we get ourselves a ride!" Arkwright said.

He ran forward suddenly and jumped onto the back of the rear coach. Following his lead, I soon saw why. As we crossed the channel, the water came up to the horses' bellies. We'd just saved ourselves a soaking. The dogs didn't seem to mind getting wet and swam strongly, reaching the far bank well before the horses.

We climbed down and walked for a while until we reached the channel of the river Kent, which proved to be about the same depth.

"I wouldn't like to be here when the tide's in!" I remarked.

"That you wouldn't, Master Ward. At spring tide the water would be deep enough to cover you three times over or more. See over there?" Arkwright asked, pointing toward the land.

I could see forested slopes with purple fells rising above.

"Those fells behind Cartmel—that's where we're heading. Soon be there now."

The crossing was about nine miles but Arkwright told me that wasn't always the case. The course of the river Kent kept shifting, so the distance to safe fording places varied. It was a dangerous place, all right, but a much shorter route than following the curve of the bay.

We reached a place called Kent's Bank where, after paying and thanking the guide, we left the flat sands and began the climb up to Cartmel, which took us almost an hour. We passed a large priory, a couple of taverns, and about thirty or so dwellings. Cartmel reminded me of Chipenden, with hungry children staring from doorways, the surrounding fields depleted of livestock. The effects of the war were widespread and would no doubt soon start to bite deeper. I thought we would stop and stay in Cartmel for the night, but it seemed that our business lay farther on.

"We're going to visit Judd Atkins, a hermit who lives up on those fells," Arkwright said without even looking at me. His gaze was fixed upon the steep slope ahead.

I knew that a hermit was usually a holy man who liked to live alone beyond the reach of people, so I didn't expect him to be pleased to see us. But was he the one who'd be able to use the severed finger in some way to locate Morwena?

I was about to ask, but as we passed the last cottage, an old woman emerged from the gloom of her front room and shuffled out toward us down the muddy path.

"Mr. Arkwright! Mr. Arkwright! Thank the Lord, you've come at last," she exclaimed, grabbing his sleeve and holding it fast.

"Let me be, old mother!" Arkwright snapped, irritation in his voice. "Can't you see I'm in a rush. I've urgent business of my own to attend to!"

For a moment I thought he would push her away and stride off, but he glared down at her, the veins starting to bulge at his temples.

"But we're all scared rigid," said the old woman. "Nobody's safe. They take what they want, night and day. We'll soon starve if something ain't done. Help us, please, Mr. Arkwright—"

"What are you babbling about? *Who* takes what they want?"

"A press-gang—though they're more like common thieves. Not content with dragging our lads off to war, they rob us of everything we've got. They've made their den up at Saltcombe Farm. The whole village is scared witless. . . ."

Was this the same press-gang that captured me? They'd talked about heading north and had fled this way when Alice scared them. It seemed likely. I certainly didn't want to meet them again.

"It's a job for the constable, not me," Arkwright said with a scowl.

"Three weeks ago they beat the constable to within an inch of his life. He's only just risen from his sickbed and will do nothing now. He knows what's good for him. So help us, please. Food's scarce enough anyway, but if they carry on like that once the winter sets in proper, we'll starve for sure. They take everything they can lay their hands on —"

Arkwright shook his head and tugged his sleeve free of the woman's grasp. "Maybe when I pass this way again, I'll see. But I'm too busy now. I've got important business that just can't wait!"

With that, he continued up the incline, the dogs racing ahead, and the old woman shuffled sadly back inside her cottage. I felt sorry for her and her village but thought it was strange that she should ask Arkwright for help. After all, it wasn't spook's business. Did she really think my master could take on an armed gang? Somebody should send a message to the High Sheriff at Caster; no doubt he'd send another constable. And what about the men of the village? Couldn't they band together and do something? I wondered.

After about an hour climbing up into the fells, we saw smoke ahead. It seemed to be coming from a hole in the ground, and I realized that the rocky bank we were crossing was the roof of the hermitage. After descending some well-worn stone steps we came to the entrance of a sizable cave.

Arkwright made the dogs sit and wait some distance away and then led the way into the gloom. There was a strong smell of wood smoke inside the cave and my eyes watered. But I could just make out the form of someone squatting before a fire, his head in his hands.

"And how are you, old man?" Arkwright called out. "Still doing penance for your sins?"

The hermit made no reply, but undeterred, Arkwright sat down on his left. "Look, I know you like to be alone so let's get this over with quickly and we'll leave you in peace. Have a look at this and tell me where she's to be found. . . ."

He opened his bag, pulled out a crumpled rag, and unfolded it on the earth floor between the hermit and the fire.

As my eyes adjusted to the poor light, I could see that Judd Atkins had a white beard and a wild mop of unruly gray hair. For almost a minute he didn't move. In fact he hardly seemed to be breathing, but at last he reached forward and picked up the witch's finger. He held it very close and turned it over a few times, seemingly rapt.

"Can you do it?" Arkwright demanded.

"Are lambs born in spring?" the hermit asked, his voice barely more than a croak. "Do dogs howl at the moon? I've dowsed for many a long year, and when I've put my mind to it, nothing's defeated me yet. Why should that change?"

"Good man!" Arkwright cried, his voice filled with excitement.

"Yes, I'll do it for you, William," the hermit continued. "But you must pay a price."

"A price? What price?" Arkwright said, astonishment in his voice. "Your needs are few, old man. That's the life you've chosen. So what can you want from me?"

"I ask nothing for myself," the hermit replied, his voice growing stronger with every word. "But others are in need. Down in the village hungry people live in fear. Free them from that and you shall have what you desire."

Arkwright spat into the fire, and I saw his jaw tighten. "You mean that lot at Saltcombe Farm? That press-gang? You expect *me* to sort 'em out?"

"These are lawless times. When things fall apart, someone must put them back together. Sometimes a farrier must mend a door or a carpenter shoe a horse. Who else is there, William? Who else but you?"

"How many are there?" Arkwright asked at last. "And what do you know about them?"

"There are five in all. A sergeant, a corporal, and three soldiers. They take what they want from the village without paying."

"A press-gang was taking people near Chipenden," I said with a frown. "They captured me and I was lucky to get away. Five of them, too, so it sounds like the same lot. I don't want to meet them again. One of them's only a boy not much older than me, but the sergeant's a nasty piece of work. They're armed with clubs and blades, too. I don't think you'd be able to take them on, Mr. Arkwright."

Arkwright stared at me, then nodded. "The odds are against me," he complained, turning to the hermit again. "There are only three and a half of us: me, two dogs, and a lad who's wet behind the ears. I've a trade of my own. I'm not the constable—"

"You were a soldier once, William. And everyone knows you still like to crack heads, especially after you've been at the bottle. I'm sure you'll enjoy the experience."

Arkwright came to his feet and looked down at the hermit, his face filled with fury. "Just make sure it's not your head I crack, old man. I'll be back before dark. In the meantime get on with it. I've wasted enough time already! Have you got a map of the Lakelands?"

Judd Atkins shook his head, so Arkwright rummaged in his bag and pulled out a folded map. He placed it in front of the old man. "Try that!" he snapped. "Her lair will be there; I'm sure of it. Somewhere close to one of the southern lakes."

That said, he left the cave and marched east at a furious pace.

# CHAPTER XIV
## A DEAD MAN!

WE hadn't traveled far from the hermit's cave when Arkwright stopped, settled himself down on a grassy bank, and opened his bag. He pulled out a bottle of red wine, drew the cork with his teeth, and started to swig from it.

I stood there unhappily for a while, wondering if this was the best

preparation for dealing with dangerous thugs, but the hermit had made a good point: Arkwright was always much more aggressive after a drink. He must have seen the look on my face because he scowled and gestured angrily for me to sit down.

"Take the weight off your feet, Master Ward. That and the misery from your face!" he exclaimed.

Sensing that his mood was worsening, I obeyed immediately. The sun was sinking toward the horizon, and I wondered if he intended to wait until after dark before attempting to deal with the press-gang. That seemed the most sensible thing to do. Either that or go in at first light while they were still groggy with sleep. But Arkwright was an impatient man who, probably by choice, often did things the hard way.

I was right. He soon finished off the wine and we were on our way again. After about ten minutes I came up alongside him. I was curious and wanted to know if he had some sort of plan.

"Mr. Arkwright—" I began tentatively.

"Shut up!" he snarled. "Speak when you're spoken to and not before!"

So I dropped back again. I was angry and a little hurt. I'd felt that I was starting to get along better with Arkwright but it seemed that little had changed. The Spook sometimes silenced me, saying that questions could come later, but he never did it so aggressively and rudely. No doubt my new master's manner could be blamed on the wine.

Soon we came to a ridge and Arkwright halted, shielding his eyes against the setting sun. I could see a house below, brown smoke drifting up almost vertically from its chimney. The house lay at the head of a narrow valley. No doubt it had once been a hill farm specializing in sheep, but now there were no animals to be seen.

"Well, that's it!" he said. "Saltcombe Farm. Let's go down and get it over with. . . ."

He strode off down the incline, making no effort to keep out of sight. Once in the valley, he made straight for the front door, which I expected to spring open at any moment as the gang raced to attack us. When he was less than twenty paces away, he came to a halt and turned to face me, nodding toward the two dogs.

"Hold their collars firmly and don't let them go," he ordered. "When I shout 'Now!' release them. But not before. Understand?"

I nodded uncertainly and gripped the dogs' collars as they strained forward. If they decided to go, there was no way I'd be able to stop them.

"What if something goes wrong?" I asked. There were five soldiers inside the house — still probably armed with blades and clubs. I remembered what the old lady had said about the parish constable. They'd beaten him to within an inch of his life.

"Master Ward," he said scornfully, "if there's one thing I can't abide, it's a pessimist. Believe that you can do something and half the battle is won before you start. I'm going to sort this lot out and then get on with my real business. Here, watch this for me," and he dropped his big bag at my feet. Then he reversed his staff so that the murderous spear was pointing downward. It suggested that he didn't want to do the soldiers any permanent damage.

With that he strode directly toward the front door and, with one kick from his heavy left boot, smashed it open. He went straight in, swinging his staff, and I heard swear-words, then shouts of pain and anger from inside. Next a big man in a ragged uniform with blood running down his forehead came running out of the door, heading straight toward me, spitting out broken teeth. The two dogs growled simultaneously, and he halted and stared straight at me for a moment. It was the sergeant with the scarred face, and I saw recognition and anger flare simultaneously behind his eyes. For a moment I thought he'd decided to attack me despite the dogs but then he turned to the right and ran up the slope.

I heard Arkwright shout "Now!" and before I could react, the dogs tore free of my grip and raced toward the open door, barking furiously.

No sooner had Tooth and Claw entered the house than the remaining four deserters left it. Three fled through the door and followed the sergeant up the hill, but the fourth jumped through a front window and headed straight toward me, brandishing a knife. It was the corporal. The dogs couldn't help me now so I raised my staff and held it diagonally across my body in a defensive stance.

As he drew closer, a mirthless smile creased his face. He halted, facing me in a crouch, the blade held wide in his right hand. "Made a big mistake in deserting, boy. I'm going to slice open your belly and take your guts for garters!"

So saying, he ran at me fast, the knife already curving toward my body. I moved faster than I could think, the practice with Arkwright paying off. My first blow was to his wrist, spinning the knife from his hand. He grunted with pain as I hit him a second time: a blow to his head that sent him to his knees. He wasn't laughing now. There was fear in his eyes. He came slowly to his feet. I could have hit him again but I let him be. He turned and with a curse set off after his companions. They were all running up the hill as if the Devil himself were at their heels.

I headed toward the house, thinking it was over, but then watched openmouthed from the doorway as Arkwright, roaring with anger, proceeded to smash everything inside into tiny pieces: furniture, crockery, and every remaining window. When he'd finished, he whistled Tooth and Claw back to heel and set fire to the house. As we climbed out of the valley, a thick plume of dark smoke obscured the setting sun.

"Nothing for them to come back to now!" Arkwright remarked with a grin.

Then, from high on the fell, someone called down to us:

"You're a dead man, Spook! A dead man! We'll find out where you live. You're dead: you and the boy! You've both got it coming to you now. We serve the king. You'll hang for sure!"

"Don't look so worried, Master Ward," said Arkwright with a wry smile. "He's all talk. If they had the stomach for it, they'd be down here fighting now, not cringing with fear up on that hill."

"But won't they report what's happened and send more

soldiers after us? You've hit one of the king's soldiers and we've destroyed all their possessions."

"The war's going badly so I doubt very much whether they've got soldiers to spare for hunting the likes of us. Besides, I'm pretty sure they're deserters. They're the ones who need fear hanging. They certainly don't behave like a proper press-gang. Beating up the parish constable wasn't part of the job when I was in the army!"

With that, Arkwright turned on his heel and set off for the cave.

"When were you a soldier?" I asked.

"Long ago. After completing my time with Mr. Gregory I went back to the mill and tried to free my mam and dad. When I couldn't do it, I was so bitter that I left the trade for a while. The army trained me as a gunner, but the land was at peace and there was nobody to shoot at, so I bought myself out and went back to being a spook. Funny how things work out. But I'll tell you one thing. I'd never have run from a battle — not like those lily-livered cowards up there."

222

"You were a gunner? You mean you fired one of those big cannon?"

"An eighteen-pounder, it was, Master Ward. The biggest cannon in the County. And I was a master gunner and sergeant to boot. To all intents and purposes, that was my gun!"

"I've seen it," I told him. "In the summer soldiers brought it up from Colne and used it to breach Malkin Tower."

"How long did it take 'em?" Arkwright asked.

"They were at it from noon to sunset, then finished the job in less than an hour the following morning."

"Did they now? No wonder the war down south is going so badly. I've seen that tower and I reckon I could breach its walls in under two hours. It's all about technique and training, Master Ward!" he said with a smile.

It was strange how cheerful and talkative he'd suddenly become. He seemed elated. It was as if the fight with the deserters had lifted his spirits.

But back at the hermitage, Arkwright's anger bubbled up again when he discovered that the hermit hadn't been able to discover the whereabouts of Morwena's lair.

"I've kept my side of the bargain, now keep yours!" he raged.

"Have patience, William," Judd said calmly. "Can crops be grown in winter? Of course not, because all things have their time. I said I haven't discovered it *yet*. Not that I won't be able to do so eventually. And I've got close enough to know that you're right. Her lair is in the southern Lakelands. But it's hard to find a witch. She's undoubtedly used her powers to cloak her whereabouts. Is she a particularly strong witch?"

Arkwright nodded. "They don't come much stronger. Her true name is Morwena but some call her Bloodeye. No doubt you'll have heard the name?"

"That I have," replied the hermit. "Both names. Who hasn't? Every mother in the County trembles at those names. Scores of children have gone missing in the last twenty years. I'll do all I can to help, but I'm tired now.

These things can't be rushed. I'll try again tomorrow when things will be more propitious. What's the weather like?"

"Turning milder and starting to drizzle," grumbled Arkwright, still far from pleased.

"You don't want to be traveling in those conditions, do you? Why don't you settle yourselves down for the night? Have you eaten?"

"Not since breakfast. I can manage but Master Ward here is always hungry."

"Then I'll heat us up some broth."

But before supper Arkwright took me out onto the dark hillside and we practiced fighting with staffs again. It seemed he was determined to keep up with my training wherever and whenever he could. A fine rain drifted into our faces as we tried to keep our balance on the slippery grass. This time he didn't deliver any blows to my body but seemed content to force me backward and test my defensive skills.

"Well, Master Ward, that's enough for now," he said at

last. "I do believe we're starting to see a faint glimmer of improvement. I saw how you dealt with that corporal earlier. You did well, lad. You should be proud of yourself. Keep at it and within six months you'll be well able to look after yourself."

His words cheered me up, and as we headed back to the cave, I began to look forward to my supper. But it proved a disappointment. The broth was bitter, and at the first mouthful I pulled my face. I wondered what was in it.

Arkwright just smiled at my distaste. "Eat it all up, Master Ward! That's the best herb soup you'll get north of Caster. Judd here is a vegetarian. The dogs'll eat better than us tonight."

The hermit gave no sign that he was insulted by Arkwright's remarks, but out of respect I made myself empty my bowl of broth and then thanked him. Whatever was in it, I had my best night's sleep since leaving Chipenden.

# CHAPTER XV
## THE DANCING FINGER

THERE was no breakfast. Soon after dawn Judd Atkins opened the lakes map and laid it on the ground near the embers of the fire.

"Right!" he said at last, staring at it. "I've had a good night's sleep and I'm feeling much better. Should be able to find her now . . ."

So saying, he pulled two items from

his breeches pocket. One was a short length of fine string; the other was the severed witch's finger. He then tied one end of the string to the finger.

The hermit saw me watching and smiled. "Before I retreated from this wicked world, I was a dowser, Thomas. Mostly I used a birch twig to find water. Many of the wells to the north of the County were found by me. Occasionally I found missing people, too. I could suspend a shred of clothing or a locket of hair above a map until my hand twitched. Sadly, many of those I located were already dead, but their families were still grateful to find a body to bury in hallowed ground. Now, let's see if I can find myself a water witch called Morwena. . . ."

Arkwright moved closer and we both watched as the hermit began a systematic search. Moving the suspended finger slowly from west to east, then east to west, he made steady sweeps across the width of the map, moving slightly farther north each time. After less than a minute his hand suddenly twitched. He paused, took a deep breath, moved his hand to the right and brought it back again very smoothly and steadily. It twitched again, this time jerking upward so that the witch's finger danced on the end of the string.

"Mark that, William!" he called, and Arkwright walked across, knelt, and made two small crossmarks. That done, the hermit continued to traverse the map. Soon his hand twitched again. Within moments the severed finger was once more dancing on the string as he identified a third location. Each time Arkwright marked the spot very carefully. The hermit continued but found nothing more to report.

All three crosses were to the west of Coniston Water: the first was on its northwest shore; the second marked a very small lake called Goat's Water; the third, farther to the north, was called Lever's Water.

"So is it all of them, old man, or are you simply not sure?" Arkwright asked, impatience strong in his voice.

"Is to be certain to be right? We must always allow room for doubt, William. It could well be all three. I'm sure she spends some time at each location," came the reply. "There could even be others farther north than you asked me to investigate. I got the strongest reaction from the Coniston shore, but I also feel that she roams the whole area west of that lake. Do you know the place well?"

"I've had cause to work up there more than once, but I don't know the lake's northern extremity, on the border of the County. They're a surly lot up there in Coniston, set in their ways, and don't take kindly to outsiders. They'd rather suffer in silence than bring in a spook from the south."

Wisely I kept my thoughts to myself, but I thought that was a bit much coming from someone as unfriendly as Arkwright, who could barely tolerate an apprentice in his house.

Just when we were about to set off, the weather closed in, the west wind driving the rain hard against the hillside so that it drummed on the roof of the cave and encroached into its entrance, at times hissing into the edge of the fire.

"You daft old man," Arkwright taunted. "Why on earth

choose a cave with an entrance facing the prevailing winds?"

"The cold and wet are good for the soul. Why do you live in a house on the edge of a swamp when you could live more healthily up in the bracing air?" Judd Atkins retaliated.

Anger flickered across Arkwright's brow but he said nothing. He lived there because it had been his parents' house, and now that his mother's spirit was trapped, he couldn't leave them. The hermit probably knew nothing of that, otherwise he would surely not have spoken so cruelly.

Because of the inclement weather, Arkwright decided to stay for one more night and then head north toward Coniston at first light. While Judd built up the fire, Arkwright took me fishing in the pouring rain. I thought he'd use a rod or a net but he had a method he called "tickling."

"Never go hungry if you can do this!" he told me.

It consisted of lying on his belly on the wet riverbank

with his arms plunged into the cold water. The idea was to tickle the belly of the trout so that it moved backward into your hand, at which point you flipped it onto the grass. He showed me the technique, but it took a lot of patience and no trout came even within reach of my hands. Arkwright caught two, however, which he soon cooked to perfection. The hermit simply sipped more of his broth, which meant that Arkwright and I got a whole fish each. They were delicious and soon I was feeling much better.

But then it was more fighting with staffs. I got off lightly, ending up with just one bruise on my arm, but Arkwright fought me to a standstill and I was exhausted. So I slept well in that cave. It was certainly more restful than the mill.

By dawn the rain had ceased and we set off without further delay, heading north toward the lakes.

The Spook had certainly been right about the scenery in this part of the County. As we reached Coniston Water and skirted its western tree-lined shore, all about us were sights to delight the eye. The slopes to the east were forested with deciduous and coniferous trees, the latter providing greenery to brighten the somber late-autumn day. The clouds were high, so there was a spectacular view of the mountains to the north, and the rain had evidently been falling as snow up there, causing their peaks to gleam white against the gray sky.

Arkwright seemed in a slightly more cheerful mood so, tired of the long silence—he hadn't spoken a word since we'd left the hermit's cave—I risked a question.

"That mountain ahead, is that the Old Man of Coniston?"

"That it is, Master Ward, as you should well know. You'll be familiar with it after our study of that map yesterday. Quite a sight, isn't it? Far higher than the fells behind Mr. Gregory's house. It attracts the eye, but sometimes places of equal significance don't stand out so much. See that bank over there?" he said, pointing across to the eastern shore of the lake.

I nodded.

"Well, that's the spot where I slew the Coniston Ripper. Right under that very bank. Probably the best thing I've done since completing my time with Mr. Gregory. But if I could catch or kill Morwena, that would top it for sure."

Something approaching a grin creased Arkwright's face, and he even began to whistle low and tunelessly while the dogs circled us, snapping at the air in their excitement.

We entered Coniston village from the south. There were few people about, but those we saw seemed unfriendly; some even crossed to the other side of the street rather than pass close to us. It was only to be expected. Most people were nervous at being close to a spook even in Chipenden, where Mr. Gregory had lived for years. My master liked to keep his distance and avoided walking through the center, and when I collected the provisions, not everybody was as friendly as the shop-keepers, who welcomed our regular custom.

On reaching a stream—marked on the map as CHURCH

BECK—we began to climb a steep track to the west, leaving behind the huddle of houses with their smoking chimneys. Above us loomed the formidable heights of the "Old Man," but just when my legs were beginning to ache, Arkwright led us off the track into a small garden that fronted a tavern. The sign proclaimed it as: THE BECK INN.

Two old men were standing in the doorway, each holding a pot of ale. They stepped aside briskly to allow us through, the alarm on their faces probably not only caused by the sight of the two fearsome wolfhounds. They could tell our trade by our clothes and staffs.

Inside, the tavern was empty but the tabletops were clean and a welcoming fire blazed in the grate. Arkwright walked to the bar and rapped loudly on the wooden counter. We heard someone coming up the steps and a rotund, jovial-looking man in a clean apron came through the open doorway to our right.

I saw him glance warily at the dogs and give Arkwright a quick up and down, but then his initial uneasy smile settled into the businesslike welcome of an experienced host. "Good day to you, good sirs," he said. "What can I offer you? Accommodation, a meal, or simply two tankards of my very best ale?"

"We'll take two rooms, landlord, and an evening meal — hot pot, if you have it. In the meantime we'll sit over there in the corner by the fire and start with a caudle."

The landlord bowed and hurried away. I took my seat opposite Arkwright, wondering what was going on. On the very rare occasions Mr. Gregory and I stayed in a tavern, we shared a room; he got the bed while I slept on the floor. Arkwright had ordered us a room each.

"What's a caudle?" I asked.

"It's something to cheer you up on a cold, damp late-autumn evening. A hot, spicy mixture of wine and gruel. Just the thing to sharpen our appetites for the hot pot."

I worried a bit when he said the word wine. The fight with the soldiers had shown me again how violent and angry Arkwright could become with wine inside him, and I feared him when he was like that. I'd hoped that he had started to curb his drinking recently, but perhaps the episode with the press-gang had given him a taste for it.

I tried to remain positive about the situation, though, and sleeping in the tavern was certainly better than spending the night under a hedge or in a drafty barn — though I knew there were often very good reasons for the things John Gregory did. For one thing, he would have expected us to fast before facing the dark, and for another, he didn't like people knowing his business. He would have approached one of the three potential lairs of Morwena without first passing through the village. In a small place such as this gossip spread like wildfire. Now we had taken rooms for the night, soon everyone in Coniston would know that a spook and his apprentice were here. And sometimes witches had allies among the community; I'd learned that in Pendle. Even a malevolent water witch such as Morwena might have informants.

For a while I struggled with myself, torn between two options: say nothing to Arkwright and suffer the consequences; or tell him my fears and risk a beating or at least a tongue-lashing. My sense of duty finally won.

"Mr. Arkwright," I began, keeping my voice low in case the landlord returned and overheard us, "do you think it's wise for us to sit here so publicly? Morwena might have supporters in the area."

Arkwright smiled grimly. "Stop your mothering, Master Ward. Do you see any spies about? Remember, when you're with me, you do things my way, and I need some rest and refreshment if I'm to face Morwena. Count yourself lucky that you'll have a full belly and a featherbed tonight. Mr. Gregory never treats his apprentices so well."

Perhaps Arkwright was right. There was no one about and we both deserved a good meal and rest after two nights camped out in the hermit's cave. I was sure Mr. Gregory would have insisted we fast before facing Morwena, but I decided not to argue with Arkwright any-more—especially if he was soon to have some wine in him. I settled back in my seat, stopped worrying, and enjoyed my caudle.

But soon the tavern began to fill, and by the time our

steaming hot pots arrived, a group of farmers were down-ing mugs of ale, and most of the tables were full of lively, genial people, joking, laughing, and filling their bellies. We got a few suspicious glances and I sensed that some people were talking about us. A few customers even turned back in the doorway on catching sight of us. Maybe they were just nervous of us or perhaps it was something more sinister.

Then things started to go wrong. Arkwright ordered a tankard of the landlord's strongest ale. He downed it in seconds and then bought another, and another. With each drink his voice became louder and his words more slurred. When he went to the bar for his seventh pint, he stumbled against someone's table, spilling the drinks and earning himself some angry looks. I sat trying not to draw attention to myself, but Arkwright seemed to have no such thoughts. At the bar he was telling the story to any-one who'd listen of how he'd defeated the Coniston Ripper.

After a while he staggered back to our table, carrying

his eighth pint. He drank it quickly, then burped loudly, drawing more glances.

"Mr. Arkwright," I said, "do you think we ought to go to bed now? We've got a busy day tomorrow and it's getting late."

"There he goes again," said Arkwright loudly so that he soon had the audience he wanted. "When will my apprentice learn that it's me who gives the orders, not the other way round. I'll go to bed when I'm good and ready, Master Ward, and not before," he snarled.

Humiliated, I hung my head. What more could I say? I thought my new master was making a big mistake getting so drunk when we had to face Morwena in the morning, but like he said, I was only the apprentice and had to obey orders.

"Happen the boy's right, though," said the landlord, coming over to clear our table. "I don't like to turn away paying customers but you've had a few too many, Bill, and you'll need your wits about you if you're really going to hunt Morwena."

I was shocked. I didn't realize my master had told the

landlord what we were planning. Who else had he told while he was at the bar?

Arkwright banged his fist loudly on the table. "Are you telling me I can't handle my ale?" he shouted.

Suddenly the room was silent as everyone turned to look at us.

"No, Bill," said the landlord amiably, clearly experienced in dealing with drunkards. "How about you come back tomorrow night when you've sorted out Morwena and you can drink as much as you like—on the house."

At the mention of Morwena, a low whispering started among the other customers.

"Right. You've got yourself a deal," said Arkwright, to my relief. "Master Ward, it's an early night for us."

I led the way to our rooms with the dogs, and he stumbled behind us up the stairs. But as I entered my room, he stepped in, too, and closed the door, leaving the dogs outside. "What do you think of your room?" he slurred.

I looked about me. The bed looked inviting, and everything, including the curtains, looked clean and well cared for. The candle beside the bed was beeswax rather than smelly tallow.

"Looks comfortable," I said. But then I noticed the large mirror on the dressing table to my left. "Should I cover that with a sheet?" I asked.

"No need. We're not dealing with your Pendle witches now," Arkwright said, shaking his head. "No, no, no," he hiccupped. "This is something different. Very different, mark my words. A water witch can't use a mirror to spy on folk. Not even Morwena can do that. Anyway, Master Ward, be grateful. Mr. Gregory never booked me a room as comfortable as this—not in all the five years I was his apprentice. But don't get too snug now. Don't get yourself as snug as a little, little bug in a rug. Let us give ourselves a couple of hours' rest, but when the church clock chimes midnight, we're off a-hunting. A-hunting we will go! Go left from the door of your room and down the back steps. I'll meet you at the outer door. Softly, softly does it!"

With those words Arkwright staggered out, closing the door behind him, but I could hear him singing, "*A-hunting we will go,"* as he struggled drunkenly to unlock his own door. So, without getting undressed, I lay down on the bed. I might be a sound sleeper, but I was good at knowing the time, even when asleep, and if I put my mind to it, I'd wake up just before the bells began to chime.

# CHAPTER XVI
## TRAIL OF BLOOD

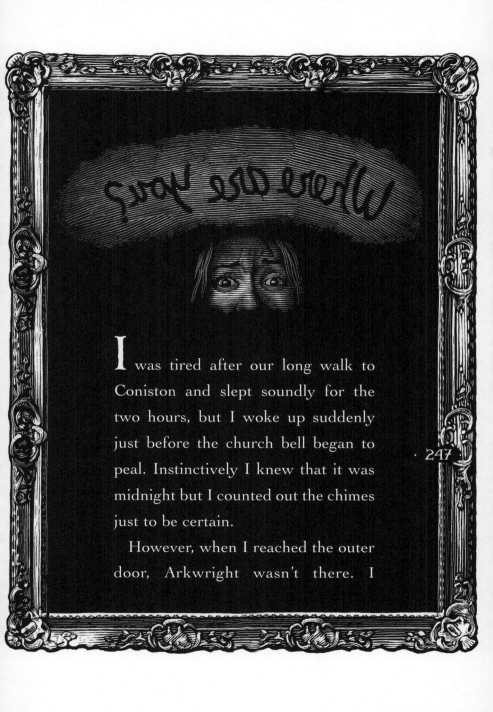

Where are you?

I was tired after our long walk to Coniston and slept soundly for the two hours, but I woke up suddenly just before the church bell began to peal. Instinctively I knew that it was midnight but I counted out the chimes just to be certain.

However, when I reached the outer door, Arkwright wasn't there. I checked outside, then went back to his room. I paused outside and listened: I could hear the sound of snoring. I rapped softly on the door, and when there was no answer, eased it open slowly. Claw and Tooth gave simultaneous low growls as I stepped into the room but then their tails began to wag.

Arkwright was lying on the bed, fully clothed. His mouth was wide open and he was snoring very loudly.

"Mr. Arkwright," I said close to his ear. "Mr. Arkwright, sir, it's time to get up."

I called his name several more times but to no avail. Finally I shook him by the shoulder, and he sat up very suddenly, his eyes wide, face twisted with anger. At first I thought he was going to hit me so I spoke quickly.

"You asked me to meet you outside at midnight but it's well after that now. . . ."

I saw understanding flicker into his eyes; he swung his legs over the edge of the bed and came unsteadily to his feet.

There were two lanterns on the bedside table and he lit

both and handed one to me. Then he staggered out of his room and down the steps, clutching his head and groaning a little. He led the way through the backyard onto the moonlit slope beyond. I glanced up at the rear of the tavern; all the upstairs windows were in darkness but the downstairs ones still cast bright shafts of light onto the ground. From within I could hear raucous voices and someone singing tunelessly.

The clouds had dissipated and the air was crisp and sharp. The two dogs followed at our heels, their eyes gleaming with excitement. It was a steady climb up the southern slopes of the Old Man until snow crunched under our feet. It wasn't very deep and the surface was just starting to freeze.

Once we reached the shore of Goat's Water, Arkwright came to a halt. The small lake had been well-named: A mountain goat would have been far more at home on its steep banks and overhanging crags than a human. The near shore was dotted with large boulders, making access difficult. But Arkwright had not stopped to look at the view. To my surprise, he bent forward very suddenly and began to vomit violently, gushing ale and hot pot onto the ground. I turned my back on him and walked away, my stomach heaving. He was ill for some time but then the retching stopped and I heard him sucking in big breaths of night air.

"Do you feel well, Master Ward?" he asked, tottering toward me.

I nodded. He was still breathing very heavily and there was a film of sweat on his brow.

"That hot pot must have been off. I'll be giving the landlord a piece of my mind in the morning, make no mistake about that!"

Arkwright took another deep breath and wiped his forehead and mouth with the back of his hand. "I don't feel too well. I think I need to rest for a little while," he said.

We found a boulder close by for him to rest against and sat together in near silence, save for his occasional groans and the odd whimper from the dogs.

After ten minutes I asked if he felt a little better. He nodded and tried to stand, but his legs seemed to buckle beneath him and he sat down again heavily.

"Should I go on alone, Mr. Arkwright?" I suggested. "I don't think you're well enough to search round here, let alone make it all the way to Coniston Water."

"Nay, lad, you can't go off alone. Whatever would Mr. Gregory say with Morwena in our midst. Another five minutes and I'll be right as rain."

But in another five minutes he was throwing up the last of the ale and hot pot and it was clear that he wasn't fit to hunt for Morwena that night.

"Mr. Arkwright," I said, "I think I'd better leave you here and take a look round myself—or we could go back to the inn and search for Morwena tomorrow night."

"We've got to do it tonight," Arkwright said. "I want to get back to the mill as soon as possible. I've been away too long as it is."

"Well, let me search round Coniston Water, then," I said. "I'll take one of the dogs with me. I'll be fine."

Reluctantly he agreed. "All right. You win. I'm not well enough to make it to Coniston Water tonight. You head back the way we came toward the northwest of the lake and search there. Keep your lantern shielded so you won't draw any unwelcome attention. If you see Morwena—or indeed anyone else acting suspiciously—don't take any chances. Just follow them at a distance. Beware of that bloodeye, and just try to find out where they go to ground. Apart from that, do nothing. Just watch and report back to me here.

"If I feel better, I'll have a look around here; then, later, we can check out Lever's Water together. And take the bitch with you," he commanded. "It'll give you a better chance if you run into trouble. Reckon you can find your way back to Coniston Water from here?"

I nodded. The map was fixed inside my head.

"Right. Good luck and I'll see you back here."

Without waiting for a reply, he bent and whispered into Claw's ear, then patted her three times. After pulling the wooden shutters across the lantern, I headed for Coniston

Water, Claw walking obediently at my side. I'd only gone a few steps when I heard Arkwright retching and groaning again. I was sure there was nothing wrong with the hot pot. The ale must have been very strong and he'd downed it far too quickly.

So with Claw at my side, I headed toward Coniston Water and the moon, which was climbing above the trees.

As I walked down the hill, retracing my steps toward the village, an eerie cry came from directly ahead. I waited, tense and alert, sensing danger. There was something familiar about the sound. It could well be some sort of warning cry or signal. But then the strange call came again, almost directly overhead, and suddenly I remembered that I'd heard it before: on the marsh just minutes before I met Morwena and she'd dragged me into the slime. Immediately I glimpsed something flying back toward Goat's Water.

Without doubt it was some sort of bird, and I resolved to ask Arkwright about it just as soon as I got the chance. It might be linked to the water witch. Some witches used either blood or bone magic, but others used familiars: creatures that became their eyes and ears and did their bidding. Maybe the strange bird was Morwena's?

Eventually I came to the village and passed quickly through its deserted streets, Claw padding at my heels. Just a few lights gleamed at upper windows. Once beyond the last house, I skirted the lake to the north shore, where I settled down within the shelter of some trees with a clear view of the shore, the lake beyond gleaming silver in the moonlight.

Time passed slowly, and although Claw and I searched high and low, I neither saw nor heard anything of note. I began to think about Alice, wondering what she was doing and whether she was missing me as much as I missed her. I thought about my master, John Gregory, too. Was he safely tucked up in his bed at Chipenden or out in the dark on spook's business like me?

Finally I decided to return to Goat's Water and Mr. Arkwright. There was no sign of Morwena here.

The climb seemed harder this time, and although the

path gradually leveled out, it was still some way around the Old Man. Soon I was crunching across snow again, following our footprints toward the lake. At last I came within view of the place where I'd left Arkwright. I was moving as quietly as possible so as not to attract the attention of anyone or anything that might be lurking on the fells, but suddenly, to my dismay, Claw started to howl and then bounded ahead of me.

It took me some time to catch up with her, and I needed my staff to help me keep my feet on the slippery surface. As I drew closer, I pulled back the shutters on my lantern so that I could see better.

Immediately my heart sank, my throat tightened with anguish and I began to tremble at the horrific sight before me. It seemed that Arkwright and Tooth had found Morwena. Or rather, she had found them. Tooth was dead, his body lying on the bloodstained snow. His throat had been ripped out. There were footprints around him — something with talons and webbed feet; something that had walked upright. There was another wide trail of blood leading to the lakeshore. While Claw whined with grief for her dead mate, I gripped my staff tightly, numb with shock, and followed that trail right to the water's edge.

The lantern illuminated Arkwright's staff at the edge of the lake; one of his boots was half in, half out of the water. The leather was ripped and it looked as if it had been torn from his foot.

At first I had no doubt what had happened: Morwena had killed Tooth and then hooked Arkwright and dragged him into the water. Then I noticed more webbed prints farther back. Lots of them. More than one water witch had been here. If Arkwright had encountered Morwena, she hadn't been alone. Had she attacked from the water while the others closed in from behind, giving Arkwright no chance of escape?

My heart lurched with fear. She could be submerged under the lake, watching me. There might be lots of witches, just waiting for their chance to attack. At any moment they might erupt from its calm surface, and I would suffer the same fate.

Claw began to howl, that tormented sound echoing back from the high crag above. In a panic I ran just as fast as I could. As each footstep carried me to safety, the howls of the dog became fainter and fainter. At one point I was afraid she might suffer the same fate as her mate. So I paused and whistled for her. I tried three times but got no response, so I pressed on toward the tavern.

Hungover as he was, Arkwright would have had little chance of defending himself. He'd been an experienced and successful spook, but he'd made a big mistake in drinking so heavily. A mistake that had cost him his life.

I reached the safety of the tavern and locked myself in my room, unsure what else to do. As soon as it was light, I intended to head back to Chipenden and tell the Spook what had happened. I couldn't honestly say that I'd liked Arkwright, but I was upset and shaken by the manner of his death. He'd been a good spook and would have taught me lots of useful—maybe vital—things. For all his bully-ing and drunken ways he'd been a powerful enemy of the dark and the County would be the worse for his passing.

But was I in immediate danger now? Doors could be broken down. If the landlord had played some part in this, the water witches would know who and where I was. Morwena might come for me herself or send other water witches to drag me back to the lake.

I remembered what Alice had said about using mirrors to communicate. The Spook wouldn't like it, but I was desperate. I had to tell them what had happened at once. Perhaps the Spook would come north to help me? Maybe meet me halfway?

Sitting on the edge of the bed, I leaned forward, placed both my palms against the cold glass of the mirror and started to think about Alice, as she'd instructed. I tried to visualize her face and thought of the conversations we'd had, the happy times spent at the Spook's house at Chipenden. I concentrated hard but nothing happened.

After a while I lay back on the bed and closed my eyes, but I kept seeing the horror of Tooth's body, the blood on the snow, and Arkwright's boot lying in the water. I sat up and put my head in my hands. Would Alice sense me somehow and use what her aunt, Bony Lizzie, had taught her? Would Alice even now be chanting at the mirror back in the Spook's house in Chipenden?

How could it work when so much distance separated Alice and me? And what if my master caught her? Would he understand that it was necessary? He might send her away; perhaps it was just the excuse he was looking for.

After about ten minutes I placed my hands against the glass again. Now I thought about the time when I'd taken Alice to stay with her aunt in Staumin. I remembered eating the delicious rabbits that Alice had caught and cooked, and how afterward she'd reached across and held my hand. Her left hand had held mine and I'd felt a little guilty, knowing the Spook wouldn't like it, but I'd been truly happy.

Immediately the mirror began to brighten, the glass warming beneath my palms, and suddenly there was Alice's face. I dropped my hands and stared back into her eyes.

Her mouth opened and she began to speak, but the

mirror was silent. I knew that witches used mirrors to spy on one another and their intended victims, but did they actually communicate by reading one another's lips? I couldn't make out what she was saying and shook my head. At that she leaned forward and the mirror began to cloud. Quickly she wrote on the glass:

## !ɘƚiɿw bns ɘdƚsɘɿᙠ

What did it mean? For a moment I was puzzled, but then I managed to decipher the message. The mirror had reversed her words. It was an instruction. *Breathe and write!* She was telling me how to speak to her.

So I leaned forward, misted the glass with my breath, and wrote quickly:

## Arkwright killed by water witch called Morwena. Help!

Alice's eyes widened and she breathed on the glass and wrote again:

Where are you?

This time I found it easier to read. *Where are you?* So I wiped the glass with the palm of my hand and breathed on it again before writing:

## Coniston.
## On way back.
## Tell Spook. Meet me at
## Arkwright's water mill.

After a few seconds I wiped the mirror again so that I could see Alice's face. She nodded and gave me a faint smile, but she looked very anxious. As I watched, her face faded until I was looking at my own reflection again.

Then I lay back on the bed and waited for dawn. The sooner I was clear of this place, the better.

# CHAPTER XVII
## PURSUIT

AT first light I prepared to leave. The bill had been paid in advance for three days, covering our rooms and breakfasts. But I wouldn't risk showing my face downstairs. Questions would be asked about my master's disappearance; perhaps the landlord or his customers were in league with Morwena. I couldn't take any risks.

So carrying my bag and staff, I slipped out by the back door and was soon heading south.

The easiest and most direct route was down the western shore of Coniston Water. I kept my distance from it, just in case Morwena or any of the other water witches were following me. But it was late afternoon, when I was already well past the lake's southern extremity, before I began to suspect that I was indeed being pursued.

There were faint but disturbing noises behind me: an occasional rustling in the undergrowth and once the distant crack of a breaking twig. At first it was hard to be sure because when I stopped, all became quiet. As soon as I walked on, the sounds continued, and gradually over the next few miles they seemed to be closing in on me. By now I was sure I was being stalked. The light was fading and I didn't relish the prospect of being hunted in the dark, so with my heart pounding, I put down my bag, released the blade from the top of my staff and turned to face my pursuer. I waited tensely, my body rigid, all my senses alert, but it wasn't a witch who emerged from the thickets to my rear. It was Claw.

She whined and came to lie at my feet, her head almost resting on my left shoe. Relieved, I let out a sigh and reached down to pat her head. I realized I was actually pleased to see her. A lot had happened since I'd been afraid to turn my back on her. If I was being pursued by witches, I now had a formidable ally.

"Good girl!" I said softly, then turned and continued on my way just as fast as I could, Claw close at my heels. My instincts told me that I was still in danger. The sooner I was back at the mill, the better, but I had a decision to make. I could take the long route east, following the wide curve of the bay, but this might enable any pursuers to overtake me or even cut me off. Alternatively I could cross the dangerous sands. That would mean waiting for the tide and the guide and would waste precious time, perhaps allowing Morwena to catch up with me anyway. It was a difficult choice but I finally opted for the sand crossing.

I was exhausted but forced myself to continue through

the night. Keeping to the lower ground, I passed to the west of the hills where we'd stayed with the hermit but was soon forced to climb again. At last I began to descend toward the bay. The distant sea gleamed in the moonlight. The tide seemed a long way out, but was it safe to cross?

I'd have to wait for dawn, then try to find the guide. I didn't know where he lived but I just had to hope that he was on this side of the bay, not on the far shore. I halted at last on the edge of a low cliff, staring out at the flat sands stretching into the distance. To the east there was a faint purple light on the horizon that hinted at sunrise but it was still well over an hour before dawn.

Claw stretched out on the frosty grass beside me but she seemed uneasy. Her ears were flat against her head and she kept growling low in her throat. At last she settled down and became quiet. My head kept nodding, but each time I jerked awake suddenly, alert for danger. The long walk had exhausted me, and without realizing it, I eventually fell into a dark, dreamless slumber.

I was probably asleep for no more than thirty minutes

when a low growl from Claw and her teeth tugging at my breeches woke me. The sky was much lighter and a stiff breeze was blowing in from the bay. I could smell the approach of rain. Out of the corner of my eye I thought I saw something move. I looked up the hill. At first I could see nothing, but the hairs on the back of my neck began to rise and I sensed danger. After persevering for a minute or so, I finally made out a figure moving down the slope toward me, keeping within the shelter of the trees. Claw growled again. Was it Morwena?

I stood up, clutching my staff. After a few moments I knew for sure that I was watching the approach of a water witch. It was something about the way she walked, a strange rolling of the body, perhaps caused by the talons and webbed toes. She was a creature more suited to water and bog than the firm surface of a grassy slope. But was it Morwena or another less dangerous witch? She was much nearer now but it was still impossible to tell.

Should I confront her? I had both my staff and my silver chain. In theory either was sufficient to deal with an ordinary water witch. But they could move very quickly indeed. If I let her get close enough, she'd hook me with her finger. I was good with my silver chain but the practice post in the Spook's garden was no match for the real thing. I'd faced Grimalkin, the witch assassin, and missed her—probably because of fear, nerves, and exhaustion. I was very tired now, and the fear was starting to build inside me.

If I failed with the chain, I'd have to keep the water witch at bay with my staff, but I would only get one opportunity. If I missed, she'd be under my guard. Would Claw try to help me then? The dog was certainly brave and loyal enough. But I remembered what had happened to her mate, Tooth.

I would be failing in my duty if I left a witch at large. What if she seized someone else because of my failure to act? A child maybe? No, I had to face her.

The witch had approached to within fifty paces when I changed my mind again. Her face was no longer in shadow and I could see that her left eye was closed. I could also see the sharp splinter of bone that pinned the two eyelids together. It was Morwena! Once she opened that bloodeye I'd be paralyzed, petrified, helpless.

Claw growled a warning but it was too late. The witch reached toward her left eye and withdrew the pin. The blood-filled eye opened very wide and stared straight at me. I was already lost. I felt the strength leave my body; the will to move leave my mind. All I could see was that red eye growing brighter and larger.

Suddenly I heard a growl and felt a hard blow to my back, which knocked me clean off my feet. I was sent sprawling facedown into the dirt, banging my forehead. For a moment I was stunned, but then I felt warm breath as Claw began to lick my face. I reached up and patted her with my right hand, realizing that I could move again. Immediately I understood. The dog had not been under the power of the witch. Morwena's bloodeye could only transfix one person or animal at a time. Claw had leaped at me, hurling me to the ground, breaking the spell of the red eye.

I came quickly to my knees but kept my eyes down. I could hear the witch's feet slapping the ground as she ran full tilt down the slope toward me. Don't look at the witch! I told myself, keeping my eyes glued to the ground. Look anywhere except at that blood-filled eye!

I was on my feet in a flash and fleeing from her toward the shore, Claw at my heels. My silver chain was still gripped in my left hand, but how could I ever hope to use it when one glance at my enemy would bind me to the spot? My legs trembled as I ran; surely I wasn't quick enough to escape her. I wanted to check over my shoulder and see how close she was but daren't for fear of that paralyzing eye. At any moment I expected to feel the witch's talons pierce my neck or stab into my throat.

"Claw!" I shouted as I jumped down onto the sands. As the dog panted at my side, I felt more and more relieved with every step. We were safe from the witch for now. I knew Morwena wouldn't be able to tolerate the salt deposited on the sands by the tide. Bare webbed feet couldn't walk on that. But how long could we stay out here? She'd be watching and waiting for when we tried to leave the sands again. And what would I do when the tide came in?

Even if I could manage to evade her and get off the sands, I knew Morwena would follow me all the way back to the mill. I was exhausted already but I knew a witch as strong as Morwena would never tire. Following around the bay with her behind me and possibly other witches lying in wait somewhere along the route would surely be a mistake.

If only the sand guide were here to guide me across. But he was nowhere to be seen. The sea looked a long way out, but I had no way of judging if it was safe to cross now. Arkwright had told me how dangerous the incoming tides were. Travelers drowned; coaches, passengers, and horses were swept away, never to be seen again.

If it hadn't been for Claw I'd have dithered there for hours, but she suddenly darted away from me toward the sea, then turned and barked. I stared at her stupidly; she ran back to my side and then away in the same direction, as if she wanted me to follow. Still I hesitated, but the third time she came back she seized hold of my breeches and tugged violently, almost pulling me over. Then she growled and raced away again.

This time I followed her. It made sense, I told myself. She must have made this crossing many times with her master and she knew the way. I should trust her instincts and follow her. Perhaps if he'd set off recently she'd take me to where the sand guide was waiting.

I walked fast, heading southeast. The sky was brightening rapidly. If I could cross the sands and reach the mill safely, the salt moat would keep Morwena and her allies out. Not only that, she'd have to go the long way round to reach Arkwright's mill, which would take her a day at least. By then, with any luck, the Spook and Alice would have arrived. My master would know how best to defeat her.

When Claw and I reached the river Kent's channel, it was starting to rain and a thick mist was descending. There seemed plenty of water down there in the gully, but it was impossible to tell how deep it was without testing it with my staff. But Claw seemed to know what she was doing and headed north, parallel with the bank. We followed the channel until it curved, at which point Claw barked, plunged down the slope and swam straight across. It was only about fifteen or sixteen paces to the other side. Holding my bag high, I tested the water with my staff before taking each careful stride. It was cold, but the deepest part came up only to my thighs, and I was soon across.

Feeling more confident now, I began to jog behind Claw. The wind was getting up, and the rain was starting to drive harder from my left. The sea was somewhere to my right. I could hear waves crashing in the distance, but the visibility was worsening by the minute and I couldn't see more than a few dozen yards ahead.

I walked on, but as the sea fog grew thicker, I began to feel more and more isolated. How many miles was it to the second river channel? I consoled myself with the thought that, once across, it wasn't more than half an hour or so to

Hest Bank and safety. We walked and walked and I began to lose all track of time. The wind had been coming from my left but now it seemed to have changed direction, driving rain hard into my back. Or had *we* changed direction? I couldn't tell. Wherever I looked, all I could see was a wall of gray mist, but I felt sure the sound of the waves was getting louder. What if we were heading out to sea?

Were we lost? I'd been afraid of the witch, but in my desperation to escape, had I put too much faith in Claw? Even if she could guide us to the far shore, why had I believed that she could possibly know about the tides? It seemed to me that the tide had already turned, but by now it was too late to retrace my steps. The sea would be sweeping in fast down both channels to cut me off. The water would be too deep for me to wade across, and the current would surely carry me away.

As I began to lose all hope, I looked at the sand at my feet and saw something that restored my confidence in Claw. There were tracks there: horses' hooves and two

274

parallel lines recently made by the wheels of a coach. I hadn't seen the coach set off, but we seemed to have caught up with it. We were following the sand guide! Claw was leading me in the right direction after all.

But when we reached the next channel, I despaired again. The water in the channel looked deep and the current was strong, water surging from right to left. The tide was coming in fast now.

Again Claw followed the bank for some way, this time to the right, which worried me because I knew that was probably taking us nearer to the sea. Soon she plunged into the water and swam across. I clambered down the bank as before and waded in. There was less distance to cover this time — maybe only ten paces — but three steps in and the water was up to my waist. Two more and it was almost up to my chest, the fierce current starting to pull me over. I struggled on, my feet sinking into the soft sand at the bottom of the channel as I tried to keep my bag clear of the water.

Just when the water reached my neck and I thought I

would be swept away, I found higher ground. A few more strides brought me out of the water, and I clambered up the bank to safety. But my ordeal wasn't over yet. The tide was now racing in over the flat sands. The mist had lifted and I could see the shore but it still seemed a long way off. The first incoming wave swept over my boots; the second well over my ankles. Soon Claw was swimming and the water was almost to my waist again. If I had to swim, I would lose my staff and my bag, which contained my silver chain.

I urged myself on as fast as I could and finally, miraculously, I reached the edge of the bay and collapsed onto the bank above, struggling for breath, my limbs trembling with exhaustion and fear.

I heard Claw give a warning growl, and I looked up to see a man with a staff standing over me. For a second I thought it was a spook but then realized it was Sam Jennings, the sand guide.

"You're a fool, boy!" he growled. "What possessed you to cross so late and without a guide? I brought a coach over well before first light. One of the horses went lame and we barely made it in time ourselves."

"I'm sorry!" I said, stumbling to my feet. "But I was being chased. I had no choice."

"Sorry? Don't waste your time apologizing to me. Think of your family who'd be left behind to grieve — your poor mother who'd have lost a son. Who was chasing you?"

I didn't reply. I'd said enough already.

He looked me up and down, glancing warily at my bag and staff. "Even if it were the Devil himself at your heels, you did a reckless thing, boy. Bill told me himself that he'd warned you about the dangers here. He's crossed the sands with me more times than I can remember. Why didn't you listen?"

I said nothing.

"Anyway, let's hope you've learned your lesson," he continued. "Look, my cottage isn't too far yonder. Come and dry yourself off. No doubt my wife could find you some hot food to warm your bones."

"Thanks for the offer," I said, "but I've got to get back to the mill."

"Off you go, then, boy. But think on. Remember what I've told you. Too many have drowned out on those sands. Don't you be another!"

I set off, shivering in my cold, wet clothes. At least I was a day ahead of the witch, and with any luck Alice and the Spook would join me soon. I hadn't told the guide that Arkwright was dead because it involved too much spook's business. It seemed to me Arkwright would be missed. For all his faults, he'd done a good job protecting those in the north of the County, and people knew and respected him almost as part of the community.

I'd just had a dangerous encounter with the sea, but the wetlands of the northern County weren't finished with me yet. In an attempt to save time, rather than heading directly for the canal and following it toward the mill, I tried a more direct approach from the north. I skirted the Little Mere, heading for the path where I'd first faced Morwena. I thought I was well clear of the bog but I was wrong. One moment I was squelching along quite happily, the next my right boot began to sink into the soft ground.

The more I struggled, the worse it got, and the soft mud quickly climbed halfway to my knee. I started to panic but then took a deep breath to calm myself. My other foot hadn't sunk in very far and must be on firmer ground. So, taking my weight on my staff, very slowly I managed to drag my right leg clear. The boot freed itself with a loud sucking sound and I almost overbalanced.

After that I was much more careful about where I put my feet. It had made me realize just how dangerous the marsh could be. At last I reached the path and pressed on more swiftly toward the mill.

# CHAPTER XVIII
## TWO MESSAGES

It was only as I approached the mill that I remembered the press-gang and how one of them had threatened to kill us. Arkwright had laughed it off at the time but I wasn't as confident.

It would be easy enough to find out where a spook lived. What if they'd already discovered the location of the mill? They could be waiting in

ambush, either in the garden or within the building.

But after cautiously crossing the moat and thoroughly checking the mill inside, including the room with the coffins, I realized my fears were groundless. No press-gang and no witches. Then, despite my weariness, I carried the five barrels of salt into the garden and tipped them into the moat, making sure that most went into the section open to the marsh. I needed to maintain the strength of the solution to keep out Morwena. Claw followed me while I did so but then barked twice, circled me three times, and bounded away into the distance—no doubt she was off hunting rabbits.

I was worried about the water pits under the mill, too. There were the skelt and the witch to consider. Did they need more salt to keep them docile? If I put too much in, I might kill them, so I decided to take a chance and leave them be for now.

Back in the kitchen, I built up the fire in the stove and dried my wet clothes; then I allowed myself a well-deserved sleep before cooking a hot meal. Those done, I decided to go upstairs to the attic room and search Arkwright's library for the book about Morwena. I hadn't read it all, and I needed to find out everything I could about her. It might make the difference between death and survival. I was nervous of ghosts strong enough to move objects, but it was still daylight and, after all, they were Arkwright's mam and dad, sad and trapped rather than malevolent.

The coffins stood side by side and the three armchairs were drawn up to the stove. I glanced at the cold ashes in the grate and shivered at the damp chill in the air, shaking my head sadly. The two ghosts would no longer have the companionship of their son.

I turned my attention to Arkwright's books. His library was just a fraction of the size of the Spook's at Chipenden, but that was only to be expected. My master had not only lived longer, giving him more time to acquire and write books; he had also inherited them from the generations of spooks who'd lived there before him.

Arkwright's shelves held many titles of local interest,

such as: *The Flora and Fauna of the North County, The Art of Basket Weaving*, and *Lakeland Paths and Byways*. Then there were his notebooks, dating from the time of his apprenticeship almost to the present. These were bound in leather and would no doubt give a detailed account of the knowledge and skills Arkwright had acquired while following our trade. There was also a Bestiary, less than a quarter the size of Mr. Gregory's but probably just as interesting. And beside it was the book about Morwena.

I decided to take it downstairs and read it by the warmth of the stove. I'd taken just one step toward the door when I felt a sudden icy chill: a warning that the unquiet dead were approaching.

A luminous cylindrical shape began to form between me and the doorway. I was surprised. Most ghosts didn't appear during daylight hours. Was it the mother, father, or even the ghost of Arkwright himself? Lingering spirits were usually bound to their bones or the scene of their death, but very occasionally a ghost was forced to wander. I just hoped it wasn't Arkwright. Some spirits are possessive after death and particularly resent intruders into their homes. They still want to live there. Some aren't even fully aware that they're dead. I couldn't help thinking that he'd be angry to find me inside his room, reading one of his books. For an intrusion such as this, I'd suffered cuts and bruises. What now?

But it wasn't Arkwright. A woman's voice called out to me. It was the ghost of Amelia, his mother.

*"My son, my William, still lives. Help him, please, before it's too late."*

"I'm sorry, Mrs. Arkwright. Really sorry. I wish I could help but I can't. You must believe me, your son really is dead," I said, trying to keep my voice as kind and calm as possible, just as the Spook advised when facing the unquiet dead.

*"No! That isn't true. Listen to me! He's shackled within the bowels of the earth, still waiting to die."*

"How can you know that," I asked her gently, "when you're a spirit bound to this place?"

She began to weep softly and the light faded. But just

when I thought she'd gone completely, the light flared to a new brilliance and she cried out in a loud, tremulous voice, *"I heard it in the howl of a dying dog; I read it in the whispers of the marsh reeds; I smelled it in the water dripping from the broken wheel. They spoke to me and now I speak to you. Save him before it is too late. Only you can do it. Only you can face the power of the Fiend!"*

And then in an instant, the column of light shifted into the image of a woman. She was wearing a blue summer dress and carrying a basketful of spring flowers. She smiled at me, and the scent of those flowers suddenly filled the bedroom. It was a warm smile but her eyes glistened with tears.

Suddenly she was gone. I shivered and made my way back to the kitchen, thinking over what had been said. Could the ghost of Arkwright's mother be right? Was he still alive? It seemed unlikely. The trail of blood had led right to the edge of the lake, and he'd lost his staff and boot. The witches must have dragged him into the water. Surely they'd have taken their chance to slay him there and then? After all, he'd been their enemy for long enough and killed many of their kind.

As for that poor ghost, she was probably just confused. That happens sometimes with spirits that are bound to the earth. Their reason flees. Memories fray and become tattered and torn.

With trepidation I thought about what lay ahead. I didn't expect Morwena and the other witches to arrive much before dawn. When they came, the moat would hopefully keep them at bay—but for how long? With luck Alice and the Spook would arrive before then. Together we could finish off Morwena forever. I certainly didn't feel capable of it alone. Then we could return to Chipenden and leave behind this terrible place of streams, lakes, and bogs. I hoped that the Spook wouldn't be too angry with Alice for using the mirror. Surely he had to see that it was justified?

I'd just picked up the book and started to read when I heard the sound of a distant bell. I listened carefully. After a few moments the sound was repeated. When it rang for the fifth and final time, I knew that it was Mr. Gilbert down by the canal with a delivery.

He must have often rung the bell when Arkwright was away on business. If I just stayed in the mill, he'd probably move on down the canal, thinking to call next time he passed. But Mr. Gilbert wouldn't yet know that Arkwright was dead, and as he'd seemed genuinely fond of the man, I felt it was my duty to go and break the bad news to him. After all, it should be safe enough. Morwena would still be miles away, and I could do with seeing a friendly face.

So, carrying just my staff, I set off for the canal. It was a bright afternoon and the sun was shining. Mr. Gilbert was heading south, and the barge was on the far side of the canal. It seemed very low in the water, suggesting that it was heavily laden with cargo. Someone was grooming the horses. It was a girl of about my own age, golden hair glinting in the sun — no doubt Mr. Gilbert's daughter. He waved to me from the towpath and pointed toward the nearest bridge, about a hundred yards to the north.

I crossed over and came back to the barge.

When I drew closer, I could see that the bargeman was holding an envelope. He raised his eyebrows. "What's wrong?" he demanded. "You look down in the mouth, Tom. Bill's not giving you that bad a time, is he?"

There was no easy way to explain what had happened so I told him simply, "I've some bad news for you. Mr. Arkwright's dead. He was killed by water witches north of the bay. They may be after me now, so take care of yourself on the water. Who knows where or when they might appear."

Mr. Gilbert looked stunned. "Who indeed!" he said. "It's a terrible business. Bill'll be sadly missed, and I fear for the County now he's gone."

I nodded. He was right. There would be nobody to replace him. Competent members of our trade were thin on the ground. The area north of Caster would become much more dangerous now. It was a significant victory for the dark.

With a regretful sigh he handed me the envelope. "This

is from Mr. Gregory," he said quietly. "He gave it to me this morning at Caster."

It was addressed to me and was in my master's handwriting. To reach Caster so soon the Spook and Alice must have set off over the fells almost immediately and walked through the night as I had. I was relieved at the thought. But why hadn't the Spook carried on to the mill? He could have got himself a ride on the barge — although the barge was now on the wrong side of the canal, as if it had come from the north rather than from Caster. But then I realized the bargeman must have used the bridge I'd just crossed to bring the horses over to this side so he could now head back south. I tore open the envelope and began to read.

Ask Mr. Arkwright to release you from his instruction for a few days. Mr. Gilbert will bring you safely to Caster, where I'll be waiting. This is a matter of great urgency. Right in the heart of that city, close to the canal, I've found something of

immense help in our fight against the dark. It
concerns you directly.

　　Your master,

　　John Gregory


The Spook seemed to know nothing of Bill's death, so
either Alice hadn't told him or for some reason he was
pretending not to know. And as he hadn't come straight to
the mill to deal with Morwena, I knew that the find in
Caster must be something very special.

　"Get yourself aboard," said Mr. Gilbert, "but first there's
somebody I'd like you to meet. My son had long overdue
chores at home, but my daughter's with me. Come here,
daughter, and meet young Tom!" he called out.

　The girl looked up from her grooming and, without
bothering to turn round, lifted her arm to wave but made
no effort to obey her father.

　"A very shy girl," Mr. Gilbert observed. "But let's be on
our way. No doubt she'll pluck up the courage to talk to
you later."

I hesitated. Leaving Claw at the mill would probably be all right; she could fend for herself for now. And I felt fine enough about leaving my bag but not the most valuable thing it contained: my silver chain. Who knew what we might face in Caster? It was a potent weapon against the dark—particularly witches—and I didn't want to be without it.

"I need to go back to the mill for something," I told Mr. Gilbert.

He frowned and shook his head. "We haven't really got time. Your master's waiting and we need to get to Caster before dark."

"Why don't you start the journey," I told him, "and I'll run and catch up."

I could tell that he didn't like the idea, but what I'd suggested was perfectly reasonable. Pulling a heavy barge, horses usually plodded along at a relatively slow pace, so I would be able to catch up and then ride and rest for the remainder of the journey.

I smiled at him politely, then set off at a run. Soon I'd

crossed the bridge and was sprinting along the banks of the river toward the house.

When I walked into the kitchen, I had the shock of my life. Alice was sitting in the chair by the stove and Claw was close to her, muzzle resting comfortably upon her pointy shoes.

She smiled up at me and patted Claw on the head. "Expecting puppies, this one," she said. "Two, I reckon."

I smiled back, relieved and glad to see her. "If that's so, their father's dead," I told her, the smile slipping away. "Morwena killed him as well as his master. It's been bad, Alice. Really bad. You can't know how glad I am to see you. But why aren't you in Caster with the Spook?"

"Caster? Don't know nothing about that. Old Gregory went off to Pendle more than a week ago. On his way to Malkin Tower, he said. He was going to look in your mam's trunks and see if they held any information about the Fiend. When I talked to you in the mirror, he still wasn't back so I left him a note and came by myself. Knew you needed help urgently."

Puzzled, I handed Alice the Spook's letter. She read it

quickly and looked up, nodding. "Makes sense," she said. "Most likely Old Gregory found something important and traveled straight from Pendle to Caster. Don't know what's happened to Arkwright yet, does he? Just sent a message to the mill and asked for you."

"You nearly missed me, Alice. Mr. Gilbert's waiting for me now. I came back only to get my silver chain."

"Oh, Tom!" Alice said, coming to her feet and moving toward me, alarm on her face. "What's happened to your ear? It looks really sore! I've got something that should help. . . ." She reached for her pouch of herbs.

"No, Alice, there isn't time now and the doctor said it'll be all right. It's where Morwena hooked me with a talon and dragged me into the bog. Claw saved me. I'd be dead but for her."

I unfastened my bag and pulled out my chain, which I then tied about my waist, hiding it under my cloak. "Why didn't you follow the canal from Caster to the mill, Alice? It's the shortest route."

"No it ain't," she said. "Not if you know what's what.

Told you before, I know this place well, don't I? Year before I met you, Bony Lizzie brought me up here and we stayed on the edge of the marsh until Arkwright came back from one of his trips north and we had to move on. Anyway, I know that marsh like the back of my hand."

"I don't expect Mr. Gilbert'll mind if you travel with me. But he'll probably have set off already and we'll have to catch up."

When Claw followed us out into the garden, Alice shook her head. "Ain't a good idea for her to go with us to Caster," she said. "City ain't no place for a dog. Better off here, where she can live off the land."

I agreed but Claw completely ignored Alice's commands that she "stay" and trotted at our heels until we were on the path beside the stream.

"You tell her, Tom. Maybe she'll listen to you. After all, she's *your* dog now!"

My dog? I hadn't thought of that. I couldn't imagine the Spook wanting a dog with us in Chipenden. Nonetheless I knelt beside Claw and patted her head.

"Stay, girl! Stay!" I commanded. "We'll be back soon."

She whimpered and rolled her eyes. It wasn't that long since I'd been terrified of her but now I felt sad at leaving her. But I wasn't lying: We'd call back here on our way to deal with Morwena.

To my surprise, Claw obeyed me and stayed behind on the path. We jogged along until we reached the canal. The barge was still waiting.

"Who's the girl?" Alice demanded as we walked toward the bridge.

"That's just Mr. Gilbert's daughter. She's really shy."

"Never seen a shy girl with hair that color," Alice said, an edge of venom in her voice.

The truth was I'd never seen a girl with quite that color hair at all. It was far brighter and more vivid than that of Jack's wife, Ellie, whose hair I'd always considered especially beautiful. But whereas Ellie's was the color of best-quality straw three days after a good harvest, this really was a most spectacular gold, now lit to brilliance by the sun.

The girl was still grooming the horses and probably felt

more comfortable doing that than talking to strangers. Some people were like that. My dad told me that he'd once worked with a farm laborer who wouldn't give you the time of day yet talked to the animals all the time.

"And who's this young lady?" Mr. Gilbert asked as we came up to the barge.

"This is Alice," I said, introducing her. "She stays with us at Chipenden and makes copies of Mr. Gregory's books. Is it all right if she travels with us on the barge?"

"Only too happy to oblige." Mr. Gilbert smiled, glancing at her pointy shoes.

Moments later we were both aboard, but the bargeman's daughter didn't join us. Her job was to lead the horses down the towpath while her dad relaxed on the barge.

It was now late afternoon, but it was pleasant to be gliding toward Caster in the sunshine. However, the thought of entering that city filled me with foreboding. We'd always avoided it previously because of the danger of being arrested and imprisoned in the castle. I wondered what it was that my master had found that was so important.

# CHAPTER XIX
## THE BARGEMAN'S DAUGHTER

THE journey south was uneventful. The strange thing was that, for most of the time, nobody spoke a word. I'd lots of things to say to Alice but I didn't utter them in the bargeman's presence. I just didn't like talking spook's business in front of him and I knew my master would have agreed. Such things were best kept to ourselves.

I already knew that Mr. Gilbert was a taciturn man and didn't expect much in the way of conversation, but then, as the castle and church spires of the city came into view, he suddenly became very talkative.

"Do you have brothers, Tom?" he asked.

"I have six," I answered. "The eldest, Jack, still lives on the family farm. He runs it with James, the next eldest, who's a blacksmith by trade."

"What about the others?"

"They're scattered about the County doing jobs of their own."

"Are they all older than you?"

"All six," I said with a smile.

"Of course they are—what a fool I am to ask! You're the seventh son of a seventh son. The last one to gain employment and the only one fitted by birth for Bill Arkwright's trade. Do you miss them, Tom? Do you miss your family?"

I didn't speak and for a moment became choked with emotion. I felt Alice rest her hand on my arm to comfort me. It wasn't just missing my brothers that made me feel that way—it was because my dad had died the previous year and Mam had returned to her own country to fight the dark. I suddenly felt very alone.

"I can sense your sadness, Tom," said Mr. Gilbert. "Family are very important and their loss can never be replaced. It's good to have family about you and to work alongside them as I do. I have a loyal daughter who helps me whenever I need her."

Suddenly I shivered. Only moments earlier the sun had been far above the treetops, but now it was quickly growing dark and a thick mist was descending. All at once we were entering the city and the angular shapes of buildings quickly rose up on either side of the canal bank like threatening giants, though all was silent but for the muffled *clip-clop* of the horses' hooves. The canal was much wider here, with lots of recesses on the far bank where barges were moored. But there was little sign of life.

I felt the barge coming to a halt, and Mr. Gilbert stood up and looked down at Alice and me. His face was in darkness and I couldn't read his expression but somehow he seemed threatening.

I looked ahead and could just make out the form of his daughter, apparently draped over the leading horse. She didn't seem to be moving so she wasn't grooming it. It was almost as if she was whispering into its ear.

"That daughter of mine," Mr. Gilbert said with a sigh. "She does so love a plump horse. Can't get enough of them. Daughter! Daughter!" he called out in a loud voice. "There's no time for that now. You must wait until later!"

Almost immediately the horses took up the strain again, the barge glided forward, and Mr. Gilbert went toward the bow and sat down again.

"Don't like this, Tom," Alice whispered in my ear. "It don't feel right. Not right at all!"

No sooner had she spoken than I heard the fluttering of wings somewhere in the darkness overhead, followed by a plaintive, eerie cry.

"What sort of bird is that?" I asked Alice. "I heard a cry like that just a few days ago."

"It's a corpsefowl, Tom. Ain't Old Gregory told you about 'em?"

"No," I admitted.

"Well, it's something you should know about, being a spook. They're night birds, and some folk think witches can shape-shift into them. But that's just a load o' nonsense. Witches do use them as familiars, though. In exchange for a bit o' blood the corpsefowl will become their eyes and ears."

"Well, I heard one when I was looking for Morwena. D'you think it's her familiar? If so, she might be somewhere nearby. Perhaps she's moved faster than I expected. Maybe she's swimming underwater close to this barge."

The canal narrowed, the buildings closing in on either side, as if attempting to cut us off from the thin oblong of pale sky above. They were huge warehouses, probably busy with the hustle and bustle of business during the day but now still and silent. The occasional wall lantern sent patches of flickering light onto the water, but there were large areas of gloom and patches of intense darkness that filled me with foreboding. I agreed with Alice: I couldn't put my finger on exactly what it was but things certainly didn't feel right.

I glimpsed a dark stone arch ahead. At first I thought it was a bridge but then realized that it was the entrance to a large warehouse and the canal went straight through it. As we glided into the doorway, the horses beginning to slow, I could see that the building was vast and filled with large mounds of slate, probably brought by barge from the quarry to the north. On the wooden quayside were a number of mooring posts and a row of five huge wooden supports, which disappeared into the darkness to hold up the roof. From each hung a lantern so that the canal and near bank were bathed in yellow light. But beyond lay the dark, threatening vastness of the warehouse.

Mr. Gilbert bent toward the nearest hatch and slowly slid it back. Until that moment I hadn't noticed that it wasn't locked, something he'd once told me was vital when carrying cargo. To my surprise, the hold was also filled with yellow light and I looked down to see two men sitting on a pile of slate, each nursing a lantern. Immediately I saw something to their left that started my whole body trembling and plunged me into a pit of horror and despair.

It was a dead man, the unseeing eyes staring upward. The throat had been ripped out in a manner that reminded me of what had been done to Tooth by Morwena. But it was his identity that scared me more than the cruel horror of his murder.

The dead man was Mr. Gilbert.

I looked across the open hatch at the creature who had taken the bargeman's likeness. "If that's Mr. Gilbert," I said, "then you must be . . ."

"Call me what you will, Tom. I have many names," he replied. "But none adequately convey my true nature. I've been misrepresented by my enemies. The difference between the words *fiend* and *friend* is merely one letter. I could easily be the latter. If you knew me better . . ."

With those words I felt all the strength drain from my

body. I tried to reach for my staff but my hand wouldn't obey me, and as everything grew dark, I caught a glimpse of Alice's terrified face and heard her give a wail of terror. That sound chilled me to the bone. Alice was strong. Alice was brave. For her to cry out in such a way made me feel that it was all over for us. This was the end.

Waking felt like floating up from the depths of a deep, dark ocean. I heard sounds first. The distant terrified whinnies of a horse and a man's loud, coarse laughter close by. As memories of what had happened returned, I felt panic and helplessness, and I struggled to get to my feet.

I finally gave up when I'd taken in my situation. I was no longer on the barge but sitting on the wooden quay, bound tightly to one of the roof supports, my legs parallel with the canal.

By a simple act of will the Fiend had rendered me unconscious. What was worse, the strengths we'd learned to depend upon had failed us. Alice hadn't managed to sniff out Morwena. My powers as a seventh son of a seventh son had proven equally useless. Time had also seemed to pass in a way that was far from normal. One moment the sun had been shining and the city spires were on the horizon; the next it had been almost dark and we'd been deep within its walls. How could anyone hope to defeat such power?

The barge was still moored at the quay, and the two men, each with a long knife tucked into his leather belt, were sitting there, big steel-toed boots dangling over the edge. But the horses were no longer harnessed. One of them was lying on its side some distance away, its forelegs hanging over the water. The other was nearer, also lying down, and the girl had her arms around its neck. I thought she was trying to help it to its feet. Were the horses sick?

But there was something different about her: Where previously her hair had been golden now it was dark. How could her hair have changed color like that? My mind was still befuddled or I would have worked out

307

much sooner exactly what was happening. It was only when she left the horse, turned, and walked toward me, her feet bare, that I began to understand.

She was cupping her hands, holding them before her strangely as she walked. Why was she doing that? And she was walking very slowly and carefully. As she drew nearer, I noticed the blood on her lips. She'd been feeding from the horse, drinking the poor animal's blood. That's what she'd been doing when I'd first glimpsed her. That's why she'd halted the barge as we journeyed south.

It was Morwena! She must have been wearing a wig. Either that or some dark enchantment had made me see her hair as golden. No wonder she'd kept her back to us. Now I could see that fleshless nose and hideous face. Her left eye was closed.

A shadow fell upon me, and I flinched back against the post. I sensed the Fiend close at my back. He didn't move into my field of vision, but his voice was an icy chill squeezing my heart so that it began to beat erratically and I could hardly breathe.

"I have to leave you now, Tom. You are not my only concern. I have other important business to undertake. But my daughter, Morwena, will take care of you. You are in her hands now."

With those words he was gone. Why hadn't he stayed? What could be so important as to call him away just when I was so completely vulnerable? He must have great faith in Morwena's power. As his footsteps faded away, the Devil's daughter came toward me, her expression cruel.

I heard the flapping of huge wings and an ugly bird swooped to alight on her left shoulder. She raised her cupped hands and it dipped its beak into them again and again, drinking its fill of what she held there: the blood of the dying horse. Having quenched its thirst, the corpse-fowl gave a shrill cry, flapped its wings, and fluttered upward, to be lost from sight.

Morwena then knelt on the wooden quay, her hands red with blood, so close that she could have reached out and touched me. I tried to keep my breath steady but my heart was hammering in my chest. She stared at me with her reptilian right eye as her tongue flicked out and licked the blood from her lips. Only when they were clean did she speak.

"You sit so still and quiet. But bravery has no place here. No place at all. You are here to die and won't escape your fate a second time!"

Now she revealed those terrible yellow-green canine teeth, and her foul breath washed over me so that it was hard not to retch. Her voice was harsh and sibilant, beginning each sentence with the hiss and splutter of liquid being poured over hot coals, ending with the gurgle of a swamp swallowing its victims, sucking them into its sodden maw. She moved her head a little closer to mine, and rather than looking me in the eye, stared at my neck.

For a moment I thought she was about to sink her teeth in before ripping out my throat. I actually flinched, and at that involuntary movement she smiled and raised her right eye to meet mine.

"I've already drunk my fill, so live a little longer. Breathe for a while and watch what's about to unfold."

I was starting to tremble and struggled to control the fear that is always a spook's worst enemy when facing the dark. Morwena seemed to want to talk. If that was the case, I could get information that might prove useful. Things looked bleak, but I'd been in difficult spots before when my chances of survival appeared slim. As my dad used to say, "While there's life, there's hope," and it was something I believed in myself.

"What *are* you going to do?" I asked.

"Destroy my father's enemies: you and John Gregory will die tonight."

"My master? Is he here?" I asked. I wondered if he was a prisoner in the other hold.

She shook her head. "He's on his way even as we speak. My father sent him a letter to lure him to this place — just as he forged the letter he placed in your hands. John Gregory believes it's a plea for help from you and now hastens here to his fate."

"Where's Alice?"

"In the hold where she's safe," Morwena hissed, that

jutting ridge of bone that served as her nose now mere inches away from my face. "But I want you in view. You're the bait that will draw your master to his *death*."

That final word was like the ugly croak of a swamp frog echoing over a stagnant bog. She quickly pulled a mottled handkerchief from her sleeve and gagged my mouth. That done, she looked up suddenly and sniffed twice.

"He's almost here!" she said, nodding toward the two men, who retreated into the shadows to lie in wait. I assumed she'd join them, but to my surprise and dismay, she approached the edge of the canal, lowered herself into the water, and disappeared from sight.

The Spook was tough and skilled with his staff. Unless he was taken completely by surprise I estimated him to be more than a match for the two armed men. But if the witch attacked from the water while he fought them, that was another matter. My master was in grave danger.

# CHAPTER XX
## NO CHOICE AT ALL

I sat there, helpless, knowing that any moment now my master would arrive; if Morwena had her way, he'd be the first of us to die. But things still weren't hopeless because, for some strange reason of his own, the Fiend had now left us. My master would not be so easy to kill. He had a fighting chance at least. But how could I help him?

315

I struggled to free myself from the thick rope that bound me to the post. It was very tight, and no matter how hard I twisted and turned it barely yielded. I heard a faint noise in the distance. Was it one of the waiting men? Or was it the Spook?

The next moment there was no doubt. The Spook was walking down the quay toward me carrying his staff and bag, his footsteps echoing. I suppose we noticed each other at exactly the same moment because no sooner had I set eyes on him than he came to a halt. He stared at me for a long time before continuing more slowly. I knew he would have worked out that it was a trap. Why else would I be tied up like that in full view? So he could either retreat and make his escape or come forward and hope that he could deal with whatever had been prepared. I knew he wouldn't leave me—so it was no choice at all.

After another twenty paces he halted again, directly under one of the huge posts that supported the roof of the warehouse. He was staring at the two dead horses. The lantern was shining full in his face, and by its light I could see that although he looked old and a little gaunt, his eyes still glittered fiercely and his senses were sharp and alert, testing the dark recesses of the warehouse for danger.

He continued toward me again. I could have nodded toward the water to warn him about the threat from Morwena. But to do so might distract him from the other threat from the darkness on his right.

Suddenly, less than twenty paces from me, he halted again, and this time he put down his bag and lifted his staff defensively, holding it with both hands at an angle of forty-five degrees. I heard the distinctive click as he released the retractable blade and then everything happened very quickly.

The two thugs burst out of the darkness from my left, their long knives glinting in the lantern light. Turning his back on the water, the Spook whirled to meet them. For a second his opponents seemed to hesitate. Perhaps they saw the wicked-looking blade at the end of his staff. Either that or the determination in his eyes. But then, as they rushed on, knives aloft, ready to cut him down, he struck. Using the thick base of his staff, he landed a terrible blow on one man's temple. The man fell soundlessly, the knife flying from his fingers, even as the Spook thrust the point of his blade toward his second assailant. As the blade pierced the man's right shoulder, he also dropped his knife, then fell to his knees and uttered a thin, high cry of pain.

The Spook angled his staff toward his fallen enemy, and for a moment he seemed about to stab downward, but then he shook his head and said something to him in a low voice. The man staggered to his feet and stumbled away into the darkness, clutching his shoulder. Only then did the Spook glance back in my direction and I was finally able to nod desperately toward the water of the canal.

I wasn't a second too soon. Morwena surged into the air with the strength of a salmon leaping up a waterfall, her arms outstretched to tear at the Spook's face, though her left eye was still closed.

My master met her with equal speed. He spun, bringing his staff in a rapid arc from left to right. It missed

Morwena's throat by a hair's breadth, and with a terrible shriek of anger she flopped back into the water less than gracefully, creating a huge splash.

The Spook froze, looking down into the water. Then, with his right hand, he reached up and tugged his hood up, forward, and down so that it shielded his eyes. He must have seen the pinned eye and realized who he was dealing with. Without eye contact Morwena would not be able to use her bloodeye against him. Nonetheless he would be fighting "blind."

He waited, immobile, and I watched anxiously as the last ripple erased itself from the surface of the canal, which became as still as glass. Suddenly Morwena surged from the water again, this second attack even more sudden than the first, and then landed on the very edge of the wharf, her webbed feet slapping hard against the wooden boards. Her bloodeye was now open, its baleful red fire directed at the Spook. But without looking up, he stabbed toward her legs and she was forced to retreat.

Immediately she struck at him with her left hand, the

claws raking toward his shoulder, but he stepped away just in time. Then, as she moved the other way, he flicked his staff from his left to his right hand and jabbed toward her hard and fast. It was the same maneuver he'd made me practice against the dead tree in his garden—the one that had saved my life in the summer when I'd used it successfully against Grimalkin.

He executed it perfectly, and the tip of his blade speared Morwena in the side. She let out a cry of anguish but leaped away quickly, somersaulting back into the water. The Spook waited a long time but she didn't attack again.

Only then did he come swiftly to my side, lean forward and tug the scarf downward to free my mouth.

"Alice is tied up in the hold!" I said, gasping. "Mr. Gilbert is dead. And that was Morwena who attacked you from the water! The Fiend's own daughter! And there could be other water witches on their way!"

"Calm yourself, lad," the Spook said. "I'll have you free in a moment. . . ."

That said, he used the staff's blade to cut through my

bonds. As I came slowly to my feet, rubbing my wrists to restore the circulation, my master pointed at the knife of one of his assailants, which was lying on the quayside.

"Free her while I stand guard," he said.

We stepped onto the barge, and staff at the ready, the Spook stood resolutely beside me while I slid back the hatch. Alice stared up at me from below. She was bound and gagged and they'd left her by the dead body of the bargeman.

"The Fiend was here. He's taken Mr. Gilbert's shape," I told my master.

"Well, there's nothing we can do for the poor man now," said the Spook, shaking his head sadly. "We'll have to leave him for others to find and bury. But cut the girl free. We need to be away from here as quickly as possible. The witch isn't badly hurt. No doubt she'll be getting ready to try again."

I could feel Alice trembling as I cut her bonds and helped her from the hold. She didn't say a word and her eyes were wide with fear. It seemed that the proximity of the Fiend had terrified her even more than it had me.

Once the three of us were standing on the quay, the Spook pointed north, then led us out of the warehouse, walking so fast that I struggled to keep up.

"Aren't we heading back to Chipenden?" I asked.

"No, we're not, lad. Not enough time to get there if Morwena gives chase. We're off to poor Bill Arkwright's house first. It's the nearest refuge. But the sooner we get away from this canal bank, the better," he said, eyeing the water warily.

"I know a quicker route to the mill," volunteered Alice. "I used to live near there with Bony Lizzie. We need to cross the canal and then keep well to the west."

"Then lead on, girl," said the Spook.

So we crossed the first bridge, left the towpath, and headed north through the darkness of the narrow cobbled streets. Caster, with its castle and dungeons, was no place for those who followed our trade; fortunately there were few people about to see our passing. At last, with a sense of relief, we left the city behind us and followed Alice across the countryside, using only the light of the stars and the pale half moon. Eventually, skirting the edge of Monastery Marsh, we reached the mill garden and crossed the salt moat.

"How long since salt was last added?" asked the Spook. They were the first words that anybody had spoken since we left the canal back in Caster.

"I did it only yesterday," I told him.

As we entered the willow garden, there came a warning growl and Claw bounded up. I reached down and patted her head and she followed at my heels.

"This dog saved my life," I said. Neither the Spook nor Alice commented, and as we reached the door, Claw went her own way down the side of the house toward the waterwheel. It was better to have her outside anyway. That way she would give warning if a witch approached the garden.

Soon we were in the mill kitchen, and wasting no time, I filled the stove with wood and got it alight. The Spook and Alice sat and watched me work. My master was deep in thought. Alice still looked terrified.

"Shall I make us some early breakfast?" I asked.

My master shook his head firmly. "Better not, lad. We could be facing the dark at any time and need to fast. But no doubt the girl would like something."

Alice shook her head even more vigorously than the Spook. "I'm not hungry," she said flatly.

"Well, in that case, we need to try to make some sense of what's been going on. I smelled a rat from the very first," asserted the Spook. "As soon as I got back to Chipenden, I read Alice's note as well as your previous letter. But I was just about to set off for the mill when the bell rang at the crossroads. It was the village smith; someone had pushed a letter under his door with my name on it. It was marked 'urgent.' It was in your handwriting, lad, but even more of a shaky scrawl than usual, as if you'd written it in a hurry. It said that you were in serious trouble and needed help. From what it didn't specify; it simply gave the address of that warehouse in Caster.

"Well, I knew you couldn't be in two places at once, but

as Caster is on the way to the mill, I went there first. I was prepared for trouble and certainly found it. But there's one thing still bothering me. How did the girl know you were in danger? How did you get word to her?"

The Spook stared at me hard, and I knew I couldn't avoid telling him the truth. So I took a deep breath. "I used a mirror," I said, bowing my head, unable to meet his gaze.

"What did you say, lad?" the Spook said, his voice dangerously low. "Did I just hear you right? A mirror? *A mirror . . . ?*"

"It was the only way I could contact you!" I blurted out. "I was desperate. Mr. Arkwright was dead, murdered by Morwena, and I knew she'd be coming for me next. I needed you. I couldn't face her alone—"

My master cut me short. "I knew I should never have let a Deane stay with us!" he said angrily, glaring at Alice. "She's led you into bad ways. Using a tool of the dark like that makes you vulnerable. As soon as you used that mirror, the Fiend would have known where you were;

anything you communicated would instantly have been known to him."

"I didn't know that," I said lamely.

"No? Well, you certainly know it now. And as for you, girl," he went on, standing up and staring hard at Alice, "you're unusually quiet. Nothing to say for yourself?"

In response Alice covered her face with her hands and began to sob.

"Being close to the Fiend scared her badly," I said. "I've never seen her so shaken."

"Well, lad, you know what her problem is, don't you?"

I shook my head. I didn't know what he meant.

"The Fiend is the dark made flesh. The Devil himself, who rules over and owns the souls of those who belong to the dark. The girl here has been trained as a witch and has come close, far too close, to becoming a creature of darkness herself. That being the case, she senses the Fiend's power and knows just how easily he could steal away her soul. She's vulnerable and she knows it. That's what makes her afraid."

"But—" I began.

"Save your breath, lad! It's been a long night and I'm too tired to listen. After what you've told me, I can hardly bear to look at the two of you so I'm going upstairs to catch up on some sleep. I suggest you two do the same. The dog should warn us if anything gets close."

When he'd gone upstairs, I turned to Alice. "Come on, he's right," I said. "Let's get some sleep."

She didn't reply, and I realized that she was already in a deep slumber. So I settled myself down in my chair, and within a few moments I'd fallen asleep myself.

A few hours later I awoke with a start. Daylight was streaming through the windows, and looking across, I saw that Alice was already awake. But what I saw her doing gave me a shock. She had my pen in her hand and was writing furiously in my notebook, muttering to herself as she did so.

# CHAPTER XXI
## HOBBLED

"ALICE! What are you doing?"
I demanded. "Why are you writing in
my book?"

She looked up, her eyes wide.
"Sorry, Tom. Should have asked you
first but I didn't want to disturb you."

"But *what* are you writing?"

"Just jotting down some things that
Bony Lizzie taught me; some things

that might help us defeat the Fiend. You're going to need all the help you can get."

I was horrified. The Spook had once told Alice that she had to tell me the things she'd been taught so that we could increase our knowledge of witch lore and the dark powers that we faced. But this was different. She was suggesting we use the dark to fight the dark and I knew the Spook wouldn't like it.

"Weren't you listening last night?" I shot back. "Using the dark is making us vulnerable."

"Don't you see that we're vulnerable already?"

I turned away.

"Look, Tom, what Old Gregory said about me last night was true. I've been as close to the dark as you can get—at least without becoming a fully fledged witch. So I was terrified, being close to the Fiend like that. Ain't no way I can tell you how I felt. You belong to the light, Tom, fully to the light, and you'll never get that same feeling. A mixture of terror and despair, it was. A sense that I deserved whatever I got. If he'd asked me to follow him, to be his creature, I'd have done it without another thought."

"I don't understand what that's got to do with any-thing," I said.

"Well, I ain't the first person to feel like that. Once, long ago, the Fiend walked the earth and witches had to deal with that. So there are ways to cope. Ways to keep him at bay. I'm just trying to remember some of them. Lizzie kept Old Nick away from her, but she never told me how she done it; it could be there in some of the things she said."

"But you'd be using the powers of the dark against him, Alice! That's the whole point. You heard what the Spook said. It was bad enough using a mirror. Please don't do something worse."

"Worse? Worse! What could be worse than having the Devil appear right in this room now and be unable to do anything about it? Old Gregory can't do nothing. Reckon he's scared. Reckon this time he's up against something just too big and dangerous for him to cope with. Surprised he ain't gone back to Chipenden, where he'd feel safer!"

"No, Alice! If he's scared, then he's got good reason for it but the Spook isn't a coward. He'll have a plan. But don't use the dark, Alice. Forget what Bony Lizzie taught you. Please don't do it. No good can come of it—"

At that moment I heard the clump of boots coming down the stairs, and Alice ripped the page out, screwed it up, and stuffed it in her sleeve. Then she quickly pushed the pen and notebook back into my bag.

As the Spook came into the kitchen, carrying Arkwright's book, she gave me a sad smile.

"Right, you two," he said. "Feeling better?"

Alice nodded and he gave her the slightest nod in return before sitting down on the chair nearest to the stove.

"I hope you've both learned something from yesterday," he continued. "Using the dark will only weaken us. Do you understand that now?"

I nodded but hardly dared look at Alice.

"Well," my master went on, "it's time to continue our discussion and decide what's to be done. I've learned a lot about the Fiend's daughter. It's a far better book than I thought Bill Arkwright capable of. I want you to start at the beginning, lad, and tell me everything that happened from the moment you came to the mill for the first time until I found you bound and gagged in the warehouse. I can see you've been in the wars," he said, glancing at my sore ear, "so take your time. Give me all the details. There might be something important."

So I began my account, leaving nothing out. When I reached the point where Arkwright gave me the letter and I decided to return to the mill, my master interrupted for the first time.

"It was as I feared. Bill Arkwright has demons inside him when he drinks. I'm sorry you suffered like that, lad, but I did intend this training for the best. He's younger and stronger than me and there are things he can teach you that I can't anymore. You need toughening up to fight the Fiend and win—we might have to try things that we've never dreamed of before."

At that Alice gave me the faintest of smiles but I ignored her and carried on with my tale. I told him about the attack of the water witch when she'd almost killed me, how we'd crossed the sands to reach Cartmel, and of our meeting with the hermit. I recounted how Arkwright had had to drive out the press-gang before the hermit would dowse for him and discover the whereabouts of Morwena. Some sections of my tale were uncomfortable to tell: particularly finding the dead dog and Arkwright's boot in the water, and, of course, using the mirror to communicate with Alice. But at last, describing how I'd crossed the dangerous sands once again and returned to the mill, I finally pushed on to the ending of my tale in the warehouse.

"Well, lad, you've had a hard time of it but it's not as bad as you think. For one thing, I have a feeling that Bill Arkwright's probably still alive. . . ."

I looked at my master in astonishment.

"Close your mouth, lad, or you'll start catching flies," he said with a grin. "You're probably wondering how I know that. Well, to be honest, I'm not absolutely sure, but I have three things that point to him having survived. The first is a hunch. Pure instinct. You should always trust your instincts, lad, as I've told you before. And they tell me that Bill is still alive. The second is the ghost of his mother. You've just told me what she said to you, and last night she said pretty much the same to me —"

"But how can she know," I demanded, "when she's bound to her bones and can't travel much farther than the mill garden?"

"Amelia is no ordinary ghost, lad. Technically she's what we sometimes term a water wraith because she suffered death by drowning. Not only that. In a rash moment she killed herself, and many who do that instantly regret it but do so when it's too late. Such troubled spirits can sometimes be in tune with the living," he answered. "Bill and his mother were very close. So her spirit senses that something really bad has happened to him; that he needs help; that he's still alive. And she told me that he's shackled within the bowels of the earth, still waiting to die — the very same words she said to you.

"And the third thing is what I've gained from reading

this book. Sacrifices to Morwena were made at the approach of the full moon. . . ."

The Spook opened the book and read aloud from it:

*"The young were cast into the Blood Pool; older offerings were chained in a subterranean chamber until the propitious moment."*

"If that's true, then where will he be? Somewhere underground back up near the lakes?"

"Could be, lad, but I know one way we might find out for sure. That hermit up at Cartmel. If he could dowse for Morwena, then maybe he could find Arkwright for us. If they're saving Bill for the full moon, we have six days to find him. But the *approach* of the full moon suggests we've less leeway. In any case we have to go north again. It's our duty to sort out that witch before she sorts us."

"The thing that's puzzling me," I said, "is why the Fiend left us. Had he stayed Morwena would have won. With him there we'd have been helpless. It doesn't make sense."

"Indeed, lad. What's more, why doesn't the Fiend just appear now, kill you, and get it over with? What's stopping him?"

"I don't know," I replied. "Maybe he's got more important business to attend to."

"No doubt he *has* other things to deal with, but you pose one of the biggest threats to him in the County. No, there's more to it than that. I found out some interesting things while I was looking in your mother's trunks. The reason the Fiend hasn't destroyed you immediately is because he's been hobbled."

"What's that?" I asked.

"Well, you should be able to work that out for yourself, lad, coming as you do from a farming family."

"You hobble a horse. Tie its legs," I said.

"That you do, lad. You tie them so that it can't stray too far. So a hobble is a limitation or impediment. The Fiend's power is circumscribed in a powerful way. If he kills you — if he does it *himself* — then he'll reign on in our world for a hundred years before he's forced to retreat back to where he came from."

"I don't understand," I said. "If that's true, why doesn't he just come and kill me now? Isn't that what he wants, to rule the world in a new dark age?"

"The problem is, for the Fiend a hundred years isn't that long. Time isn't the same for him and a century might seem hardly more than the blinking of an eye. Oh no, he wants to rule for much longer than that."

"So am I safe?"

"No. Unfortunately it says in your mam's book that if he gets one of his children to kill you, then he can rule on in the world, and that's why he's sent his daughter to do the job."

"Does he have many children?" Alice asked.

"That I don't rightly know," he said. "But if Morwena can't defeat Tom—and let's face it, she's failed twice already—and if the Fiend has no other children to help, then there is a third way he'll try to destroy you. He'll try to convert you to the dark—"

"Never!" I shouted.

"You say that, but already you've used the dark and weakened yourself with those mirrors. If he can win you over to the dark, his dominion will last until the end of the world. So that's the one that really worries me, lad. He's powerful, yes. Really powerful. But also crafty. That's why we can't afford to compromise with the dark in any way."

"Who created the hobbles?" I asked. "Who has the strength to limit the Fiend's power in that way? Was it my mam?"

The Spook shrugged. "I don't know, lad. I found no evidence that it was she who'd done it—but yes, that was my first instinct. Only a mother would put herself at risk like that to protect her child."

"What do you mean?"

"There are always things that oppose the dark and circumscribe its power. My guess is that whoever managed to do so paid a terrible price. Such things are not achieved without something being given up in exchange. I searched that trunk carefully but could find nothing at all to explain it."

If it was my mam who had tried to protect me, I suddenly felt worried for her. What price had she paid to help me? Was she suffering in Greece now as a result?

Alice must have sensed my fears and moved closer to me to offer me some comfort. But the Spook had no time for such emotions.

"We've talked and rested enough," he said. "It's time for action. We're off to Cartmel now. If the tides are right, we could be safely across the bay before nightfall."

Within an hour we were on our way. I was really hungry but had to make do with a mouthful of crumbly County cheese to keep up my strength. My master offered some to Alice but she refused.

On the Spook's instructions I left my bag at the mill, but once again tied my silver chain around my waist under my cloak.

As we left the garden, Claw bounded after us; the Spook looked at her doubtfully.

"Shall I send her back?" I asked.

"No, lad, let her follow," he said to my surprise. "I'd rather not have an animal tagging along, but she's a hunting dog, well able to follow a trail, and might be useful in helping us find her master."

So it was that the three of us and Claw set off to try and find Bill Arkwright. The odds against us were great. We had Morwena and the other water witches to contend with, not to mention the power of the Fiend. Hobbled or not, there was no reason why he wouldn't intervene in some way to make it easier for his servants to destroy us.

But my two other worries were my mam and Alice. Had Mam hobbled the Fiend to protect me? And was Alice drifting steadily toward the dark? I knew she meant well and was doing it for the best of reasons, but was she in fact going to make things worse? The Spook had always feared that one day she would return to the dark; if she did so, I didn't want her to drag me with her.

# CHAPTER XXII

## WIDDERSHINS

WE arrived at Hest Bank to face a wait of several hours before the tide went out. But, in the company of half a dozen travelers, two coaches, and the sand guide, we made the crossing of the bay relatively quickly and safely.

After a steady climb we reached the hermit's cave just before dusk. All was

silent within. Judd Atkins was sitting cross-legged facing the fire; his eyes were closed and he hardly seemed to be breathing. My master led the way in, almost tiptoeing forward until he was facing the hermit across the flames.

"I'm sorry to bother you, Mr. Atkins," he said politely, "but I believe you're acquainted with Bill Arkwright and that he visited you recently. Well, I'm John Gregory and he was once an apprentice of mine. Bill's gone missing and I'd like your help in trying to find him. He was taken by a water witch, but even so, it might well be that he's still alive."

For a moment the hermit neither acknowledged the Spook nor spoke. Was he in a deep sleep or a trance of some kind?

My master pulled a silver coin from his breeches pocket and held it out. "I'll pay you, of course. Will this suffice?"

The hermit opened his eyes. They were bright and alert and quickly flicked from the Spook to Alice and then me, before returning to gaze steadily at my master. "Put away your money, John Gregory," he said. "I've no need of it.

Next time you cross the bay give it to the guide. Tell him it's for the lost. The money goes to help the families of those who've drowned trying to make the crossing."

"Aye, I'll do that," said the Spook. "So you'll help?"

"I'll do my best. At this distance it will be impossible to say whether he's alive or dead, but if there's anything left of him, I'll find it. Have you a map? And something that belongs to the man?"

My master reached into his bag, pulled out a map, unfolded it carefully, and spread it on the floor next to the fire. It was much older and more tattered than Bill Arkwright's but covered much the same area.

The hermit caught my eye and smiled. "Well, Thomas, dead or alive, a man is much easier to find than a witch."

The Spook reached into his pocket and pulled out a thin gold ring. "This belonged to Bill's mam," he said. "It was her wedding ring and she took it off before she died and left it to Bill with a note telling him how much she loved him. It's one of his most treasured possessions but he only wears it twice a year: on the anniversary of her death and on what would have been her birthday."

I suddenly realized that it was the gold ring I'd seen on top of his mam's coffin. The Spook must have taken it from Arkwright's room with just this in mind.

"If he wears it at all, it'll do the trick," said Judd Atkins, coming to his feet. He tied a piece of string to the ring, which he suspended over the map, moving steadily from right to left, each pass taking him farther north.

We watched him in silence. He was very thorough and it took him a long time. Eventually he reached the latitude of the lakes. Soon his hand jerked. He moved down a bit and repeated his sweep until his hand twitched again at exactly the same point. It was well over five miles east of Coniston Water, somewhere on the Big Mere, its larger sister lake.

"He's somewhere on that island," the hermit said, pointing to it with his forefinger.

The Spook peered at it closely. "*Belle Isle*," he said. "Never been there. Know anything about it?"

"I've passed by there more than once on my travels," the

hermit replied. "There was a murder about a mile south of that island some years ago. A fight over a woman. The victim was weighted with stones and thrown into the lake. I found the body by dowsing. As for the island itself, nobody visits it anymore. Got a bad reputation."

"Haunted?" asked the Spook.

Judd shook his head. "Not to my knowledge, but people keep away and certainly avoid it after dark. It's heavily wooded and there's a folly hidden by the trees. Otherwise it's deserted. You'd most likely find William there."

"What's a folly?" I asked.

"It's usually some sort of small ornamental building without any apparent purpose, lad," the Spook answered. "Sometimes they're built in the shape of towers or castles. They're meant to be looked at, not lived in. That's how they get their name: It's a piece of foolishness built by someone who doesn't have to worry about working for a living. Someone with time on their hands and more money than sense."

"Well, that's where William Arkwright is," asserted the

hermit. "But whether alive or dead, I just can't be sure."

"How would we get out to the island?" asked the Spook, folding up his map.

"With difficulty," answered Judd, shaking his head. "There are ferrymen who make a living taking passengers across the lake, but few will want to land anyone there."

"Well, we can but try," said the Spook. "Thank you for all your help, Mr. Atkins, and I'll certainly give something to the sand guide to support the bereaved."

"Then I'm more than glad to have been able to help," said the hermit. "Now you're welcome to shelter here for the night. In the way of sustenance, though, I've not much to offer but a share of my broth."

Preparing to face the dark, the Spook and I declined the offer of food. To my surprise, Alice once again did the same; she usually had a healthy appetite and liked to keep up her strength. However, I said nothing, and we soon settled ourselves down, grateful to spend the night close to the hermit's fire.

❂ ❂ ❂

I awoke at about four in the morning to find Alice looking at me across the embers. The Spook was breathing slowly and deeply, fast asleep. The hermit was in exactly the same position as before, eyes closed, head bowed—but whether he was sleeping or not was hard to tell.

"Sleep deeply, you do, Tom," Alice said, her eyes wide and serious. "Been staring at you hard for nearly half an hour. Most people would've woke up in two minutes."

"I can wake up any time I choose," I told her with a smile. "I usually wake up if something's threatening me. But you're no threat, Alice. Did you want me to wake up? Why?"

Alice shrugged. "Couldn't sleep and just wanted to talk, that's all," she said.

"You all right?" I asked. "You didn't have any supper. That's not like you."

"Right as I'll ever be," she answered quietly.

"You need to eat," I said.

"Ain't eating much yourself, are you? Just a nibble of Old Gregory's moldy cheese ain't going to put much meat on your scrawny bones."

"We're doing it for a reason, Alice. Soon we're going to face the dark and it helps to fast. It really does. But *you* need something. You've had nothing at all for more than a day now."

"Leave me be, Tom. Ain't none of your business."

"'Course it's my business. I care about you and don't want to see you get ill."

"Doing it for a reason, I am. Ain't just a spook and his apprentice that can fast. For three days I'm going to fast, too. I'm going to do what Lizzie taught me. Did it a lot when she needed to build up her power. It could be the first step toward keeping Old Nick at bay."

"And what then, Alice? What else will you do? Something else from the dark, is that it? Do that and you'll be no better than the enemies we face. You'll be a witch using the powers of a witch! Stop this now while you still can! And stop involving me. You heard what Mr. Gregory said: The Fiend would like nothing better than to bring me over to the dark."

"No, Tom, that ain't fair. I ain't a witch and I never will

be. I'll be using the dark, that's true enough, but I'm not leading you toward the dark. I'm just doing what your mam told me to!"

"What? Mam wouldn't tell you to do that."

"Don't know how wrong you are, Tom. '*Use anything!*
*Use anything!*' she said. '*Anything you can to protect him.*'
Don't you see, Tom? That's why I'm here: to use the dark against the dark to make sure that you survive!"

I was stunned by her words and didn't know what to say. But Alice wasn't a liar, I was sure of that. "When did Mam tell you to do this?" I asked quietly.

"When I stayed with your family last year—when we fought off Mother Malkin together. And she's talked to me once since. When we were in Pendle during the summer, she spoke to me from a mirror. . . ."

I stared at Alice in astonishment. I'd had no contact with Mam since early spring when she'd left for Greece. And yet she'd spoken to Alice! And used a mirror to do so!

"What did Mam say to you, Alice? What was so urgent

that she had to talk to you through a mirror?" I demanded.

"It's like I said before. Back in Pendle, it was, when the covens were getting ready to open the portal and let the Fiend into the world. Your mam said you'd be in great danger and now was the time I had to get ready to protect you. I've been doing my best to get ready ever since, but it ain't easy."

I glanced toward the Spook, then lowered my voice. "If the Spook finds out what you're trying to do, he'll send you away. Be careful, Alice, because it could happen. He's worried about us already because we used a mirror. Don't give him the slightest excuse, please. . . ."

Alice nodded, and for a long time we didn't speak and just sat there gazing into the embers of the fire. After a while I noticed that the hermit was staring at me. I looked back at him and our eyes locked. He didn't even blink and I felt embarrassed, so I asked him, "How did you learn to dowse, Mr. Atkins?"

"How does a bird learn to build a nest? Or a spider spin

its web? I was born with the gift, Thomas. My dad had it, too, and his dad before him. It tends to run in families. But it's not just a talent for finding water or missing people. It can tell you *about* people. About where they come from and their families. Would you like me to show you?"

I wasn't sure and didn't know what to expect, but before I could reply, the hermit stood and walked around the fire toward me, pulling a piece of string from his pocket. He tied a small piece of crystal to it and held it above my head. It started to rotate slowly in a clockwise direction.

"You come from a good family, Thomas—that's clear enough. You have a mother and brothers who love you. Some of you have been separated but you'll all be together very soon. I see a big family occasion. A gathering of great importance."

"That would be nice," I said. "My mam's away and I haven't seen four of my brothers for over three years."

I glanced toward the Spook, grateful that he was still fast asleep. He would be annoyed that the hermit was predicting the future. By now Judd Atkins had left me and approached Alice. She flinched as he held the string above her head. It began to rotate but in the opposite direction; it was moving widdershins, against the clock.

"It pains me to say it, girl," said the hermit, "but you come from a bad family, a clan of witches—"

"Ain't no secret, that," Alice said with a scowl.

"There's worse," said the hermit. "You'll be reunited with them soon and with your father, who loves you very much. You are special to him. His special girl."

Alice jumped to her feet, eyes blazing with anger. She raised her hand and for a moment I thought she was going to scratch the hermit or strike him in the face. "My dad's dead and buried. Been in the cold ground for years!" she snapped. "So is that what you're saying? That I'll be dead myself soon? Ain't nice, that! Ain't a nice thing to say to anyone!"

With that she left the cave. When I turned to follow her, Judd Atkins came up to me and put a hand on my shoulder. "Let her go, Thomas," he said with a sad shake of his head. "You two can't ever be together. Did you see the way the string circled differently for each of you?"

I nodded.

"Clockwise and widdershins. Light against dark. Good against evil. I saw what I saw and I'm sorry to say that it's true. Not only that—I couldn't help overhearing part of your conversation. Anyone who's prepared to use the dark like that, for whatever reason, can't be trusted. Can a lamb sit safely beside a wolf? Or a rabbit befriend a stoat? Take care or she'll drag you down with her! Let her go and find yourself another friend. It can't be Alice."

I went after her anyway but she had disappeared into the darkness. I waited at the cave entrance until she returned about an hour before dawn. She didn't speak and flinched away when I approached. I could tell that she'd been crying.

# CHAPTER XXIII
## A WITCH BOTTLE

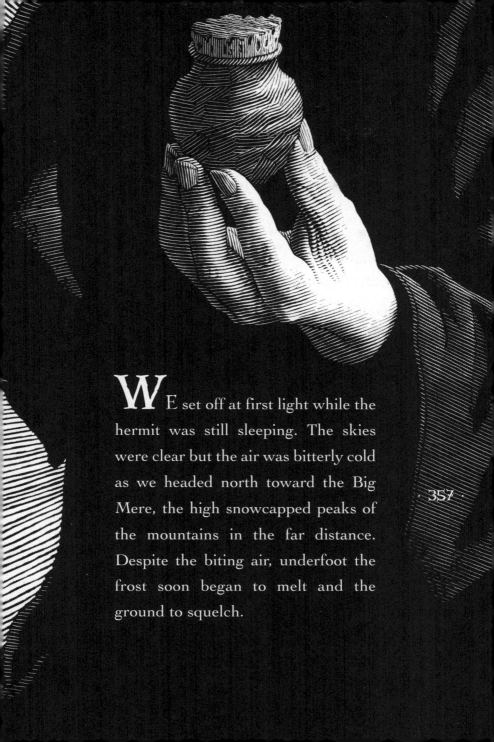

WE set off at first light while the hermit was still sleeping. The skies were clear but the air was bitterly cold as we headed north toward the Big Mere, the high snowcapped peaks of the mountains in the far distance. Despite the biting air, underfoot the frost soon began to melt and the ground to squelch.

As we crossed the river Lever by a small wooden bridge and journeyed up the western shore of the lake, the going became more difficult, the narrow path meandering through a dense forest of conifers, with steep slopes rising to our left.

We might well have been three stray sheep, judging by Claw's behavior. She kept circling us, then bounding on ahead before returning to shepherd us from behind. It was something she'd been taught by Arkwright: She was alert for danger, checking every direction for possible threats to her little flock.

After a while I dropped back and walked with Alice. We hadn't spoken since we'd disagreed in the night.

"Are you all right, Alice?" I asked.

"Never better," she said, a little stiffly.

"I'm sorry we argued," I said.

"I don't mind that, Tom. I know you were only trying to do what's best."

"We're still friends?"

"Of course."

We walked along in silence for a while until she said, "I've got a plan, Tom. A plan to keep the Fiend away from us."

I looked at her sharply. "I hope this doesn't involve the dark, Alice," I said, but she didn't answer my question.

"Do you want to hear my plan or not?"

"Go on, then," I said.

"Know what a witch bottle is?" she asked.

"I've heard of them, but I don't know how they're supposed to work. The Spook doesn't believe in them." Witch bottles were defenses against witchcraft, but the Spook thought they were just something used by the superstitious and weak-minded.

"What does Old Gregory know?" Alice said scornfully. "Do it right and it works, don't you worry. Bony Lizzie swore by 'em. When an enemy witch uses her dark powers against you, there's a way to put a stop to it. First you need some of her urine. That's the hard part but it don't have to be too much. Just a bit, which you put into a bottle. Next you put bent pins, sharp stones, and iron nails into the urine, cork up that old bottle, and shake it well.

Then you leave it in the sun for three days, and on the night of the next full moon you bury it under a dung heap.

"Then the job's as good as done. Next time she goes to the toilet she's in agony. It's just like she's weeing hot pins! All you have to do then is leave her a note telling her what you've done. In no time at all she'll take the spell off you. But you keep the bottle hidden just in case you have to use it again!"

I laughed without mirth. "So is that what you're going to use against the Fiend, Alice?" I mocked. "His piss and a few bent pins?"

"We've known each other quite a while, Tom, and I think that by now you know I ain't stupid. Your mam ain't stupid either. You ought to be ashamed, laughing like that. It was an ugly laugh. You were nice when I met you. You wouldn't have laughed at me like that then, whatever I'd said. You were too kind and well-mannered. Don't change, Tom, please. You need to get harder but not like that. I'm your friend. You don't hurt your friends, no matter how scared you are."

At those words my throat constricted so that I couldn't speak and tears welled in my eyes. "I'm sorry, Alice," I said at last. "I didn't mean it. You're right. I *am* scared but I shouldn't take it out on you."

"That's all right, Tom. Don't bother yourself, but you didn't let me finish. I was going to say that I intend to use something similar. But not urine. It's blood that I'll be using. So we need to get ourselves some special blood. I don't mean *his* blood—how could we get that? The blood of his daughter, Morwena, should do the trick! Once we get some I'll do the rest."

Alice pulled something from the pocket of her coat and held it up in front of me. It was a very small earthen jar with a cork in the end.

"They call this a blood jar," she said. "We need to get Morwena's blood into this and mix it with a little of yours. Then the Fiend'll be forced to keep away. You'd be safe, I'm sure of it. Don't need to be much. Just a few drops of each would do—"

"But it's dark magic, Alice. If the Spook finds out, he'll

send you away forever or even put you in a pit in his garden. And think of yourself. Of your own soul. If you're
not careful, you could end up belonging to the Fiend!"

But before I could say anything more, the Spook called
my name and waved me forward to join him. So I ran to
catch up, leaving Alice behind.

We walked on, the path now running very close to the
shore of the lake, and the Spook kept eyeing the water
warily. No doubt he was thinking of the threat from
Morwena or the other water witches. They could attack
from the water at any time. But I was relying on Alice or
Claw to give us some warning.

Had Morwena been following since we left the mill,
keeping her distance and just waiting for an opportunity
to attack? Both sides of the lake were thickly forested.
She could be moving through the dense tree cover or even
swimming below the surface of the still water. The winter
sun was bathing the countryside with its pale light and the
visibility was good: I didn't sense danger at all. But once
night fell it would be a very different matter.

How wrong could I have been? Danger was all around, for the Spook came to a sudden halt and pointed to a tree on our right, less than fifty paces from the lakeshore. My heart lurched with fear as I saw what was carved into its trunk.

"It looks to be freshly cut," my master said. "Now we've got another enemy to worry about!"

It was the mark of Grimalkin. In the summer she'd been sent by the Malkins to hunt me down and I'd tricked her and barely escaped with my life. But now she was back. Why had she left Pendle?

"Have they sent her after me again?" I asked fearfully. "She's not another daughter of the Fiend, is she?"

The Spook sighed. "It's impossible to say, lad, but not to my knowledge. Something's afoot, though. Last week, when I traveled to Pendle, I kept my distance from the witch-clans, confining my visit to Malkin Tower. But something was brewing. I passed several cottages that had been burned out and there were bodies rotting in Crow Wood—from all three clans: Malkins, Deanes, and Mouldheels. It looked like there'd been some sort of battle. The dark may be at war with itself. But why's Grimalkin come north? It may not be for you at all, but it does seem something of a coincidence that the two of you should both be here. Anyway, she's put her warning mark close to the shore so let's be extra vigilant."

Late in the afternoon we came within sight of Belle Isle. As we drew nearer, I saw that it was far closer to the lakeshore than I'd expected, its nearest point probably no more than a hundred and fifty yards out.

There were jetties close by from where ferrymen plied their trade, but while they'd have taken us to the far shore of the lake for a pittance, not even a silver coin could hire a boat for the short trip to the island.

When asked why, each man was evasive. "Not a place to be, night or day. Not if you value your sanity," warned the third ferryman we approached. Then, probably tired of the Spook's persistence, he pointed toward a dilapidated rowing boat tied up among the reeds. "Woman who owns that boat might just be daft enough to take you."

"Where will we find her?" asked the Spook.

"Back there about a mile and you'll be at the door of her cottage," the man said with an ugly laugh, pointing vaguely north along the bank. "Daft Deana, she's known as. But Deana Beck is her real name! She's the best you'll get for that job!"

"Why's she *daft*?" the Spook demanded with a frown. It was clear that he was annoyed by the man's attitude.

"Because the old girl doesn't know what's good for her!" retorted the ferryman. "No family to worry about, has she? And so old she doesn't care for living that much. Nobody with even half the sense they were born with goes near that hag-ridden isle."

"There are witches on the island?" asked the Spook.

"They visit from time to time. Lots of witches, if you look close enough, but most sensible folk turn the other way. Pretend it isn't happening. You go and speak to Daft Deana."

The ferryman was still laughing as we walked away. Soon we arrived at a small thatched cottage set against a steep, wooded incline. The Spook rapped at the door while Claw padded to the water's edge and stared out across the lake toward the island. After a few moments there was the sound of bars being drawn back, and the door opened no more than the width of the suspicious eye that regarded us from within.

"Be off with ye!" growled a gruff voice that didn't sound a bit like that of a woman. "Vagabonds and beggars aren't wanted here."

"We aren't here to beg," explained the Spook patiently. "My name is John Gregory. I need your help and for that I'm prepared to pay well. You're highly recommended."

"Highly recommended, am I? Then let's see the color of your money. . . ."

The Spook reached into his cloak, pulled a silver coin from his pocket, and held it toward the gap in the doorway.

"That in advance and the same again when you've done the work."

"What work? What work? Spit it out! Don't be wasting my time."

"We need to get across to Belle Isle. Can you do that? That and get us back safely?"

A gnarled hand emerged slowly into the daylight and the Spook dropped the coin into the palm, which instantly closed tightly. "I can certainly do that," said the voice, softening a little. "But the trip won't be without danger. Best come inside and warm your bones."

The door opened wide and we were confronted by the sight of Deana Beck: She was dressed in leather trousers, a grimy smock, and big hobnailed boots. Her white hair was cropped short, and for a moment she looked like a man. But the eyes, which flickered with intelligence, were soft and female and the lips formed a perfect bow. Her face was lined with age but her body was sturdy and she looked strong and robust, well able to row us out to the island.

The room was empty but for a small table in the corner. The hard stone floor was strewn with rushes and Deana hunkered close to the fire and gestured that we should do the same.

"Comfortable, are ye?" she asked when we'd settled down.

"My old bones prefer a chair," answered the Spook dryly. "But vagabonds and beggars can't be choosers."

She smiled at that and nodded. "Well, I've managed all my life without the comfort of a chair," she said, her voice now much lighter and with a lilt to it. "So tell me now, why do ye want to go out to the island? What brings a spook to Belle Isle? Are you here to deal with the witches?"

"Not directly, unless they get in our way," admitted the Spook. "Not on this occasion anyway. A colleague of mine has been missing for days, and we've good reason to believe he's somewhere out there on the island."

"And what makes you so sure?"

"We consulted a dowser: Judd Atkins from Cartmel."

"I met the man once," Deana said, nodding. "He found

a body in the lake not too far from here. Well, if Atkins says he's out there, then he probably is. But how did he get there? That's what I want to know."

The Spook sighed. "He was abducted while trying to deal with a water witch. It could well be that some locals are involved as well—either from Coniston or one of the other villages."

I watched Deana Beck's face carefully to see what her reaction would be. Was she mixed up in this? Could we trust her?

"It's a hard life up here," she said at last. "And you have to do what you can to survive. Most just turn a blind eye, but there are always some that have dealings with the dark forces that lurk in water. They do what has to be done in order to ensure their own safety and the needs of their families. When the breadwinner dies, his family have a hard time of it. They sometimes starve."

"And what about you, Deana Beck?" demanded the Spook, staring at her hard. "Have you dealt with the dark?"

Deana shook her head. "No," she said. "I'll have no truck with witches. None at all. Never had a family of my own and I've led a long and lonely life. I don't regret it, though, because now I've no kin to worry about. Just having to care for yourself makes you less afraid. It makes you stronger. The witches don't scare me. I do what I want."

"So when can you row us out there?" asked the Spook.

"As soon as darkness falls. We wouldn't want to be going there in daylight. Anybody might be watching — maybe those who put your friend on the island in the first place, and we wouldn't want to meet them."

"That we wouldn't," said the Spook.

Deana offered to share her supper but the Spook declined for all of us. I was forced to watch her tuck into a piping hot rabbit stew while my mouth watered and my stomach rumbled. Soon it would be dark and we'd face whatever was out there on the island.

# CHAPTER XXIV
## THE FOLLY

WEARING long waders that reached up to her thighs, Deana Beck led us along the lakeshore, a lantern in each hand. The moon wasn't yet up and there was scant light from the stars, but she didn't light the lanterns. The dark would help to shield us from anyone who might be lying in wait ahead or watching from the island. I

walked beside the Spook, carrying my staff and his bag; Alice was a few paces behind. Claw continued to trot around us, her black coat now making her almost invisible. When she came close, only the light padding of her feet gave away her position.

After a few moments we reached Deana's boat; she waded out and pulled it back from the reeds toward the landing stage. Claw leaped in first, causing it to rock slightly, but then Deana gripped the edge of the jetty to steady it while we climbed aboard, the Spook first, Alice last. Ahead, our destination looked dark and threatening, its shroud of trees like the humped back of a huge crouching monster awaiting the arrival of its prey.

Deana rowed toward the island with big slow sweeps of the oars, which made hardly a sound as they entered the water. The air was still and soon the moon began to rise, illuminating the distant mountains and lighting the lake to silver. But still the trees looked dark and ominous. The sight of Belle Isle disturbed me, sending a chill down the back of my neck.

The crossing took just a few minutes and soon, after beaching the rowing boat on the shingle, we disembarked and stood on the water margin, where a number of twisted, ancient yews blocked out the moonlight.

"Thanks for your help, Deana," the Spook told the old ferrywoman, his voice hardly more than a whisper. "If we're not back within the hour, you get yourself home and come back for us just before dawn."

Deana nodded and picked up one of the lanterns and gave it to the Spook. As I was already burdened with my staff and the Spook's bag, she handed the other one to Alice. Claw immediately raced ahead and was quickly lost from sight in the darkness. Leaving Deana with her boat, we followed the dog into the gloomy trees. From shore to shore, the island was no more than three hundred yards across at its widest point and three quarters of a mile long. In daylight we could have searched it thoroughly from one end to the other, but in the dark this was impossible, so we made directly for the folly, where the hermit thought we might find Bill Arkwright.

The island was densely wooded; the majority of trees were conifers, but we soon reached a stand of deciduous trees, their branches stark and leafless, and there, in their midst, was the folly.

It wasn't at all what I'd been led to expect. In the moonlight I could see two separate buildings rather than one, perhaps no more than fifteen strides apart: twin ugly, squat, square towers constructed from gray stone encrusted with lichen, each no more than twenty feet high. They reminded me of sepulchres—mausoleums to house the bones of the dead. Each had a flat roof with no castellation at all, but there were some decorative features. Whereas the lower walls were plain blocks of stone, from about twelve feet above the ground to the roof of each tower I saw a multitude of gargoyles: skulls, bats, birds, and all manner of creatures that might have been copied from the pages of some demonic bestiary.

The first building had no door and just one high narrow slit in each wall to serve as a window. So how could you get inside? And if you couldn't, what was the point of it?

It wasn't even pleasing to look at. Arkwright couldn't be inside that sealed tower, yet Claw was already circling it, sniffing and whining, and when we moved on to the next, she remained behind.

I then realized that to call them "twin" buildings wasn't strictly accurate. Although the second structure had identical slits for windows and its own selection of gargoyles, it also had a stout wooden door. This was padlocked, but since Andrew, the Spook's locksmith brother, had provided us both with keys easily able to cope with such a barrier, the Spook had it open within seconds. We lit both lanterns before stepping cautiously inside, the blades on our staffs at the ready. Descending along three walls, thirty or so stone steps led us below ground toward a pool of water.

At the bottom the Spook walked away from the water toward the far corner. I reached his side and stared down at what he'd found. It was a boot.

"Is it Bill's?" he asked.

"It's his," I said with a nod.

"So where is he now?" asked the Spook, thinking aloud rather than asking me. He turned back toward the water, walked to its edge, held his lantern high and peered down.

I followed his gaze. The water was surprisingly clear but deep, and I could see two things: a further steep and narrow flight of underwater steps, and at the foot of them what looked like the mouth of a dark tunnel.

"What have we here?" muttered the Spook. "Well, lad, look at the direction of that tunnel. Where do you think it goes?"

There wasn't much doubt about it. "Toward the other building," I answered.

"That it does. And I wonder what it contains? What better prison than a building without a door! Follow me, lad. . . ."

I did as he said, with Alice close at my heels. Once outside my master crossed to the other tower, halted below the nearest window and pointed up at it. "Stand on my shoulders and see if you can climb up and see inside. Use the lantern but try and shield it with your body so we don't attract any unwelcome attention. We wouldn't want anyone to see it from the mainland."

He crouched below the window and I stepped up onto his shoulders, holding the lantern between my body and the wall while resting my right hand against the stones to steady myself. As the Spook straightened his body, I struggled to keep my balance, but I was then able to climb to the window using the gargoyles as hand- and footholds. Holding the lantern made it more difficult but at last I was in position facing the window. I leaned forward against the wall and rested my chin on the lantern, peering through the slit. All I could see inside was a pool of water, seemingly identical to the one in the other tower; the far wall had a wide crack below ground level. The foundations were probably damp and had moved.

I clambered down and we moved to the next wall. "Not sure my poor old back and knees can take much more of this," grumbled the Spook. "Make it quick, lad!"

I did as he commanded but it was not until I peered through the fourth window slit that I saw someone bound with rope, slumped against the far wall close to the pool. I couldn't see his face but it certainly looked like Arkwright.

"There's someone tied up," I whispered excitedly. "I'm sure it's him."

"Right, lad," said the Spook. "Now check the roof. There could be a way in from the top. It's worth a try. . . ."

I climbed another few feet, then reached up, got a grip on the edge of the roof, and pulled myself up. A thorough check revealed that it was solid stone. There was no way in. So after a quick glance through the trees toward the silver water of the lake, I lowered myself back over the edge and, with the Spook's help, soon reached the ground.

We trudged back to the other building, descended the steps again and stared gloomily at the surface of the pool. There was only one way to get Arkwright out and that was through the water tunnel.

"Mr. Arkwright taught me to swim," I told my master, trying to fill my voice with more confidence than I felt. "Now's the time to put it to good use. . . ."

"Well, if you can swim, lad, that's more than I can do. But how *well* can you swim?"

"About five widths of the canal . . ."

The Spook shook his head doubtfully.

"Too dangerous, Tom," Alice said. "This is more than just swimming. It's diving and going through that dark tunnel. Ain't able to swim or I'd come with you. Two of us would have a better chance."

"The girl's right, lad. Maybe Deana could do it or knows someone who can swim well enough to get through there."

"But would we be able to trust them?" I asked. "No. I can do it. I've got to try at least."

The Spook didn't try to stop me but looked on silently, shaking his head as I took off my boots and socks, followed by my cloak and shirt. Finally I tied my silver chain about my waist again and prepared to wade into the water.

"Here," my master said, handing me a knife from his bag. "Tuck this into your belt. You'll need it to free Bill.

And take this for him as well," he said, handing me a water bottle.

"Got something else that might help . . . ," Alice said.

With these words she pulled a leather pouch from the pocket of her skirt and undid the fine cord that bound it to reveal a collection of dried herbs within. She'd used herbs before to treat the sick successfully, once helping to heal my hand when it had been burned. But never had I seen such a multitude and diversity of herbs. It seemed that, unbeknown to me, Alice had been gathering materials and developing her healing skills.

She held a leaf out toward me. "Put a bit of this under his tongue. Should revive him—that's if he ain't too far gone."

The Spook stared at her hard for a moment, then nodded, so I tucked it into my breeches pocket and fastened the knife and the water bottle to my belt.

"And take care, lad," my master warned. "This is dangerous. Any doubts, don't go through with it. Nobody will think any less of you."

I nodded my thanks and started to walk down the steps. The water was cold and took my breath away, but once it came up to my chest I felt better. With a faint smile back at Alice, I swam away from the steps, took a deep breath, and attempted to dive to the underwater tunnel.

I didn't get very far. The water resisted and forced me back up to the surface. Either I wasn't using the strokes I'd been taught properly or I simply wasn't strong enough. I sucked in another deep breath and tried again. Moments later I was sputtering on the surface, feeling a little foolish. I'd never be able to get Arkwright out. We'd have to ask Deana after all.

I swam back to the side until my feet were on the steps again. But suddenly I remembered something that Arkwright had said.

*"When a diver wants to go deep, the easiest way is for him to hold a big stone so the weight takes him down quickly. . . ."*

"Alice, run back to the shore and bring me back two of the heaviest stones you can carry!" I told her.

She and the Spook looked at me with puzzled faces.

"A weight in each hand will take me straight to the bottom and I'll be able to pull myself into the tunnel."

Alice returned in less than five minutes with two heavy stones. Holding them against my chest, I walked down the steps until the water was to my waist then, after taking a deep breath, jumped forward.

The water closed over my head and I sank quickly into the gloom. The tunnel was directly ahead so I dropped the stones and frog-kicked into it, scraping my shoulder against the side. Two more kicks and it grew absolutely black. I began to panic. What if we were wrong and this passageway didn't lead into the next building after all?

I tried to use my arms as Arkwright had taught me, but the tunnel was too narrow and I jarred my elbows badly. By now I was desperate to breathe and I kicked again and again, the urgency building in my chest. I tried to calm myself. On the surface I could hold my breath for much longer than this. So what was the difference? As long as I didn't panic I'd be all right.

Another two kicks and, to my relief, I was out of the

tunnel and rising upward, the water growing somewhat lighter. I had a sense of something big to my right, but the next second my head broke the surface and I released the breath I'd been holding, taking in two big welcome gulps of air. I used my arms and legs to paddle on the spot and keep afloat. It was dark in the tower, but looking upward, I could see the four narrow windows. Three were faint but the fourth was lit by the moon. Hopefully my eyes would soon adjust and there'd be enough light to see what I was doing.

I took a couple of strokes and then stubbed my toes against steps. Moments later I was out of the water, standing on flags, the water dripping from me, keeping perfectly still while I waited for my night vision to improve. Slowly the inside of the tower became clearer. I could see what appeared to be a shapeless bundle of rags against the wall. It had to be Arkwright. I took three cautious steps in that direction. Then I thought I heard a murmur of voices from somewhere above. Surprised, I looked up toward the window.

"Tom!" someone called.

It was Alice's voice. I knew she must have stood on the Spook's shoulders and climbed the gargoyles to the window. "You all right?" she asked.

"Fine, Alice. So far so good. I think I've found him."

"Got something for you," Alice called. "A candle. Try to catch it. Ready?"

The next moment it was falling toward me. I took two quick steps, grabbed at it but missed. It hit the ground, but despite the gloom it didn't take me long to find it. I picked it up and looked at the window again.

"Throwing down your tinderbox next," she called. "Don't drop this, Tom. Don't want it to break."

I didn't want it to break either. It meant a lot to me because it was my good-bye present from my dad when I first left home to become the Spook's apprentice. It was a family heirloom.

I sensed rather than saw it falling toward me but somehow I caught it, and it was but the work of a minute to ignite the tinder and light the candle. I pushed the

tinderbox safely into my pocket and approached
Arkwright. I could see his face now, but was he all right?
Was he breathing?

"It's him," I called out to Alice and the Spook. "He doesn't
look too good but I'll try and get him through the tunnel."

"Good!" shouted Alice. "Well done. We'll see you in the
other tower."

I heard them walk away, but just then something made
me glance into the water. It was clear and I could see right
to the bottom as before. Now I realized what I'd glimpsed
as I emerged into the pool of water. It was a second tunnel. But where did it lead? To the lake? The thought was
terrifying. It was another way into the tower. A water
witch would be able to reach me without having to get
past the Spook and Alice.

And there was something else. To my astonishment, the
surface of the water suddenly brightened and a shape
started to form. Someone was using a mirror to reach me.
Could it be Alice? Had she given the Spook the slip for
just such a purpose? Of course, it didn't have to be a

mirror. The surface of a puddle, pond, or lake could achieve the same end. But then I saw that it wasn't Alice after all and fear gripped my heart.

It was the witch assassin. . . .

But for a scarf worn loosely about her neck, Grimalkin was dressed exactly as on our last encounter: the same short black smock tied at her waist, her skirt divided and tightly strapped to each thigh. Her lithe body was bound with leather straps carrying a multitude of sheaths, each containing a deadly weapon.

My eyes fixed in terror upon one item in particular: the scissors that she used to torture her defeated enemies; sharp implements that could snip bone and flesh. Last time I'd tricked her, wounding her while I pretended to surrender. I'd flicked my staff from one hand to the other, just as the Spook had taught me. But next time we met, she wouldn't be deceived so easily. She knew what I was capable of.

I looked at the necklace of human bones around her neck: bones from those she'd hunted down, defeated, and tortured. She lived for combat, thrived on bloodshed. It was said that she had a code of honor and liked the struggle to be difficult, that she never tried to win by guile. But I'd deceived her. In fear for my life I'd behaved in a way she could only hold in contempt.

But to my utter astonishment she smiled at me and leaned forward. Her mouth opened and the surface of the water became cloudy. She was using a mirror and was about to write on it. What? A threat? A warning of what she intended to do to me next time we met?

Get out quickly!
Soon our enemies will enter
the lake tunnel!

I stared at the message in astonishment. Why would Grimalkin warn me? Wouldn't she be happy to see me captured and killed by witches? What did she mean by "*our* enemies"? Water witches? Was it a trick? A repayment for my deceit?

The image faded and disappeared. I was puzzled, but

whether she spoke the truth or not, I still had to rescue Arkwright.

I had no time to waste, and after positioning my candle on the flags nearby, I knelt beside the slumped figure. To his right was a jug half full of water. Bound as he was, someone must have been coming in to keep him alive for Morwena. I leaned closer and could hear fast, shallow breathing. I called his name. He groaned but didn't open his eyes. So, drawing the knife from my belt, I began to cut through his bonds: first the feet, then the hands.

That done, I tried rubbing his hands and face in an effort to revive him, but still his eyes remained shut. Next I held my water bottle against his lips and poured some into his mouth. He choked a little but managed a couple of gulps. Then I broke off a piece of the leaf Alice had given me and pushed a small piece under his tongue. Finally I placed him flat on the ground on his side, in an effort to make him comfortable. It was only then that I noticed the marks on his neck. They were big yellow scabs, three of them, and one was still weeping matter. I'd never seen anything quite like them before. And then I remembered what Arkwright had told me about skelts. I wondered if one had been feeding from his neck. The witches could have been using a skelt in their rituals.

There was nothing more I could do now, so after fastening the water bottle to my belt again, I sat down beside him, my head in my hands, trying to think things through. I realized that this was only the beginning of my problems. I had no heavy stones to help me make a fast descent to the mouth of the tunnel. Would I be able to swim down? I certainly hadn't managed it before. Arkwright was a very strong swimmer and, if fit, would no doubt be able to pull me through after him. But he looked worse than I'd expected. Far worse. How was I going to get him back to safety?

It was then that my eye was drawn to the wide crack in the far wall, the one I'd noticed previously from above. The tower was constructed of stone blocks both above and below ground. If one of the stones was split and I could work it loose, that would be enough, perhaps, to carry both of us down to the tunnel mouth. Could I pull one out of the wall? It was worth a try. So, picking up the candle, I went to examine the stones close-up.

The vertical crack was more extensive than it had looked: at least three stones had been split, so placing the candle at my side, I started to work on the most promising, which was about two feet from the ground. By rocking it back and forth, I managed to loosen it farther and soon tugged the bigger half out. As I did so, I realized that Arkwright was beginning to stir. Slowly he sat up and blinked in the candlelight, then frowned and pulled something from his mouth. It was the leaf I'd placed under his tongue.

"Alice gave me that. It's what brought you round. . . ."

"So you swam through the tunnel to reach me?" he asked.

I nodded.

"Then we should both be grateful that I threw you into the canal!" he said with a smirk, his strength slowly seeming to return.

"How are you feeling?" I asked.

"Terrible, but there's no time to waste. Who knows what will come through those tunnels next. We need to swim back through. Normally I'd let you go first but I feel as weak as a kitten and I'd better try to get through that tunnel while I still can. Count to ten, then follow me through. . . ."

So saying, Arkwright walked shakily to the edge of the water, took a deep breath and dived straight in, making hardly a splash, his weight taking him down toward the opening.

Peering into the water, through the turbulence caused by his descent, I watched him give a strong kick, propelling himself into the tunnel. Another second and he'd disappeared from view. Even in his weakened state he was a far stronger swimmer than I was.

I picked up the knife and tucked it into my belt, then tied my silver chain about my waist again. I would give him another ten seconds or so to get through and then I'd follow. I thought about the tinderbox in my pocket. The water wouldn't do it any good but I couldn't just leave it behind. I continued to stare down as the ripples slowly faded away and the surface of the water became as smooth as glass, reflecting back my own face. I prepared to enter the water myself, clutching the large piece of stone. But then I recoiled in horror. Something was coming out of the other tunnel—the one that led to the lake.

# CHAPTER XXV
## GRIMALKIN

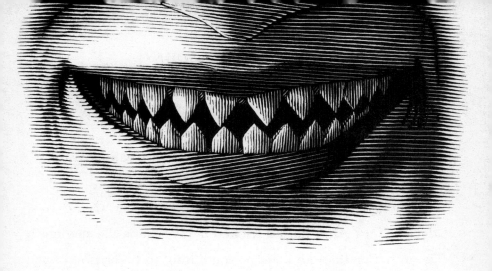

THE figure rose quickly to the surface and a female head surged clear of the water, the eyes locking with mine, water cascading from her hair. But it wasn't a water witch. It was Grimalkin! I took two rapid steps backward but she made no attempt to leave the water and attack me.

"You needn't fear me, child. I've

not come for you. I seek someone else tonight."

"Who?" I demanded. "My master?"

She shook her head and smiled grimly, treading water. "Tonight I hunt the Devil's daughter, Morwena."

I looked at her in disbelief. Was she just trying to deceive me? After all, I'd tricked her; perhaps she saw me as no better than an insect—something to be crushed by any means possible. But maybe she was telling the truth. The Pendle clans had often fought against one another, witch against witch. Perhaps they also warred against witches who lived in other parts of the County?

"Is Morwena an enemy of the Malkins?" I asked.

"She's the daughter of the Fiend and he is now my sworn enemy. For that she must die."

"But you were up on Pendle Hill the night the clans brought the Fiend through the portal," I accused. "How can he be your enemy now?"

Grimalkin smiled, showing her pointed teeth. "Don't you remember how difficult it was to unite the clans for that?" she reminded me. "Malkins, Deanes, and

Mouldheels only rarely come together. And there was dissent even within each clan. It was feared by some that once through the portal into this world, the Fiend would be too difficult to control. And that has proved to be so. He has demanded our allegiance. Commanded us to be subservient to his will.

"At the Halloween sabbath the Fiend appeared in his fearsome majesty to those who offered him obeisance. But some did not attend. And I am among those who will not kneel to him. Now the clans are divided as never before. It is not just one clan against its rival. Malkin fights Malkin and Deane fights Deane. The dark is at war with itself.

"Witches are entering the tunnel even as we speak. They know you are here. I'll return and face them. But go quickly—I may not be able to stop them all."

With those words she sank back into the water and reentered the tunnel that led to the lake.

Whether or not she was telling the truth, I was leaving anyway and right now! I picked up the stone again, held it close to my chest, took a deep breath, and jumped into the water. There was a tremendous splash and I sank rapidly. Even as I released its weight and kicked hard into the darkness, I glimpsed something emerge from the other tunnel. A water witch? Or Grimalkin?

Swimming through that dark passageway seemed far easier this time. At least I now knew that it led to the next tower and that I wouldn't reach a dead end and be trapped in the darkness. The water began to lighten. I'd almost reached the end of the tunnel. One last kick would carry me through. But then something seized my ankle.

I kicked again, trying to get free. The grip tightened and I felt myself being pulled back. Now my lungs were bursting. Was it Grimalkin, about to take her revenge? If it was a water witch, I would drown while she drained my blood. That was how their victims died. Weakened. Unable to fight back. Water rushing into the lungs. Grimalkin would probably just slit my throat.

I pulled the knife from my belt and tried to relax. Don't fight. Let her pull you back. Wait your chance. . . .

Over my shoulder I glimpsed open jaws, huge canine teeth ready to bite. It was a water witch! So I thrust my knife toward that ferocious face. The water made it difficult, slowing my arm, but the blade made contact and I pushed it home just as hard as I could. For a second nothing happened. Then my ankle was released. Close behind, I could see two figures struggling. I glimpsed leather belts, sheaths, and blades adorning the body of one and knew that it was Grimalkin. Quickly I turned and kicked myself clear of the tunnel, rising swiftly.

As I broke the surface, I tried to call out a warning about the witch but began to cough and splutter. The Spook, Alice, and Arkwright were staring down at me anxiously. Claw was growling low in her throat. My master had his staff at the ready, the blade pointing toward the water. Alice waded down the steps and gripped my right arm, helping me out. Seconds later I was back on the flags, the blade still in my hand. I looked back. There was blood in the water, rising in dark ribbons from the tunnel.

"A witch!" I shouted at last. "There's a witch in the

tunnel! There's another underwater route into the tower! From the lake!"

We stared down into the water but she didn't emerge.

"Are you hurt, lad?" the Spook asked, his eyes flicking anxiously from the water to me and back again.

"It's not my blood," I told him. "It's hers. But there could be more witches."

I dressed quickly and pulled on my boots. Then we left the tower, the Spook locking the door behind us.

"This should slow 'em down," he said, pocketing his key again. "I very much doubt *they'll* have a key to this lock. Prisoners were no doubt brought into this tower by human accomplices, then transferred later by the short connecting tunnel. The lake route would be no good. Humans wouldn't survive underwater that long."

"No doubt you're right," Arkwright agreed. "But I was out cold until I woke up in the other tower."

We hurried toward the boat as fast as we could but were hampered by Arkwright, who was considerably weakened and kept having to pause to catch his breath.

At any moment we expected another attack and Claw kept circling, alert for danger. At last we reached the shore, where Deana Beck was waiting for us. At first it looked like we'd have to make two trips, but the Spook wouldn't hear of it. The boat sat dangerously low in the water but we made the crossing safely.

"You're welcome to spend the night back at the cottage," Deana offered.

"We thank you for the offer, but you've done enough already," said the Spook. "No, we'll be on our way just as fast as we can."

The ferryman had called Deana Beck "Daft Deana," though she seemed as sensible as any woman I'd ever met. By "daft" he'd really meant "too brave." She'd certainly risked her life to row us out to Belle Isle. If the witches found out that Deana had helped us, her days on this earth would be numbered.

Our journey south was relatively slow, but the attack we feared never came. I didn't know how many witches had entered the tunnel from the lake, but I'd either killed or badly wounded the one who'd seized my ankle. Perhaps Grimalkin had slain the rest—or at least delayed them, giving us a chance to get away.

Just before nightfall we halted among the trees. By now we were clear of the lake, and the threat of attack by water witches had abated.

After nibbling a little cheese from the Spook's supply, Arkwright immediately fell into a deep sleep. He was exhausted after his ordeal, and walking in bare feet wasn't helping. But despite his pale cheeks and gaunt face he was breathing slowly and deeply.

Alice touched his forehead with her fingertips. "Ain't that cold considering what he's gone through. Neck could get infected, though." She looked up at the Spook. "Want me to see what I can do?"

"If you think you can help him, by all means go ahead," he replied, but I could see him watching her very carefully. She held out her hand for the water bottle and my master handed it to her. From her pouch she drew a small piece of leaf—an herb I didn't recognize—dampened it, and pressed it against Arkwright's neck to cover the wounds.

"Did Lizzie teach you that?" asked the Spook.

"Some of it," she answered. "But when I stayed at the farm, Tom's mam taught me lots of things as well."

The Spook nodded in approval at Alice's reply.

There was a silence and I decided to tell him about Grimalkin. I knew he wouldn't like the idea of her being involved in any way and I wondered what he'd make of it.

"Mr. Gregory," I said, "there's something I should tell you. Grimalkin used a mirror to warn me about the witches. Then she came to the surface of the pool to talk to me. She even fought off some of the witches and helped me to escape. . . ."

The Spook looked at me in surprise. "Mirrors again? When was that, lad?"

"Back in the second tower. I saw her image in the water. She said something strange—that the water witches were '*our* enemies.'"

"I would never want to admit to having anything in common with the dark," said the Spook, scratching at his beard, "but as the Pendle clans seem to be at war, perhaps that conflict extends to fighting water witches up north. But why Grimalkin would try to help *you* puzzles me. After what you did last time you met, I'd have thought she wanted you dead!"

"But if Grimalkin's really on our side, that's got to help. And we need all the help we can get!" I said.

The Spook shook his head firmly. "There's no doubt that witches being at odds with one another can only weaken them and further our cause. But I keep telling you: We can't side with any of them. The Fiend may well try to compromise you and thus bend you slowly toward the dark—so slowly that you might not even realize that it's happening!"

"I'd never serve the dark!" I said angrily.

"Don't be so sure, lad," the Spook continued. "Even your own mother once served the dark! Remember that. It could happen to you."

I had to bite my lip to stop myself giving an angry retort. The silence lengthened. The Spook stared at me hard. "Cat got your tongue, lad? Could it be that you're sulking? Can't you stand to hear a few home truths?"

I shrugged. "I can't believe you think I could end up on the side of the dark. I thought you knew me better than that!"

"I just worry about it, lad. That's all. It's a possibility we face. That you might be corrupted. I'll say this to you now, and I don't ever want you to forget it. Don't keep secrets from me. Tell me everything, no matter how badly you think I'll take it. Is that clear? *Everything!* These are dangerous times and I'm the only person you can truly trust," he said pointedly, looking in Alice's direction. "Do you understand?"

I could see Alice watching my face very carefully. I felt sure she was wondering whether I'd tell him that she was preparing to use a blood jar to keep the Fiend at bay. If the Spook knew that, he'd send her away. That or worse. He might even consider her an enemy. He bound witches in pits, and Alice had once come very close to suffering that fate.

I knew a lot hinged on my reply. The Spook was my master but Alice was my friend and an increasingly powerful ally against the dark.

"Well?" said the Spook

"I understand," I told him.

"That's good, lad."

He nodded but didn't comment and the conversation came to an end. We took turns to stand guard, watching for danger. Arkwright slept on so we decided to spend the night in the same spot.

But my sleep was fitful. What I'd just done filled me with fear and uncertainty. My dad had brought me up to be honest and truthful, but Mam, although she was an enemy of the dark, had told Alice to use anything to keep me safe from the Fiend. *Anything . . .*

# CHAPTER XXVI
## THE UNTHINKABLE

DESPITE the danger from the dark, we needed to build up our strength, so at dawn, before continuing south, we breakfasted on rabbits caught and cooked by Alice. Although Arkwright was somewhat better, our progress was still slow and we were further delayed by a detour to Cartmel to buy him a new pair of boots.

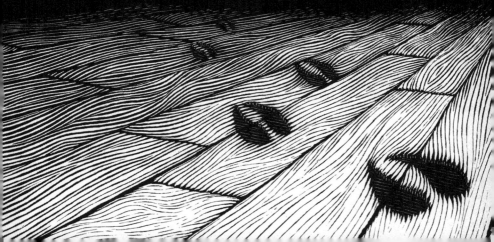

On finally reaching the coast, we had a long wait for the tide to reach full ebb. The Spook kept his promise to the hermit, and in addition to paying the guide, contributed three silver coins to the fund to support the families of those who'd drowned.

We approached the mill at dusk. But at the edge of the moat Claw warned us that something was very wrong. Her hackles rose and she began to growl. Then Alice sniffed three times and turned to me, alarm on her face.

"Something nasty ahead. Don't like it, Tom!"

Arkwright looked down at the moat and frowned. Then he knelt, dipped his forefinger into the murky water, and touched it briefly to his lips.

"The salt concentration's high. Nothing from the dark could cross that. Maybe something's got out."

I remembered the water witch and the skelt, both captive in pits under the house. Had they escaped?

"I tipped five barrels of salt into the moat," I told him. "But I didn't put any into the pits."

"Even so, Master Ward, there should still be enough in

there to keep them docile. If anything's got loose, it must've had some serious help!" said Arkwright.

"Aye," the Spook agreed, "and that moat would be no barrier to the most powerful creature from the dark: the Fiend himself!"

Arkwright nodded, and the three of us followed in his wake as he strode across the moat. He led us to the house toward the waterwheel, with Claw at his side. Suddenly he halted. There was a body lying facedown on the ground. He turned it over with his new boot.

The man's throat had been torn out, yet there was little blood to be seen. His body had been drained, probably by a water witch. But then I looked at the corpse's face, which was frozen in horror and pain. The mouth was open, the front teeth broken stumps. It was one of the press-gang: the sergeant, who'd fled the house first and run toward me before changing his mind at the sight of the dogs.

"It's one of a gang of deserters I'd a run-in with north of the bay," Arkwright said to the Spook. "They made what I thought were empty threats. Said they'd find me and sort me out. Well, this one got sorted out all right. In the wrong place at the wrong time just about sums it up."

He walked on and halted at the porch and I heard him utter a curse. When we drew level, I saw why. The front door had been ripped from its hinges. It might well be the work of a water witch.

"We need to search the house first to see if anything's still lurking inside. It's not the deserters we need to worry about. It's what killed them," Arkwright said.

He lit two candles and handed one to Alice. My master left his bag just inside the door and moved cautiously into the first room, his staff in his right hand, his silver chain in his left. Carrying the other candle, Arkwright was unarmed and so was Alice, but I had my staff at the ready.

Claw began to growl as we crossed the bare wooden floorboards, and I expected something to rush at us from the shadows at any moment. That didn't happen but we saw something that brought us to a sudden halt.

Burned into the floor was a series of footprints, nine in all, and each had the shape of a cloven hoof. They began in the middle of the room and ended just short of the kitchen door. It suggested that the Fiend had materialized there, taken those nine steps and then disappeared again. So where was he now? It sent a chill right to my heart. He might appear again at any moment.

But there was nothing to do but go on, and without a word we nervously entered the kitchen. Here Arkwright reached across the sink to the window ledge and grasped the large knife he'd shown me during our first lesson together. The door that gave access to the stairs was wide open. Was there something up in one of the bedrooms?

After commanding Claw to stay in the kitchen and guard our backs, Arkwright led the way up, with the Spook at his shoulder. I stood with Alice on the landing while they searched, waiting tensely, listening to their boots clumping through each bedroom. Again there was nothing. After that there was just the large room at the top of the house that housed Arkwright's library. No sooner had they entered it than Arkwright let out a loud cry of anguish. Thinking he was hurt or under attack, I rushed up the stairs to help.

As soon as I entered the room, it was clear why he'd cried out. The coffins of his mam and dad had been hurled from their trestles and smashed. Bones were heaped on the floorboards. And there were more cloven hoofprints burned into the boards.

Arkwright was beside himself with grief and rage, shaking from head to foot. Only gradually did the Spook manage to calm him down.

"The Fiend did this," my master told him. "He did it to rile you. He wants a red mist of anger to cloud your judgment. Stay calm for all of our sakes. When this is over, we'll put your parents to rights again, but now we need to check the pits."

Arkwright took a deep breath and nodded. We left Claw in the kitchen, and instead of using the trapdoor, we went outside again and approached the door next to the waterwheel.

"You stay outside, lad," the Spook whispered. "Bill and I will deal with this!"

I obeyed as Alice, giving me a little wave, followed them inside. But they'd been gone for less than a minute when something gleamed in the darkness to my right. There was a loud, angry hiss and two menacing eyes stared back into mine. I watched apprehensively as something resembling the leg of an enormous insect slowly emerged from the shadows.

It was gray, multi-jointed, and very long indeed. The leg of something thin but monstrous. A second limb followed and next came a head. And what a head! Something I'd never seen even in my scariest nightmares: a very thin snout, the nose flat, the ears laid back against the bony, elongated head, and close-set eyes that stared right into mine. It was the skelt.

I tried to call out but I couldn't even manage to open my mouth. As it moved closer and closer, its eyes never left mine and I felt the strength leaving me. I was like a rabbit transfixed by the gaze of a deadly stoat. My brain didn't seem to be working properly and my body was paralyzed.

Upright, it would have been taller than me. In addition to that narrow head, its long tubular body had two segments that were hard and ridged, like those of a crab or lobster, and barnacle-encrusted like the bottom of a boat. Its eight legs, however, were more like those of a spider, its movements delicate and precise, its joints creaking and crepitating as it moved.

Suddenly the skelt surged toward me, all eight legs a flickering blur, and scuttled right up my body, hurling me backward to the ground. I was winded by the fall and now its weight was pressing against me. Its scrabbling legs lay across my arms and legs, pinning me so that I was helpless. I stared up into the ugly, toothless snout, which opened just inches from my face, the creature enveloping me in a stench of dank, moldering loam and rot from stagnant pools. And from the widening mouth a long tube of translucent white bone began to extend toward me. I remembered how Arkwright had told me that a skelt had no tongue; instead it used this bone-tube to pierce its victim and suck up its blood.

Something forced my head back and there was a sudden excruciating pain in my throat. The sharp tube that protruded from the mouth of the skelt suddenly changed color and became red. It was sucking my blood and there was nothing I could do. The pain intensified. How much would it take? I began to panic. It might continue to feed until my heart stopped.

It was then that I heard the noises of running feet and a cry of dismay from Alice. There was a sudden loud *thwack* followed by a crunching sound. The skelt suddenly withdrew the bone-tube from my throat and rolled away from me.

The paralysis had left me, and I struggled onto my knees in time to see Arkwright holding a bloodstained stone in both hands, then lifting it high before bringing it down hard on the skelt's head. There was a cracking, crunching noise again, which ended with a sickening squelch; the skelt's whole body twitched, its legs going into a death spasm. Then it lay still, a pool of blood and fluid spreading out from its head, which had cracked open like an egg. I lurched to my knees, about to thank Arkwright but he spoke first.

"An interesting creature, Master Ward," he observed drily as Alice and the Spook helped me to my feet. Breathing hard and fast after the exertion, he placed the stone down beside the dead skelt. "Very rare, as I once told you. Not many people are fortunate enough to see one at such close proximity."

"Oh, Tom, I shouldn't have left you," Alice cried, squeezing my hand. "I thought it would still be inside under the mill."

"Well, no real harm done in the end," observed Arkwright. "Thank Alice for that, Master Ward. She sensed that something was wrong out here. Now let's get back inside and check the other pit."

As we'd expected, the water witch had escaped—or more likely been freed. The bars were bent apart and there were webbed witch footprints in the soft earth leading away. Smaller prints than those made by the skelt.

"No doubt this is the work of the Fiend," said the

Spook. "He likes to demonstrate his power."

"But where's the witch now?" Arkwright asked.

Claw was summoned and she made a thorough search of the garden; the two spooks followed her closely, weapons at the ready.

"She ain't here, Tom, that's for sure," Alice told me. "Would have sniffed her out myself otherwise."

"Not if the Fiend's close by, though," I said with a shiver. "Neither of us suspected Morwena on the barge."

Alice nodded and looked really scared.

"But where could the witch be hiding?" I asked.

"She's probably across the moat and escaped into the marsh," Alice said. "Old Nick could've carried her over. Salt ain't going to stop him, is it? Too strong, he is, for old tricks such as that!"

When the search proved fruitless, we retreated to the kitchen, where I made up the fire in the stove. Threatened by the dark, we didn't eat but at least we were warm and took turns to keep watch. Claw was put on guard outside to warn us if anything approached from the marsh.

"Best if we leave the body until morning," Arkwright suggested.

"Aye, we'll lay him to rest then, if we get the chance," the Spook agreed. "How many deserters were there?"

"Five in all," I replied.

"My guess is that the witch was already free when they crossed the moat into the garden," Arkwright added. "Could be that when she attacked and pinned down her prey, the others fled."

No one spoke for a while. Alice seemed preoccupied. I began to feel very uneasy. The Fiend's daughter was somewhere out there just waiting her chance. And now there was another water witch free. If she'd escaped across the moat helped by the Fiend, what was there to stop the reverse occurring? Surely he wouldn't find it too difficult to bring them to us? Not to mention the fact that he might pay us a visit himself.

The others placed the chairs close to the stove and made themselves as comfortable as they could. I sat on the kitchen floor, resting my shoulders and head against the wall. It wasn't very comfortable, but despite that and my fear of an attack, I finally managed to drift off into a shallow, fitful sleep. I woke up suddenly. Somebody was shaking my shoulder and a hand was firmly clamped over my mouth.

I looked into the eyes of the Spook, who gestured urgently toward the far corner of the room. The candles had burned low and the kitchen was gloomy. Alice and Arkwright were already awake; they were sitting beside me, staring into that same dark corner, where something strange and eerie was happening even as we watched. A shape was beginning to materialize, shifting slowly from a faint ashen gray to a flickering silver. It became more distinct—until without doubt I was looking at the Fiend's daughter: her face cadaverous and gaunt; her angular, fleshless nose jutting from between her malevolent eyes; the left lid transfixed by that sliver of bone; the right eye serpentine and cruel.

"I thirst," she cried, revealing her large canine teeth. "I thirst for your sweet blood. But I will let you live. All shall live but one. Just give me the boy and the rest may go free."

It was an image rather than the actual presence of the witch in the room. Although she was apparently standing less than seven paces away, she seemed to call to us from a great distance and I could hear the sighing of the wind in the background.

"My father will pay well for what I ask," she cried, her voice like the grating of a shingle beach under an ebb tide. "Give me the boy so that Amelia can be at peace. It's my father who binds her soul, preventing her from passing on. But surrender the boy and he'll release her and both she and Abraham will be free to choose the light. Just give me the boy and it'll be done. Send him alone out onto the marsh. Send him to me now."

"Go back from whence you came, evil hag!" cried the Spook. "We'll give you nothing. Nothing but death. Do you hear me? That's all that awaits you here!"

Arkwright remained silent but I thought that Morwena's cruel words must be like a blade twisting inside him. Above all things he wanted peace for his mam and dad. But despite the way he had treated me, I had faith in him. I believed that he served the light and would be strong enough to resist any temptation that the Fiend's daughter might dangle before him.

The image of Morwena seemed to shimmer and blur; she touched her finger to her left lid and her eye opened wide. But fortunately that baleful eye was powerless, for its bloodred color was transmuted into silver.

Now she began to chant, her voice reaching a high eldritch note. There was rhythm, intonation, and rhyme, the whole filled with a terrible power. But what exactly was being chanted? What did it mean? It sounded to me like the "Old Tongue"—that spoken by the first men who lived in the County.

My limbs seemed to be growing heavy and I felt strangely hot and cold at the same time. I tried to stand but couldn't. Too late I knew what the Fiend's daughter was doing. Those ancient words were a curse, an act of powerful dark magic that was sapping our strength and our will.

Out of the corner of my eye I saw that the Spook had somehow managed to rise to his feet. He pulled back his robe and reached into his breeches pockets. Then he hurled something straight at that evil apparition — something white from his right hand, something dark from his left: a mixture of salt and iron, usually so effective against creatures of the dark. Would it work this time — when the substance of our enemy wasn't even present in the room?

Immediately the chanting ceased and the image vanished as suddenly as a snuffed candle flame. I felt relief flood through me and staggered unsteadily to my feet. The Spook shook his head wearily.

"That was close," said Arkwright. "For a moment I thought it was all over with us."

"Aye, I wouldn't dispute that," said the Spook. "Never have I come up against a witch with such power. I suppose it comes from that dark Devil blood that runs in her veins. The County will be a far better place if we can put an end to her. But now I think we should all try to stay awake for the rest of the night. If she repeats that and only one of us is on watch, she might somehow, even at a distance, slay us in our sleep."

We did as the Spook suggested, but first I built up the fire again and left the door of the stove open so that it radiated heat directly into the room. We lit another two candles so that the light might last us until morning. I also filled my pockets with salt and iron from my bag so that I had one more weapon ready to use against the dark. But once settled down, nobody spoke. I looked sideways at Alice but she was staring at the floorboards and looked terrified. Both the Spook and Arkwright looked grim and determined but I wondered how they felt inside. After all, what could anyone do against power such as the Fiend's? As for Arkwright, he must be pondering what the witch had said—that it was her father's dark power that prevented his poor mam from crossing to the light.

What could he hope to do about that? Nothing. Nothing at all. If that were true, their spirits were trapped in the mill until the world itself came to an end.

The first thing that warned me of danger was the silence. It was intense. I could hear nothing. Nothing at all. The second was that I was unable to move. I was sitting on the floor as before, resting my head against the wall. I tried to turn my head and look at Alice, but my body refused to obey. I tried to speak to warn the others of my fears but couldn't even open my mouth.

I could see a candle on the floor opposite, set within reach of the Spook. Moments earlier the flame had been flickering but it was now perfectly still. It looked as if it had been carved from metal; it seemed to reflect light rather than cast it. On my left was the stove with its open door; I could see the flames within but each was static. Then I realized that I wasn't breathing. In a panic I tried to take a breath but nothing happened. Yet I felt no pain. My body wasn't crying out for air. My insides seemed too still and quiet. Had my heart stopped beating? Was I dead?

But then I remembered that I'd felt a little like this before—on the barge as we traveled toward Caster with the Fiend in the guise of the bargeman. Then the Devil had been tampering with time; it had passed too quickly. But I knew that this was different. I knew exactly what had happened: The Fiend had halted time itself.

I heard a noise from the shadows in the far corner of the room: a thump followed immediately by a sizzling, hissing sound. It was repeated twice more.

Suddenly I could smell burning. Wood smoke. The floorboards. And then I saw that although time had stopped and everything within the room seemed to be frozen into immobility, one thing *was* moving. And what else could move but the Fiend himself?

I couldn't see him yet—he was invisible—but I could see his footprints advancing toward me. Each time one of his unseen feet made contact with the floorboards, it burned the shape of a cloven hoof into the wood, which glowed red before darkening with a spluttering hiss. Would he make himself visible? The thought was terrifying. I'd been told by Grimalkin that to inspire awe and force obeisance he'd appeared in his true majestic shape to the covens at Halloween. According to the Spook, some people believed his true form was so terrible that anyone who saw it would instantly drop dead. Was that just a scary bedtime tale or was it real? Would he do that to me now?

Something began to materialize — no gray or silver phantasm but a solid-looking shape. However, it was not the terrifying apparition I'd feared. Once again, the Fiend had taken the shape of Matthew Gilbert, the bargeman, who now stood before me in boots and jerkin, exactly as I'd first seen him, smiling the same friendly, confident smile.

"Well, Tom," he said, "as I told you the last time we met, the difference between *fiend* and *friend* is only one letter. Which one shall I be to you? That's the choice you must make in the next few minutes. And upon that decision rests your own life as well as the fate of your three companions."

# CHAPTER XXVII
## A Hard Bargain

"**M**OVE your head, if you wish," the Fiend said with a smile. "It will make things easier. You'll be able to see better and I don't want you to miss a thing. So what is it to be? Friend or foe?"

I felt a lurch as my heart began to thump very hard in my chest and I sucked in a big breath. I turned my head slightly, instinctively checking to see that Alice was all right. She was still and quiet but her eyes were wide with fear. Could she also see the Fiend? If so, she was still frozen in time just like the Spook and Arkwright. Only the Fiend and I seemed able to move, but I felt very weak and knew I lacked the strength to climb to my feet. Yet I opened my mouth and found I could speak. I turned my gaze back toward my enemy and gave him my answer.

"You're the dark made flesh. You can never be my friend."

"Don't be so sure about that, Tom. We are closer than you think. Far closer. Believe it or not, we know each other very well. Let's take a question that each human being considers at some time in his or her brief life. Some answer it quickly and hardly ever think about it again. Some are believers. Some skeptics. Some debate it in anguish for the duration of their lives. It's a simple question, Tom, and this is it. Do you believe in God?"

I believed in the light. As for God, I wasn't sure. But my dad had believed, and maybe, deep down, the Spook also believed, though he hardly ever talked about such things. He certainly didn't believe in an authoritative old man with a white beard, the deity of the Church.

"I'm not sure," I answered truthfully.

"Not sure, Tom? Why, it's as plain as the nose on your face! Would God allow so much evil into the world?" the Fiend continued. "Disease, starvation, poverty, war, and death—that's all you poor humans have to look forward to. Would such a God let the war continue? Of course not. Therefore he simply cannot exist. All those churches, all that worship by devout but misguided congregations. And all for what? For nothing! Nothing at all! Their prayers go out into the void and are unheard.

"But if *we* ruled, together we could change everything and make this world a better place for all. So what do you say? Will you help me to do that, Tom? Will you stand at my side? We could achieve so much together!"

"*You* are my enemy," I said. "We could never work together."

Suddenly I began to shiver with fear. I remembered the

hobbles that the Spook had told me about—the limitations placed on the Fiend's power that the Spook had read about in Mam's books. The Fiend wanted me to work with him so that he could rule here until the end of the world. If he killed me himself, he'd only rule for a century. So would he do that now: kill me anyway because I'd refused?

"Sometimes it's very difficult to rule, Tom," the Fiend said, stepping closer. "Sometimes hard, painful decisions have to be made. As you refuse my offer, you give me no alternative. You must die so that I can bring about a better world for all humanity. My daughter awaits you in the marsh. There you must kill or be killed."

So he'd decided to let her kill me instead. That way the hobbles would be nullified and he would grow in power until he finally ruled the world.

"Her against me?" I protested. "No! I'll not go out to meet her. Let her come to me."

I thought of her out there in the marsh at her strongest, of the peril of that blood-filled eye. I'd be helpless, fixed to the spot within seconds. Then slain, my throat ripped out like the bargeman's.

"You're in no position to make the rules, boy. Go out there and face her if you want your companions to live," said the Fiend. "I could slay them in a second while they're powerless before me. . . ."

He leaned forward and rested his hand lightly on Alice's head. Then he spread his fingers. It was a big hand and seemed to be expanding even as I watched. Now the whole of Alice's head was enclosed by the span of that huge hand.

"All I have to do is clench my fist, Tom, that's all; her head will be crushed like an eggshell. Should I do it now? Do you need to see how easy it is for me?"

"No! Please!" I cried out. "Don't hurt her. Don't hurt any of them. I'll go to the marsh. I'll go right now!"

I lurched to my feet, snatched up my staff, and moved toward the door. There I paused and looked back at my enemy. What if I released the blade in my staff and attacked him? Would I have a chance? But it would be futile and I knew it. The instant I moved toward him I'd be frozen in time again, just as helpless as the Spook, Alice, and Arkwright.

I nodded toward them. "If I survive or I win . . . ? Will you let them live?"

The Fiend smiled. "If you win, they will live — at least for a while. If you die, I will kill them, too. So you fight for the lives of these three as well as your own."

I knew my chances of defeating the Fiend's daughter on the marsh were slim. How could my staff and chain be strong enough against her powers? And Alice, the Spook, and Arkwright would die with me. But there was something I might achieve before that happened. One last thing to be bought with my death. It was certainly worth a try.

"One more thing," I said. "Give me that and I'll go to the marsh now. Life is short and everybody has to die sometime but it's a terrible thing to be tormented afterward. Arkwright's mam and dad have suffered enough. Whether I win or lose, will you release Amelia's soul so that they can both go to the light?"

"Win *or* lose? You drive a hard bargain, Tom."

"No harder than the task you set me. You expect me to die. That's what you want. Is that fair? At least give me what I ask so it won't all have been for nothing."

He stared hard at me for a moment and then his face relaxed. He'd made his decision. "Then so be it. I'll grant your wish."

Without a backward glance, I left the kitchen, ran through the other room and out into the night. As I moved farther into the garden, I felt a change. Outside the house time was moving forward normally. But it wasn't a good night to venture out onto the marsh.

A thick mist had descended, the visibility was down to about ten paces. Overhead the orb of the moon was just visible, so there wasn't much depth to the mist, but that wouldn't help me on the marsh, where the land was low and flat. How I wished I could have Claw with me but I assumed she was frozen in time like the others.

I paused on the edge of the moat and took a deep breath. Once across it, I would face the Fiend's daughter.

She would be waiting out there; the darkness and mist would be to her advantage. I advanced onto the marsh cautiously. It was a pity I'd only practiced being hunted by the dogs once, otherwise I'd now know the meandering paths much better.

Deep, stagnant water or treacherous bog lay on either side of the paths. I'd seen the way Morwena leaped out of the water like a salmon. I had to be prepared for a similar attack now. The threat might come from either side of any path I trod. As for weapons, I had my staff and I now felt in the pocket of my cloak and my fingers closed over the silver chain. It was reassuring to feel it there. Finally I had salt and iron, but that could be used only as a last resort, when staff and chain were no longer an option and both hands were free.

Suddenly an eerie sound echoed over the marsh. It was the unmistakable cry of the corpsefowl, the witch's familiar. She had an extra pair of eyes free to soar into the sky; the bird would be searching for me now. No doubt the Fiend had already told his daughter that I was on my way.

The bird's cry had come from the west, somewhere close to the mere where I'd met Morwena and been hooked through the ear. So I took the most southerly of the paths available to me. I didn't want to meet the witch near the deep water.

Despite the slippery ground, I began to walk faster, growing more and more nervous with each step. Then, suddenly, I saw something ahead. There was a body lying on the path. I didn't want to retrace my steps so I approached it cautiously; it might be a trap of some sort. But it was a man lying facedown with his head twisted to the left. He was quite dead. His throat was torn out just like the one near the mill. He was wearing a uniform; it was another of the press-gang.

The Fiend's daughter might be close by now, ready to attack, so I moved on quickly. I'd been on the path for no more than two or three more minutes when I heard another sound, directly ahead. What was it? Not the corpsefowl this time. I halted and peered into the mist. All I could see were large clumps of reed and the faint line of the path twisting through them. So I continued more slowly this time.

I heard it again and halted immediately. It was a sort of croaking cry followed by a gurgle. It sounded as though someone was in pain. As if they were choking. I advanced a step at a time, my staff at the ready, until I could just make out a horizontal shape on the path ahead. Was it somebody creeping toward me? Two more steps and I could see that it wasn't moving. It looked like a long bundle of rags. Was it another of the soldiers? Then I saw it more clearly.

There was a witch on the path, lying on her back, one hand trailing in the water. Her eyes and mouth were wide open: the former were fixed and staring but looking at the sky, not toward me; the mouth showed the four long, sharp canines of a water witch. Was it the one who'd escaped from the pit under the mill? Was she hurt — or dead?

I hesitated. I was very close to her now. What if she was only pretending? Just waiting until I got close enough for her to grab hold of me? And then a voice spoke to me out of the darkness, one that I recognized only too well.

"Well, child, we meet again!"

My knees turned to water. Beyond the body, facing me, was Grimalkin.

Now she would get her revenge. Perhaps she'd saved me in the folly just so that she could savor this moment. I wished the ground would swallow me up. I feared the *snip-snip* of those terrible scissors. I eased the silver chain out of the pocket of my cloak and readied it. I'd missed her last time, but I'd been exhausted and I'd cast on the run. My left hand was shaking with nerves but I forced myself to breathe evenly. I would be brave like my master, the Spook. Even if I died, I could still be brave. I could do it. I'd trained long and hard for this moment.

I looked her in the eye and prepared to throw. She wasn't like Morwena and at least I *could* look into her face. It was a beautiful face but stern and cruel, and her mouth was slightly open, the lips painted black. And I could see the savage teeth that she'd filed to sharp, cruel points.

"Put away your chain, child," she said softly. "I've not come for you. This night we fight together against our enemy."

It was only then that I noticed that she brandished no weapon; all her blades were sheathed.

I lowered my chain. I believed her. After all, she'd warned me about the water witches in the tunnel, then helped me fight them off. My mam had always told me to trust my instincts and I felt that Grimalkin was telling the truth. It seemed to me that this was to our advantage. Despite what the Spook had said, if the dark fought against the dark, it would surely be weakened.

Grimalkin pointed at the dead body of the witch. "Don't worry, child," she said softly. "She won't bite. Just step over her body. Hurry. We have little time!"

I stepped over the witch, and ten more paces brought me face to face with the assassin. As before, she was bristling with weapons, the sheaths carrying knives of various sizes, not to mention the scissors. But there were two changes: Her hair was pulled back tightly from her brow and tied at the nape of her neck with a black silk scarf; secondly, she was very dirty, her face and bare arms and legs streaked with mud, and she stank of marsh slime.

"What do you seek here, child? Your death?" she demanded, opening her black-painted lips to show her pointed teeth again. "The Fiend's daughter is close. Within minutes she'll be here."

I shook my head. "I've no choice. The Fiend made me come here; otherwise he'll kill my master, Alice, and Arkwright. If I slay his daughter, he'll spare their lives."

She laughed softly. "You're brave," she said, "but foolish. Why try to fight her here? Water is her element. If you begin to win, she'll flee deeper into the marsh where you can't reach her. And give her half a chance and she'll drag you into the water. No! This isn't the way. We must lure her onto higher, drier ground. I've seen you run and you're fast, almost as fast as me. But how sure are your feet over this terrain? Now, if you are to survive, you must match me step for step."

Without another word, she turned and began to run

down the path that would take us deeper into the marsh. I followed at her heels, running faster and faster across the treacherous ground. Once I almost lost my footing and came close to falling into the bog; on two occasions Grimalkin began to pull away from me into the mist, and only by making a huge effort did I manage to keep her within sight.

At last we began to climb out of the marsh. Ahead was a small rounded hill with the ruin of a small abbey at its summit. It was Monks' Hill. Three stunted sycamores grew among the rubble. In places hardly a stone stood upon a stone, but Grimalkin led us to a low wall and we settled down with our backs to it so that we could gaze upon the swamplands. Above us the moon shone from a cloudless sky, lighting the ruins and the hillside to a silver.

We were above the mist, which now lay undulating below, obscuring the marsh and the path. We were sitting upon an island rising from a calm sea composed of white cloud. For a long time we didn't speak. After my exertions I was happy just to allow my breathing to return to normal, and it was the witch assassin who spoke first.

"It is to Alice Deane that you should give thanks that you don't face your enemy here alone."

I turned toward Grimalkin in astonishment. "Alice?" I asked.

"Yes, your friend Alice. Afraid that the Fiend and his daughter were about to slay you, she summoned me north to come to your aid. We've been in contact many times during the past month. Mostly by mirror."

"Alice used a mirror to contact *you*?"

"Of course, child. How else do witches communicate over long distances? I was surprised at first but she persisted and slowly won me round. How could I refuse one whose mother was a Malkin? Especially when our cause is now the same."

"So did you come looking for me on the island?"

"You or the Fiend's daughter. But I was never on that island until we spoke. I watched you from the mainland shore, saw the witches preparing to enter the water, and warned you. I'd been watching you for days. John

Gregory wouldn't welcome my presence so I kept my distance."

"The Fiend expects me to face her alone. Will he know that you're here?"

Grimalkin shrugged. "He might. He can't see everything, but when his daughter sees me, then he will know."

"So won't he intervene? He could appear right here, up on this hill."

"That's something you needn't fear. He'll keep his distance. Where I am you won't see him."

"You're able to make him keep away?"

"Yes—because of what I did years ago."

"What was that? Alice has been trying to find the means to keep him away. How's it done? Did you use a blood jar? Or have you hobbled him in some way?"

"There may well be more than one way but I chose the most usual method for a witch. I bore him a child—"

"You had a child by the Fiend?" I asked in astonishment.

"Why not? That's what some witches do—if they have the nerve for it. And if they're desperate enough to be free of his power. Give him a child, and later, after his first visit to see his offspring, he must leave you alone. Most children of the Fiend and a witch are either monsters or other witches. The mother of the one we face was the witch Grismalde. They say she was very beautiful but dwelt in mud caverns and roamed the darkest bowels of the earth and so stank accordingly. But the Devil's tastes are sometimes strange.

"Yet by some chance my own body managed to cheat him. My child was neither monster nor witch. He was perfectly human, a beautiful baby boy. But when the Fiend saw him, he was beside himself with anger. He picked up my child, his son, and dashed out his brains against a rock. The blood of that innocent bought my freedom but it was a high price to pay.

"After his death I was a little mad with grief. But the trade that I then chose saved me. Through the cruelty demanded of a witch assassin, I found myself again. Time has passed and memories fade but what the Fiend did can never be forgotten. There are two reasons why I fight by your side tonight. The first is because of my need for revenge. The second is because Alice Deane asked me to protect you against Morwena. Tonight we'll begin by slaying the Fiend's daughter."

For a few moments I turned over in my mind what Grimalkin had just told me. But suddenly she placed her finger against her lips to indicate the need for silence and stood up.

Almost immediately the eerie cry of the corpsefowl echoed over the marsh. Seconds later the plaintive cry came again, much louder and nearer. I heard the beating of wings as a large bird flew straight up out of the mist, gaining height as it approached. It had seen us; now the Fiend's daughter would know exactly where we were.

Grimalkin reached into a leather sheath and drew forth a knife with a short blade. In one smooth, powerful movement she hurled it at the bird. End over end it spun. The creature twisted away too late. The blade buried itself deep in its breast, and with a loud wailing screech the corpsefowl fell into the sea of mist, to be lost from view.

"I rarely miss," Grimalkin said with a grim smile, settling herself down on my left again. "But I missed when I hurled my long knife at you. Or rather, it was on target but then you plucked it from the air. The Fiend tampers with time, slowing, stopping, or speeding it up to meet his needs. But I think that night you did it, too. Just a little but enough to make a difference."

She was referring to our meeting in the summer, when she'd hunted and caught me on the edge of Hangman's Wood as I was fleeing to the refuge of my mam's room. After pinning her shoulder to a tree with the Spook's staff, I'd turned to run but she'd thrown her knife at the back of my head. I'd turned to watch it spin end over end as it sped toward me through the air, then reached up and caught it, saving my own life. Time had indeed seemed to slow, but never for one moment had I thought that I might be responsible.

"Stand up now," Grimalkin commanded, her voice sharp. "It's almost time. The moment of danger is close. Very soon our enemies will be here."

"Enemies?" I asked. "Is there more than one?"

"Of course, child. The Fiend's daughter will not be alone. She has called others to her aid. Water witches from far and wide are converging upon this hillock. They have been approaching since dark. The struggle is imminent."

It was time to face the witches. Soon, one way or the other, it would be over.

# CHAPTER XXVIII
## THE FIGHT ON THE MARSH

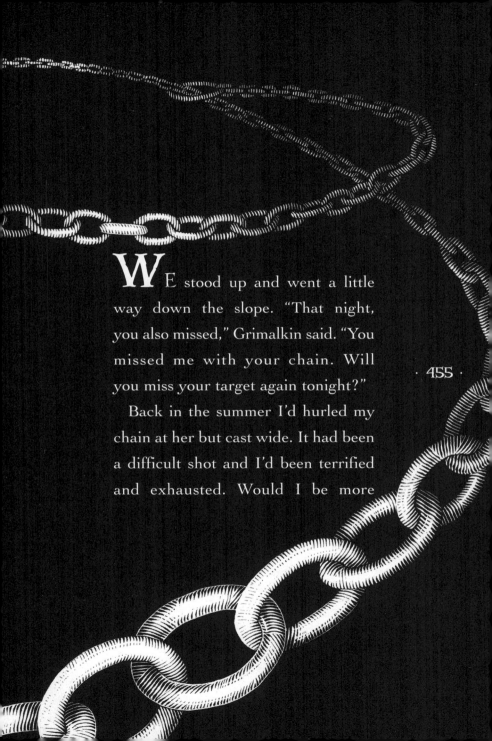

W E stood up and went a little way down the slope. "That night, you also missed," Grimalkin said. "You missed me with your chain. Will you miss your target again tonight?"

Back in the summer I'd hurled my chain at her but cast wide. It had been a difficult shot and I'd been terrified and exhausted. Would I be more successful tonight against the Fiend's daughter?

"I'll do my best," I told her.

"Then let's hope your best is good enough. Now listen well while I explain what's about to happen. Water witches will attack, surging up from the marsh below. So use your staff—but keep your chain in reserve. It may make all the difference. We must face the blood-filled eye of Morwena, but it can be used against only one enemy at a time. If she comes at me, then use your chain against her. Until then hold it in reserve. Fight the others with your staff. Understand?"

I nodded.

"Good. The second thing to our advantage is that Morwena will be reluctant to venture onto this hill, where the ground is relatively dry and firm underfoot. So hopefully she'll hang back."

Once again I nodded, nerves now beginning to overtake me. I could feel a trembling in my knees and hands and butterflies in my stomach. I took a deep breath and fought to control myself. I needed a steady left hand to cast the silver chain.

The first attack took me completely by surprise. But for the slap of clawed, webbed feet on the grass, it was silent and terrifyingly fast. A water witch ran straight out of the mist toward Grimalkin, claws at the ready, dank hair streaming behind her, face contorted into a mask of hatred.

But Grimalkin was even quicker. She pulled a knife from her belt and hurled it straight at her attacker. I heard a soft thud as it buried itself in the witch's chest. She fell back with a groan and slid down the slope to be enveloped by the mist.

Now they attacked in force. I would have been hard pressed to deal with just one, such was their speed and ferocity. Up out of the mist they surged—six or seven of them in all—shrieking as they came, talons outstretched, faces twisted in fury, some wielding short blades. Only when the nearest were no more than five paces away did I remember the retractable blade in my rowan staff. I found the recess and pressed, hearing a satisfying click as the blade emerged and locked into position.

I thrust, parried, and turned again and again, spinning on my heels to keep them at bay, sweat running down my face and into my eyes as I used all the skills that Arkwright had taught me. But despite my best efforts, I would quickly have been overwhelmed but for Grimalkin. Now I saw why the witch assassin was, in combat, the most feared of all the Pendle witches.

Each deadly economical movement of her body was a killing stroke. Each blade slipped from a leather sheath found a new resting place in the flesh of an enemy. Talon against talon, blade against blade, she was matchless. She spun and slew, a wheel of death, cutting down those who opposed us until seven dead bodies lay on the slope beside us.

Then she sucked in a deep breath and remained absolutely still, as if listening, before placing her left hand lightly upon my shoulder and leaning toward me.

"There are more emerging from the marsh now," she whispered, her mouth very close to my ear. "And the Fiend's daughter is with them. Remember what I said.

Use your chain against her. Everything depends on that. Miss and we're both finished!"

A lone witch attacked from the mist. Twice Grimalkin hurled blades and found a target before the two collided in a fury of tangled limbs, gouging fingers, and sharp teeth. Neither witch uttered a sound as they rolled away from me in the silent fury of combat, down the hill, and into the mist.

Suddenly I was alone on the hillside, listening to the hammering of my own heart. Should I go down and help Grimalkin? What if other witches had now set upon her? But before I could make a decision, it was my own turn to come under attack. Another water witch stepped out of the mist. She didn't race toward me at speed like the others but padded softly up the hill, step by careful step. Her mouth gaped wide to reveal four immense yellow-green fangs. In appearance she was very similar to Morwena: The triangular bone that served as a nose made me feel as if I were facing something more dead than alive. But despite her slow, careful advance, I was still mindful of the speed she was capable of. I knew she would attempt to hook one of her talons into my flesh, and above all I feared the upward sweep that would attempt to pierce my upper throat and wrap her fingers around my teeth, a grip from which it would be impossible to break free.

The witch attacked suddenly; she was fast but I matched her, bringing my staff across in a short arc that missed her left cheek by less than an inch. She snarled and a low growl of anger rose in her throat. But I jabbed at her again and she took a step backward. Now I was on the offensive and each careful, calculated jab drove her down the hillside, closer to the edge of the thick mist.

Then, too late, I guessed what she intended: to drag me into the mist and marsh, where she'd have the advantage.

The attack was sudden. She'd just been playing with me. With her right hand she struck out like a snake. Two fingers hooked up toward my throat, the talons extended. I tried to twist away but felt a glancing blow and then I was being tugged forward. I lost my balance and rolled down the slope, my staff flying out of my hands. The witch rolled with me but then we broke apart and I felt no pain in my throat or jaw. She'd missed and hooked her talon into the collar of my sheepskin jacket, and now the fall had torn it free.

I rose onto my knees and glanced about me. I hadn't reached the bottom of the slope but the witch had rolled much farther. The mist was thinner now and I could make out my staff. It was out of reach, but four paces would see me armed again. Then I glanced to my right and saw something that made my blood run cold. Grimalkin was standing over the body of a witch she'd slain but she was rooted to the spot, completely immobile, staring at Morwena, who was moving up the slope toward her, talons extended. I stood and reached into my pocket for my chain, easing it around my left wrist.

It was clear that Grimalkin was in thrall to that blood-filled eye. Within moments she would be dead. If I missed, then Morwena would kill Grimalkin and turn her attention to me.

This was the moment of truth. Would all those months

of training in the Spook's garden pay off? This was far more difficult than casting toward the practice post. Nerves and fear played a significant part. I'd sometimes used the chain successfully against witches, but I'd often failed, too. The enormity of what depended upon this darkened my mind with doubts. If I missed, it was over. And I would get only one chance!

The first step was to *believe* I could do it. Think positively! The Spook had told me that the key to controlling the body was first to control the mind. So I did just that. I raised my left arm, sucked in a deep breath and held it.

I concentrated, staring hard at my target, Morwena, who was almost within arm's length of Grimalkin now. Time seemed to slow. Everything became utterly silent. Morwena was no longer moving. I wasn't breathing. Even my own heart seemed to have stopped.

I cracked the silver chain and cast it toward the witch. It formed a perfect spiral in the air, shimmering in the moonlight; it seemed to be the only thing moving. It fell over her, tightening itself against her teeth and arms so that she toppled to her knees. Sound rushed back into my ears. I breathed out and heard Grimalkin let out her own great sigh of relief before easing a long blade from her belt and advancing purposefully toward her enemy.

Concentrating on casting the silver chain at Morwena, I'd neglected the threat to myself. Suddenly a water witch was beside me, her taloned finger hooking up toward my jaw. Faster than I could ever have believed, my left arm parried the blow, but we locked together and fell hard before rolling farther down the hill.

I was immediately fighting for my life again. Witches are physically strong, and in close combat even a grown man would be in serious trouble. I fought, punched, and struggled, but she gripped me tightly and began to drag me toward the water. I'd kept my promise to Grimalkin and used my chain against Morwena. But in doing so, I'd lost the chance to retrieve my staff, the only thing that gave me a fighting chance against a witch such as this. The only other weapons at my disposal were salt and iron but my arms were pinned to my sides.

The next moment we rolled into the water. I just had time to close my mouth and hold my breath and then my head went under. I struggled even harder, and we spun round again and my face emerged for a second or so, allowing me to take one more breath. Then the water closed over me again, and I felt myself being drawn down. My new swimming skills were useless. The water witch had me in her grip and it was too strong. Down and down I sank, into the depths. I fought to hold my breath but my lungs were bursting and there was a darkness over my eyes.

How long I fought to be free I don't know, but my struggles grew weaker and at last the water rushed into my mouth and up my nose and I began to drown. The final thing I remember is a feeling of resignation. I'd done my best but it was all over now and I was finally dying. Then it grew dark and I stopped struggling.

But my battle in this world wasn't over. I awoke to find myself on the hillside again, coughing and choking while somebody pressed and pounded my back. I thought I was being sick but it was water, not vomit, that was gushing from my nose and mouth.

It seemed to go on for a long time, until gradually the pounding stopped and I found myself breathing without choking, although my heart was beating so fast I thought it might burst. Then someone rolled me onto my back and I was looking up into the face of Grimalkin.

"You'll live, child," she said, pulling me up into a sitting position. "But it was a close thing. I only just reached you before the witch dragged you into the really deep water."

I realized that I owed my life to a malevolent witch. Whatever the Spook thought, we were on the same side. So I thanked her. It was what my dad would have expected.

Then I saw that the line of dead bodies lying on the edge of the marsh included the Fiend's daughter. She was still bound by my silver chain.

"I'm sorry I wasn't more help," I said. I just got the words out before a coughing fit took me.

Grimalkin waited patiently until it finished before speaking again. "You did enough, child. When you cast your chain at Morwena, you ensured our victory. So now come and reclaim it. I can't touch silver."

Grimalkin helped me to my feet. I felt weak and began to shiver violently. My clothes were saturated, my body chilled to the bone. As I walked toward the line of supine bodies, I saw what Grimalkin had done and was almost sick. She had cut the heart from each dead witch and placed it near the head. She saw the appalled look on my face and rested her hand on my shoulder.

"It had to be done, child, to ensure that none of them is able to return. Hasn't your master taught you that?"

I nodded. Strong witches such as these could be reborn again or might be powerful enough to walk the earth while dead and do untold harm. To prevent this you had to cut out the heart; it then had to be eaten.

Grimalkin lifted the body of the Fiend's daughter by the hair while I removed my chain. It was covered in blood. There was a faint noise in the distance and Grimalkin looked up. It was repeated: the bark of a hunting dog. Claw was on her way. If the Fiend had kept his word, the normal progress of time would now be restored to the mill.

"I no longer have the stomach for such things, so make sure the dog eats the hearts—all of them," Grimalkin said. "I'll go now before the others come. But one last thing: How old are you, child?"

"Fourteen. I'll be fifteen next August. On the third of that month."

Grimalkin smiled. "Life is hard on Pendle, and consequently children must grow up quickly. On the Walpurgis Night sabbath following his fourteenth birthday, the boy child of a witch-clan is considered to have become a man. Go to Pendle soon after that feast and seek me out. I guarantee your safety and I will give you a gift. It will be well worth having."

It was a strange thing for her to say. Walpurgis Night was the last day of April. I couldn't imagine myself visiting Pendle to receive a gift from Grimalkin. I knew what the Spook would think of that!

With that the witch turned swiftly on her heel, ran back up the hill, leaped over the low wall, and was lost to view.

Within five minutes Claw arrived. I watched as she began to devour the hearts of the witches. She was ravenous, and by the time the Spook, Arkwright, and Alice arrived she'd almost finished the last one.

I remember Alice offering to wash the blood from my silver chain. Then the world grew suddenly dark and the Spook was helping me to my feet. Shivering violently, I was taken back to the mill and put to bed. Whether from swallowing stagnant marsh water or from the scratches on my throat probably caused by the water witch's talons, I quickly developed a dangerous fever.

# CHAPTER XXIX
## WHERE I BELONG

I learned afterward that Alice tried to help with one of her potions but that the Spook forbade it. Instead, the local doctor visited the house again and gave me medicines that made me vomit until I thought my stomach would tear. It was almost five days before I was able to leave my sickbed. Had I known at the time that Alice wasn't being allowed to treat me, I would have protested.

The Spook recognized her skills with potions, but it was only after I'd recovered that I found out why he'd kept her away from my bedside. It was a blow to my heart. The worst possible news.

As soon as I was on my feet, we had a long discussion in the upstairs sitting room. The coffins of Bill Arkwright's mam and dad were no longer there; they'd been buried on the edge of a local churchyard where he could visit them. The Fiend had kept his word and their spirits had gone to the light. Now that the unquiet dead no longer haunted the mill, it had a new atmosphere of tranquility.

Arkwright was very grateful for what I'd done. He began the discussion by thanking me to the point where it became embarrassing. Next it was my turn to speak but I had little to tell the gathering, other than to describe how the fight on the marsh had unfolded. They knew the rest already. And the Spook knew too much. Far too much.

His face stern and tinged with anger, he explained that,

although their bodies had been frozen in time, their minds had been free and they had somehow been able to see what I saw and listen to the discussion between the Fiend and me. They knew the task I'd been set and the bargain I'd made both for their lives and the release of Arkwright's parents. That was terrible enough as they feared the outcome on the marsh and were aware of the imminence of their own deaths. But, cheated of that, the Fiend had later maliciously told them other things: facts designed to drive a wedge between the Spook and me and, even worse, create a gulf between us and Alice that could never be crossed.

"I was already saddened and worried by the fact that you used the mirror to talk to the girl. It showed me the bad influence she's had on you. Far worse than I'd expected . . ." lamented the Spook.

I opened my mouth to protest but he gestured angrily for silence. "But now there's more. That sly and deceitful girl has been in contact with Grimalkin for nearly a month."

I looked across at Alice. Tears were streaming down her

face. I suspected that the Spook had already told her what was going to happen as a consequence.

"And don't try to tell me that good came from it," the Spook continued. "I know that Grimalkin saved your life — saved all our lives — by fighting alongside you on the marsh, but she's evil, lad. She belongs to the dark and we can't compromise; otherwise we'll end up no better ourselves and we might as well be dead as suffer that. Alice belongs in a pit, and as soon as we get back to Chipenden, that's where she'll go!"

"Alice doesn't deserve that!" I protested. "Think of all the times she's helped us in the past. She saved your life when you were seriously hurt by that boggart near Anglezarke. You would have died but for Alice."

I stared hard at him but his expression was unrelenting and a torrent of words poured from my mouth before I could stop them.

"If you do that, if you bind Alice in a pit, I'll leave. I won't be your apprentice anymore! I couldn't work with you after that!"

One part of me meant every word; the other was horrified. What would Mam think of the threat I'd just made?

"That's your choice, lad," said the Spook sadly. "No apprentice of mine is forced to complete his time. You wouldn't be the first to walk away. But you'd certainly be the last. I won't take on another apprentice if you go."

I tried one more time. "You do realize that the Fiend told you those things about Alice deliberately? That he *wants* you to put her in a pit? That it serves his purpose because without Alice we'll be weakened?"

"Don't you think I haven't gone over all this in my mind already, lad? This is no easy decision and I don't make it lightly. And I do remember that your mam believed in the girl, too, so you don't need to remind me of that. Well, anybody can be wrong. But my conscience tells me what to do. I know what's right."

"You could be making a big mistake," I told him bitterly, feeling that nothing I said would change his mind. "The biggest mistake you've ever made."

There was a long silence then but for the sound

of Alice weeping. Then Arkwright spoke up.

"It seems to me that there's another way," he said quietly. "There's clearly a strong bond between Master Ward and this girl. And I'll say this to you, Mr. Gregory: If you carry out your threat, you'll lose an apprentice. Perhaps the best you've ever had. We'll all lose someone who could be a dangerous foe to the Fiend. Because without our training and protection, Tom will be seriously vulnerable and might never reach his full potential.

"And there's something else very close to my own heart. The lad made a bargain with the Fiend that freed my mam's and dad's spirits from over fifteen years of suffering. But without the help of Grimalkin he wouldn't have been able to win. And without Alice summoning her the witch assassin wouldn't have stood at Master Ward's side. So even I owe the girl something."

I was astonished by Arkwright's defense of Alice. I'd never heard him talk with such eloquence and passion. Suddenly I was filled with hope.

"From what I've been told, the girl had a bad upbringing,

a training in witchcraft that very few people of even the strongest character would have been able to recover from. That she did recover and has contributed so much shows you her mettle. I don't think we're dealing with a witch here. And certainly not a malevolent one. But maybe, like all of us, she's both good and bad inside, and you know only too well that light and dark fight a war within each of our hearts. I should know: At times my thoughts have been darker than most people's. And I've had to struggle long and hard to limit my drinking. So let Alice go free. You wouldn't be releasing a witch into the world. You'd be releasing a girl who I think will prove to be a strong-minded woman; she'll still be on our side whatever the methods she may sometimes choose to employ. As I said, there's a middle way," he continued. "Don't put her in a pit. Instead, why don't you just send her away to make her own way in the world? Just banish her. Do that for us all. It's a way out of this mess."

There was a long silence, then the Spook looked at me.

"Would that be lenient enough for you, lad? Could you live with that? If I did that, would you continue as my apprentice?"

The thought of not seeing Alice again was more than I could bear but it was far better than her being condemned to spend the rest of her life in a pit. I also wanted to continue as the Spook's apprentice. It was my duty to fight the dark. I knew that my mam would want me to carry on.

"Yes," I said softly, and the moment I spoke Alice stopped sobbing. I felt so bad, I couldn't even look at her.

"Right, girl," said the Spook. "Collect your things and get you gone. Keep well away from the lad and don't ever come within five miles of Chipenden again! Return and you'll know exactly what to expect."

Alice didn't reply and I suddenly realized that she'd been silent throughout and hadn't uttered even one word in her own defense. That wasn't like Alice! Now, silently, her face grim, she left the room.

I looked at the Spook. "I need to say good-bye to her," I told him. "It's something I've got to do!"

He nodded. "If you must. But make it short, lad. Don't linger. . . ."

I waited for Alice at the edge of the garden. She smiled sadly as she approached through the drooping willows, carrying her few belongings in a bundle. It was starting to rain: a cold drizzle, the kind that soaks you to the bone.

"Thanks for coming to say good-bye, Tom," she said, wading through the moat. Once across she held my hand very tightly, her left hand squeezing mine in such a grip that I thought my bones would break as well as my heart.

"I don't know what to say," I started.

She silenced me. "Ain't nothing you can say. We both done what we thought was best—and I always knew what Old Gregory thought about me using the dark. It was a risk worth taking to protect you. I don't regret it for a minute— though it breaks my heart to think I'll never see you again."

We walked in silence until we reached the canal bank. Then she released my hand, pulled something from the pocket of her coat, and held it out toward me. It was the blood jar.

"Take it, Tom. Fiend can't touch you if you keep this close. It's got Morwena's blood in it. Keep you safe, it will!"

"How did you get her blood? I don't understand."

"Don't you remember? I washed your chain. But first I put some in the bottle. Don't take much. Just add a few drops of your own blood to it and it'll do the trick!"

I shook my head. "No, Alice. I can't take it —"

"Oh, please, Tom, please. Just take it. Take it for me. Not trying to scare you. But you'll be dead soon without this. Who'll keep you safe if I'm not there? Old Gregory can't, that's for sure. So take the bottle so I can sleep at night knowing that you're safe."

"I can't take it, Alice. I can't use the dark. Please don't ask me again. I know you mean well, but I just can't accept it. Not now. Not ever."

She looked down at the towpath, replaced the bottle in her pocket, and started to cry silently. I watched the tears run down her cheeks and start to drip from the end of her chin. One part of me wanted to put my arms round her but I daren't. Do that and I'd never be able to let her go. I had to be strong and keep her at a distance.

"Where will you go, Alice? Where will you stay?"

She lifted her tear-lined face toward me, her expression a blank. "I'll go home," she said. "Back to Pendle. Back where I belong. I was born to be a witch and that's what I'm going to be. It's the only life I can live now. . . ."

Then Alice put her arms round me and pulled me close, almost squeezing the breath from my body. And before I could move, her lips were pressed against mine, kissing me hard. It only lasted a couple of seconds, then she turned and ran off down the towpath, heading south. It hurt me to watch her go. My own eyes filled with tears and I sobbed deep in my throat.

The clans were divided against themselves now, some in support of the Fiend, others in opposition. But because of what she'd done before—and also the blood that ran through her veins, half Deane and half Malkin—Alice had many enemies in Pendle. Her life would be in danger as soon as she set foot there.

What hurt me most of all was that I knew she didn't want to go. She didn't really want to become a witch — I was sure of that. Alice was just saying it because she was upset. Before our last visit to Pendle she'd been afraid of returning. I knew she felt no differently now.

Alice had said that Pendle was where she belonged. That wasn't true but the danger now was that, under the influence of the dark forces there, she might eventually become a fully fledged malevolent witch. In time, despite Arkwright's optimism, she could belong to the dark.

# CHAPTER XXX
## THE BLACK BARGE

AFTER another week at the mill the Spook set off for Chipenden without me. It seemed that I had no choice but to stay with Arkwright and complete my six months of training.

It was hard, and to add to the ache in my heart there was physical pain. Long before the end of my time there I was covered in bruises from head to

foot. Our practice sessions with staffs were brutal, with no quarter given. But in time I sharpened my skills, and despite the difference in size and strength between me and Arkwright, gradually I began to give as good as I got. On at least two occasions my speed almost enabled me to get the better of him, and when the doctor visited the mill, it wasn't only my injuries that he tended.

Arkwright had changed. Now that his mam and dad had gone to the light, a lot of his pain and anger had dissipated, too. He drank rarely and his temper was much better. I much preferred the Spook as my master, but Arkwright taught me well, and despite his rough ways, I learned to respect him. In addition to the training I received, we went out to deal with the dark together sometimes—once far to the north beyond the County's border.

Time passed: A cold winter gradually gave way to spring, and at last it was time for me to return to Chipenden. By now Claw had two puppies: a dog and a bitch, which Arkwright named Blood and Bone. On the morning I left they were play-fighting together in the garden while Claw guarded them jealously.

"Well, Master Ward, at one time I thought you'd be taking the bitch back with you to Chipenden, but fond as she is of you, I think she dotes on those two whelps more!"

I smiled and nodded. "I don't think Mr. Gregory would be too happy if I took Claw back. Not to mention the fact that dogs and boggarts probably don't mix!"

"Better keep her here, then, and save your bacon!" Arkwright joked. Then his face grew serious. "Well, we've certainly had our ups and downs, but it all seems to have turned out for the best. The mill's a better place following your visit, and I hope you've learned things that'll stand you in good stead."

"I have," I agreed. "And I've still got the lumps to prove it!"

"So if you're ever in need, remember that there'll always be a place for you here. You could complete your apprenticeship with me if it proved necessary."

I knew what he meant. Things might never be quite the same between me and the Spook. Although he'd acted for the best, I still thought he was wrong in his treatment of Alice. The fact that he'd sent her away would always be an unspoken barrier between us.

So I thanked Arkwright one final time and soon, having crossed the nearest bridge to the far bank of the canal, I was strolling south toward Caster, bag and staff in hand. How I'd once looked forward to this. But things had changed. There would be no Alice to greet me in Chipenden, and despite the fact that it was a fine spring morning, with the sun shining and the birds singing, my heart was right down in my boots.

My intention was to leave the canal bank long before Caster, then pass to the east of the city before making my way across the high fells. I suppose I must have been deep in thought. I was certainly worrying about the future. Whatever the cause, I didn't notice it happening until it was too late. But what could I have done anyway?

A sudden shiver ran the length of my spine, and I looked about me and saw that it was dusk and growing darker by the minute. Not only that, but there was a chill in the air, and when I looked back over my shoulder, a thick gray mist was swirling toward me down the canal.

Then out of that mist, a black barge slowly approached. No horses pulled it and its movement through the water was completely silent. As it drew nearer, I realized that it was no ordinary craft. I'd seen the barges that carried Horshaw coal and they were black with grime; this one was highly polished and there were black wax candles in the prow, burning with fierce flames that didn't flicker. More candles than on a church altar on a holy day.

The barge had neither deck nor hatches and steps led directly into the darkness of a deep, cavernous hold. One glance told me that such depth was impossible because most canal barges are flat-bottomed and canals them-selves are not so deep. Yet the manner in which the strange vessel glided through the water was abnormal, and again I had that strange feeling of being in a dream in which the normal rules of life no longer apply.

The barge halted alongside me and I looked into the depths of that impossible hold and saw a seated figure surrounded by a cluster of even more candles. Although no command was uttered, I knew what I must do. So, leaving my bag and staff on the towpath, I stepped aboard and went slowly down the steps as if in the grip of a nightmare, a cold fear twisting at my stomach while my whole body began to tremble.

In the depths of that hold the Fiend, in the shape of the bargeman, was seated on a throne of the same dark polished wood as the barge. It was intricately carved and adorned with evil creatures straight out of the Bestiary in the Spook's library at Chipenden. His left hand rested on a fierce rampant dragon, its claws lifted aggressively toward me; his right lay upon a fork-tongued snake whose sinuous body trailed down the side of the throne to coil three times around the claw-footed leg.

He smiled the smile of Matthew Gilbert, but his eyes were cold and venomous. I'd assisted Grimalkin to slay his daughter. Had he summoned me to take his revenge?

"Sit down, Tom. Sit at my feet," he said, gesturing to the

space before the throne, and I had no choice but to obey, sitting cross-legged upon the planks to face him. I looked up into his face, which was no longer smiling, and felt utterly powerless and at his mercy. And there was something else that I found disturbing. I had no sense of being in a barge upon a canal. I felt as if I were falling, dropping like a stone, the ground hurtling up toward me.

"I sense your fear," said the Fiend. "Calm yourself. I'm here to teach you, not destroy you. And if I wanted you dead, there are many others who would be delighted to do me that service. I have other children. And many others who've sworn allegiance to me. You couldn't hope to evade them all.

"I kept my word," he continued. "I allowed your companions to live—something I needn't have done because you didn't defeat my daughter alone but had the help of the assassin Grimalkin. But nevertheless, I did it as a gift to you, Tom, because one day we are going to work together, despite your present reluctance. In fact we are already far closer than you think. But just so that you know exactly what it is you're dealing with, I'm going to reveal a secret.

"You see, there is one of my children whose identity only one other person in this world knows. A special child of mine who will one day achieve great things in my service. I speak of my beloved daughter Alice Deane. . . ."

For a moment I couldn't take in what he'd just said. I was stunned. His words spun within my mind like black crows in a storm wind and then dived to plunge their sharp beaks into my heart. *Alice* was his daughter? He was saying that Alice was his daughter? That she was no better than Morwena?

Monsters or witches—those were the offspring of the Fiend. And if one was born human and untainted, he slew it on the spot, as he had done with the child of Grimalkin. But he had allowed Alice to live! Could it be true?

*No*, I told myself, trying to keep calm. He was just trying to divide us. I remembered what Mam had once said about the Spook, Alice, and me:

*"John Gregory's star is starting to fade. You two are the*

*future and hope of the County. He needs you both by his side."*

How could Mam have been so wrong? Or perhaps she *wasn't* wrong at all. One of the Fiend's names was "the Father of Lies." So most likely he was lying now!

"You're lying!" I shouted at last, all my fear of him fleeing, to be replaced by outrage and anger.

The Fiend shook his head slowly. "Even the Pendle clans don't know it, but it's the truth nonetheless. Alice's *real* mother is bound in a pit in John Gregory's garden at Chipenden. I speak of Bony Lizzie. When her child was born, it was immediately given into the safekeeping of a childless couple—the father a Deane, the mother a Malkin. But when Alice was older and ripe for training in the dark arts, their usefulness was over. On the night they died, Lizzie came to claim her daughter. That training would have continued but for the intervention of you and your master."

Bony Lizzie—Alice's mother! Could it be possible? I remembered the first time I'd seen Lizzie. She was supposed to be Alice's aunt and I'd immediately noted the strong family resemblance. They had the same features, very dark hair and brown eyes, and although older, Lizzie had been as pretty as Alice. But she was quite different in many other ways. Her mouth twisted and sneered as she talked, and she hardly ever looked you in the eye.

"It's not true. It can't be—"

"Oh, but it is, Tom. Your master's instincts have proved correct as usual. He's always doubted Alice, and this time, but for your feelings and the intervention of Arkwright, would have bound her in a pit next to her mother. But nothing I do is without careful thought and calculation. That is why I agreed to your request to free Amelia's soul. How grateful William Arkwright was! How useful he proved. How eloquent! And now Alice is free at last, beyond the influence and watchful eye of John Gregory, able to return to Pendle, where she will eventually assume her rightful place as leader and unite the clans once and for all."

For a long time I didn't speak and a feeling of nausea came upon me, the sense of falling intensifying. But then a thought suddenly came into my head to lift my spirits. "If she's your daughter," I said, "then how is it that she's fought so hard against the dark? How is it that she struggled against the witch-clans in Pendle, risking her life to stop them bringing you through the portal into this world?"

"That's easy, Tom. She did it all for you. You were all that mattered to her, so she became what you wanted and put aside most of her training in witchcraft. Of course, she can never really let it go. It's in her blood, isn't it? Families make you what you are. They give you flesh and bone then mold your soul into their beliefs. Surely you've been told that before? But things are different now. Her hopes are over. You see, until the night before John Gregory sent her away, Alice didn't know who she really was. We kept it from her until the moment was right.

"That night she tried to contact Grimalkin. Tried to thank her for what she'd done in saving you. She used a pool of water at midnight. But mine was the face that stared back at her. And then I appeared right beside her and named her as my daughter. She didn't take it well, to say the least. Terror, despair, then resignation—that was the sequence of responses. I've seen it all before. Being who she is, Alice now has no hope of continuing as your friend. Her life at Chipenden is over and she knows it. She can no longer be at your side. That is, unless I choose to intervene and make it possible. Everything changes eventually, but sometimes things move in a spiral and we may return to the same point but on a different level."

I looked at him and locked my gaze with his. Then I answered, the words coming without thought. "The same point but a different level? For you that could only be downward. Down toward the dark."

"Would that be so bad? I am the lord of this world. It belongs to me. You could work alongside me to make it better for everyone. And Alice could be with us. The three of us together."

"No," I said, struggling to my feet and turning toward the steps. "I serve the light."

"Stay!" he commanded, his voice full of authority and anger. "We haven't finished yet!"

But although my legs felt as heavy as lead and the sense of falling made it hard to keep my balance, I managed to take one step and then another. As I began to climb, I felt unseen forces tugging me down but I continued to fight my way upward. When my eyes were able to see beyond the edge of the barge, I was terrified. For rather than the canal bank, beyond the barge there was nothing. I was gazing into absolute blackness, into nothingness. But I took another step, and then another, until the world as I knew it suddenly shimmered into view and I jumped down onto the towpath.

I picked up my bag and staff and continued in the same direction as before. I didn't look back but sensed that the black barge was no longer there. The mist had gone and above my head the sky was bright with stars. I walked and walked mindlessly, too numb for thought.

# CHAPTER XXXI
## WHOSE BLOOD?

Eᴀʀʟʏ morning and I was climbing above Caster, heading south toward Chipenden. I reached the Spook's house late in the evening. I found him sitting on the bench in the western garden, deep in thought, staring toward the distant fells.

I sat down beside him without a word, unable to meet his eyes. He

placed a hand on my shoulder and patted it twice before standing up.

"It's good to see you back," he said in a kindly voice. "But I can see that something has affected you badly. Now look at me and spit it out. Whatever it is, you'll feel better if you get it off your chest, lad. Just start at the beginning and go on. . . ."

So I told him everything: the sudden appearance of the sinister black barge; what the Fiend had said about Alice being his own daughter; my struggle to escape. I even told him how Alice had been prepared to use the dark to protect me using a blood jar. How she'd got Morwena's blood and had intended to mix mine with it to keep the Fiend away. That Mam had used a mirror, telling Alice to use *anything* to keep me safe.

Finally I explained how I felt. That I hoped with all my heart that the Fiend *had* lied and that Alice wasn't his daughter.

As I finished, my master sighed deeply; it was a long time before he spoke.

"My head's spinning with what you've just told me, lad. I find it particularly hard to believe what you said about your mam: Whatever she was in the past, in my judgment she's now a powerful servant of the light. Maybe the girl lied about that? Alice would do anything for you, and no doubt she wanted to save you at any cost. She knew you wouldn't like her methods so maybe she said that about your mam just so you'd accept it. Does that make sense?"

I shrugged. "It's possible," I admitted.

"So let's take it one more step. I'm asking you now: How can you be sure, lad? How can you be certain that Alice isn't exactly who the Fiend says she is?"

"I'm sure," I said, trying to fill my voice with conviction. "It can't be true. . . ."

"Look into your heart, lad. Are there no doubts there at all? Nothing that worries you in the slightest way?"

There *was* something that had been bothering me, and I'd been thinking about it all day as I walked back to Chipenden. The Spook was staring at me hard, so I took a deep breath and told him.

"There's something I never told you before," I said. "When Alice frightened those soldiers away and rescued me, she used something she called Dread. But her head was covered with snakes and I felt cold when she approached. She looked like the most frightening witch I'd ever seen. Did I see the truth of things by the moonlight that night? Did I see her as she really is?"

The Spook didn't answer.

"And there's another thing," I continued. "The way Alice behaved when you sent her away. She didn't say a single word in her defense. That's not like her. The Fiend claimed to have told her the night before and he said she was resigned. And that's what she looked like to me. As if she'd given up and all the fight had gone out of her. She knew who she was and there was nothing she could do about it."

"You could well be right," said the Spook. "But the Fiend would certainly lie to suit his own purposes. There's actually one other thing that worries me, lad. You say

Alice got some of Morwena's blood. That would be difficult. When did she get it?"

"After Morwena was dead. When she washed my chain—"

"I saw her wash your chain, lad, but she didn't put any
blood into a jar. I could be mistaken, though she was just
a few feet away when she did it. But she believed in the
jar, and I've had an unpleasant thought. Maybe she used
her *own* blood! She was desperate to keep you safe, and if
she knew she was the Fiend's daughter, then she'd be confident that her own blood would work just as well. . . ."

I buried my face in my hands, but the Spook put his
hand on my shoulder. "Look at me, lad."

I looked into his eyes and saw sadness. "None of that is
proof. I could be wrong. Maybe she did save blood from
the chain. So I'll tell you this: I'm undecided myself.
There's one other person who knows the truth and that's
Bony Lizzie—but witches lie, too. If Bill Arkwright were
here in my shoes, he'd drag Lizzie from that pit and make
her talk. But I don't hold with that. Besides, people will
say anything to avoid being hurt.

"No, we'll just have to be patient. Time will deliver the truth into our hands, but in the meantime you must promise me to have no contact at all with the girl. If she *is* the Fiend's daughter, I've made the biggest mistake of my whole life. Not only did I spare her the pit because you pleaded for her, I've given her a home and let her share our lives for far too long. She's had all that time to corrupt you. Too many opportunities to undermine everything I've tried to teach you. What's more, whether or not she's the Fiend's daughter, I still think she's a dangerous influence. She may well try to reach you either in person or using a mirror. You must resist that, lad. You must have no contact with her at all. Will you do that for me? Do you promise?"

I nodded. "It'll be difficult," I said, "but I'll do it."

"Good lad! I know it will be hard because you two had become very close. Too close for my liking. But the biggest danger is that the Fiend will try to compromise you and draw you toward the dark. It could happen gradually, bit by bit so you hardly notice. And he'd most likely use the girl to achieve it.

"Now, then, things aren't all bad. I do have some good news. A letter arrived for you just two days ago."

"A letter? Who from? Is it from Jack?"

"Why don't you come back to the house and find out?" the Spook said mysteriously.

It was good to be back. I realized just how much I'd been missing my life at Chipenden. The Spook told me to sit myself down at the kitchen table. Then he went upstairs and came down carrying an envelope, which he handed to me with a smile. One glance and my smile became even broader than his.

*To my youngest son, Thomas J. Ward*

It was from Mam! News of her at last! Eagerly I tore it open and began to read.

*Dear Tom,*
*The struggle against the dark in my own land has been*

long and hard and is approaching a crisis. However, we two have much to discuss and I do have further things to reveal and a request to make. I need something from you. That and your help. Were there any way at all to avoid this, I would not ask it of you. But these are words that must be said face to face, not in a letter, and so I intend to return home for a short visit on the eve of midsummer.

I have written to Jack to inform him of my arrival so I look forward to seeing you at the farm at the appointed time. Work hard at your lessons, son, and be optimistic, no matter how dark the future seems. Your strength is greater than you realize.

Love,

Mam


"Mam's coming back to visit at midsummer," I told the Spook, handing him the letter excitedly. It was now the tenth of April. In just over two months I'd see her again. I wondered what she wanted to tell me.

The Spook read the letter, then looked up at me, his face

very serious, and began to scratch at his beard, deep in thought.

"She says she wants my help. And something from me. What do you think she means?" I asked, my mind still whirling.

"We'll just have to wait and see, lad. It could be anything; it's a bridge that can be crossed only when we come to it. But when you go to the farm, I'll go, too. There are things I need to say to your mam, and no doubt she'll have words of her own for me. But until then we have work to do. How long have you been my apprentice now, lad?"

I thought for a moment. "About two years . . ."

"Aye, two years, give or take a week or so. In the first I taught you about boggarts. In the second we've studied witches, including six months' sound training from Bill Arkwright concerning the ones that lurk in stagnant water. So now we've arrived at your third year of study and we're about to begin a new topic, which is 'The History of the Dark.'

"You see, lad, those who fail to learn the lessons of

history are doomed to make the same mistakes as others before them. We're going to examine the different ways the dark has manifested itself to people during the centuries leading up to our own. And we're not just going to confine ourselves to County history. We'll be broadening our horizons and looking to accounts from other lands. You'll also begin your study of the Old Tongue, the language of the first men who came to the County. It's a lot harder than Latin and Greek, so you'll have your work cut out!"

It all sounded interesting. I couldn't believe that in six months I'd be halfway through my apprenticeship. A lot had happened: good things, bad things, scary things, and sad things. And with or without Alice, my training would go on.

After that we had our supper—one of the best the boggart had ever cooked. Tomorrow was going to be a busy day. The first of many to come.

ONCE again, I've written most of this from memory, using my notebook when necessary.

It's three weeks since I arrived back at Chipenden, and the weather's starting to get much warmer; the mists and cold weather up at Arkwright's mill are now just a memory.

Yesterday I had a letter from my brother Jack. He's as excited as me at the news of Mam's visit. All's well at the farm and my other brother James is doing really well as a blacksmith and getting lots of business.

I should be happy, but I keep thinking about Alice, wondering how she's doing and whether or not the Fiend told the truth about her. So far she's tried to contact me twice, using the mirror in my bedroom. Each time, just as I've been about to climb into bed, I've noticed the glass begin to lighten and caught a glimpse of Alice's face.

It's been hard. I've really wanted to breathe on the glass and write to say I'm worried about her and ask if she's safe. Instead, I've thrown myself into bed, turned my face to the wall, and kept my promise.

He's the Spook and I'm only the apprentice. He's still my master and everything he does is for the best. But I'll be glad when Mam gets back. I'm really looking forward to seeing her again. I'm intrigued by what she wants to ask me and I also want to find out what she thinks about Alice. I want to know the truth.

*THOMAS J. WARD*

# The Journal of
# THOMAS J. WARD

# Skelts

*Skelts* look like huge insects. Have long, thin multijointed legs and, despite size, can fold themselves into very narrow spaces. Segmented bodies hard and ridged like crustaceans and usually barnacle-encrusted. They live in or close to water. Often in caves. Emerge to feed on the warm blood of mammals. Have long snouts but toothless. Most noticeable feature is long, narrow sharp-ended bone tube. They insert it into their prey in order to suck their blood.

Skelts are greatly prized by water witches. They use the creatures in their rituals. They allow them to drink the blood of a sacrificial victim over a period of days. Once the victim is dead, they then dismember the skelt alive and eat it raw. This triples the power of the blood-magic gained.

Skelts relatively rare. Need to be studied and notes made. To do this, keep in water pit with strong salt solution.

# Wights

A *wight* is another creature used by witches, usually as guardian of some secret place. Wights are created using dark magic. A drowned sailor's soul is bound to his body, which does not decay but becomes bloated and extremely strong. Although blind (their eyes devoured by fishes), they have keen hearing and locate victims whilst still submerged. Once seized, prey is dragged into deep water and drowned whilst being slowly dismembered.

# Wormes

(NOTE: The word "worme" is spelled with an "e" to mark it as different from the common earthworm.)

—Frederick Harper

*Wormes* are dangerous creatures that range in size from that of a small dog to the size of a house. Some have legs, most have tails, and all are vicious and bad-tempered. Have long jaws and a mouth full of fangs that can bite off a head or an arm in the twinkling of an eye. Can also spit a deadly poison that is quickly absorbed through the victim's skin, with rapidly fatal results. Some wormes even have short, stubby wings, and because steam often erupts from their jaws sometimes mistakenly believed to be firebreathing dragons.

Mainly water dwellers, and although they prefer deep lakes, occasionally make do with a marsh or a river. Wormes rare in the County but are to be found in its most northerly regions, ranging from the lakes down almost as far as Caster.

# Boogles

*Boogles* are elemental earth spirits. Found in caves and tunnels. Mostly harmless, but make miners very nervous. Take the form of grotesque shadows that move really slowly. Sometimes they whisper or sigh.

FROM

# THE LAST APPRENTICE

## CLASH OF THE DEMONS

·BOOK SIX·

I awoke suddenly with an urgent sense that something was wrong. Lightning flickered against the window, followed almost immediately by a tremendous crash of thunder. I'd slept through County storms before, so it wasn't that which had woken me. No, I had a feeling that some kind of danger threatened. I jumped out of bed, and suddenly the mirror on my nightstand grew brighter. I had a glimpse of someone reflected in it, and then it quickly vanished. But not before I'd recognized the face. It was Alice.

Even though she'd trained for two years as a witch, Alice was my friend. She'd been banished by the Spook

1

and had returned to Pendle. I was missing her, but I'd kept my promise to my master and ignored all the attempts she'd been making to contact me. But I couldn't ignore her this time. She'd written a message for me in the mirror, and I couldn't help but read it before it faded away.

## Danger! Maenad assassin in garden!

What was a maenad assassin? I'd never heard of such a thing. And how could an assassin of any kind reach me when it had to cross the Spook's garden—a garden guarded by his powerful boggart? If anyone breached the boundary, that boggart would let out a roar that could be heard for miles and then it would tear the intruder to pieces.

And how could Alice know about the danger anyway? She was miles away, in Pendle. Still, I wasn't about to ignore her warning. My master, John Gregory, had gone off to deal with a troublesome ghost, and I was alone in the house. I had nothing with me that I could use in self-defense. My staff and bag were down in the kitchen, so I had to get them.

Don't panic, I told myself. Take your time and stay calm.

I dressed quickly and pulled on my boots. As thunder boomed overhead once more, I eased open my bedroom door and stepped out cautiously onto the dark landing. There I paused and listened. All was silent. I felt sure that nobody had entered the house yet, so I began to tiptoe down the stairs as quietly as I could. I crept through the hallway and into the kitchen.

I put my silver chain in my breeches pocket and, taking up my staff, opened the back door and stepped out. Where was the boggart? Why wasn't it defending the house and garden against the intruder? Rain was driving into my face as I waited, carefully searching the lawn and trees beyond for any sign of movement. I allowed my eyes to adjust to the dark, but I could see very little. Even so, I headed for the trees in the western garden.

I'd taken no more than a dozen paces when there was a blood-curdling yell from my left and I heard the pounding of feet. Someone was running across the lawn, directly toward me. I readied my staff, pressing the recess so that, with a click, the retractable blade sprang from the end.

Lightning flashed again, and I saw what threatened. It was a tall, thin woman brandishing a long, murderous blade in her left hand. Her hair was tied back, her gaunt face twisted in hatred and painted with some dark pigment. She wore a long dress, which was soaked with rain, and rather than shoes, her feet were bound with strips of leather. So this is a maenad, I thought to myself.

I took up a defensive position, holding my staff diagonally, the way I'd been taught. My heart was beating fast, but I had to stay calm and take the first opportunity to strike.

Her blade suddenly arced downward, missing my right shoulder by inches, and I whirled away, trying to keep some distance between myself and my opponent. I needed room in order to swing my staff. The grass was saturated with rain, and as the maenad came at me again, I slipped and lost my balance. I almost toppled over backward but managed to drop down onto one knee. Just in time I brought up my staff to block a thrust that would have penetrated deep into my shoulder. I struck again, hitting the maenad's wrist hard, and the knife went spinning to the ground. Lightning flashed overhead, and I saw the fury in her face as, weaponless, she attacked again. She was shouting at me now, mad with rage—the harsh guttural sounds contained the odd word that I recognized as Greek. This time I stepped to one side, avoided her outstretched hands with their long, sharp nails, and gave her a tremendous thwack to the side of her head. She went down on her knees, and I could have easily driven the point of my blade through her chest.

Instead I transferred my staff to my right hand, reached into my pocket, and coiled the silver chain around my left wrist. A silver chain is useful against any servant of the dark—but would it bind a maenad assassin? I asked myself.

I concentrated hard, and the moment she came to her feet, she was illuminated by a particularly vivid flash of lightning. Couldn't have been better! I had a perfect view of my target and released the chain with a crack! It soared upward to form a perfect spiral, then dropped around her body, bringing her down on the grass.

I circled her warily. The chain bound her arms and legs and had tightened around her jaw, but she was still able to speak and hurled a torrent of words at me, not one of which I understood. Was it Greek? I thought so—but it was a strange dialect.

It seemed the chain had worked, though, so wasting no time, I seized her by her left foot and began to drag her across the wet grass toward the house. The Spook would want to question her—if he could understand what she was saying. My Greek was at least as good as his, and she made little sense to me.

Against one side of the house was a wooden lean-to where we kept logs for the fire, so I dragged her in there out of the rain. Next I took a lantern down from the shelf in the corner and lit it so that I could get a better look at my captive. As I held it above her head, she spat at me, the pink viscous glob landing on my breeches. I could smell her now—a mixture of stale sweat and wine. And there was something else, too. A faint stench of rotting meat. When she opened her mouth again, I could see what looked like pieces of flesh between her teeth.

Her lips were purple, as was her tongue—signs that she'd been drinking red wine. Her face was streaked with an intricate pattern of whorls and spirals. It looked like reddish mud, but the rain hadn't managed to wash it off. She spat at me again, so I stepped back and hung the lantern on one of the ceiling hooks.

There was a stool in the corner, which I placed against the wall, sitting well out of spitting range. It was at least another hour until dawn, so I leaned back and closed my eyes, listening to the rain drumming on the roof of the lean-to. I was tired and could afford to doze. The silver chain had bound the maenad tightly, and she'd no hope of setting herself free.

I couldn't have been asleep for more than a few minutes when a loud noise woke me. I sat up with a jerk. There was a roaring, rushing, whooshing sound, which was getting nearer by the second. Something was coming toward the lean-to, and I suddenly realized what it was.

The boggart! It was rushing to attack!

I hardly had time to get to my feet before the lantern went out and I was blown onto my back, the impact driving the breath from my body. While I gasped for air, I could hear logs being hurled against the wall, but the loudest sound of all was that of the maenad screaming. The noise went on in the darkness for a long time; then, but for the pattering of heavy rain, there was silence. The boggart had done its work and gone.

I was afraid to light the lantern again. Afraid to look at the maenad. But I did it anyway. She was quite dead and very pale, drained of blood by the boggart. There were lacerations to her throat and shoulders; her dress was in tatters. On her face was a look of terror. There was nothing to be done. What had happened was unprecedented.

Once she was my bound captive, the boggart shouldn't have so much as touched her. And where had it been when it should have been defending the garden?

Shaken by the experience, I left the maenad's body where it was and went back into the house. I thought about trying to contact Alice with the mirror. I owed her my life, and I wanted to thank her. I almost weakened, but I'd made a promise to the Spook. So, after struggling with my conscience for a while, I simply had a wash, changed my clothes, and waited for the Spook to return.

He came back just before noon. I explained what had happened, and we went out to look at the dead assassin.

"Well, lad, this raises a fair few questions, doesn't it?" my master said, scratching at his beard. He looked seriously worried and I couldn't blame him. What had happened made me feel very uneasy, too.

"I've always felt confident that my house here at Chipenden was safe and secure," he continued, "but this makes you think. Puts doubts in your mind. I'll sleep less

9

easily in my bed from now on. Just how did this maenad manage to get across the garden undetected by the bog-gart? Nothing's ever gotten past it before."

I nodded in agreement.

"And there's another worrying thing, lad. Why did it attack and kill her later, when you had her bound with your chain? It knows not to behave like that."

Again I nodded.

"There's something else I need to know—how did you know she'd gotten into the garden? It was thundering and raining hard. You couldn't possibly have heard her. By rights, she should have entered the house and killed you in your bed. So what gave you warning?" asked the Spook, raising his eyebrows.

I'd stopped nodding and was now gazing at my feet, feeling my master's glare burning into me. So I cleared my throat and explained exactly what had happened.

"I know I promised you I wouldn't use the mirror to talk to Alice," I finished, "but it happened too quickly for me to do anything about it. She's tried to contact me before, but I've always obeyed you and looked away—until now. It was a good job I did read her message this time, though," I said a little angrily, "otherwise I'd be dead!"

The Spook stayed very calm. "Well, her warning saved your life, yes," he admitted. "But you know how I feel about you using a mirror and talking to that little witch."

I bristled at his words. Perhaps he noticed, because he let the matter drop. "Do you know what a maenad assassin is, lad?"

I shook my head. "One thing I do know—when she attacked, she was almost insane with fury!"

The Spook nodded. "Maenads rarely venture from their homeland, Greece. They're a tribe of women who inhabit the wilderness there, living off the land, eating anything from wild berries to animals they find wandering across their path. They worship a bloodthirsty goddess called the Ordeen and draw their power from a mixture of wine and raw flesh, working themselves up into a killing frenzy until they are ready for fresh victims. Mostly they feed upon the dead, but they're not averse to devouring the living. This one had anointed her face to make her appear more ferocious, probably with a mixture of wine and human fat, and wax to hold the two together. No doubt she'd killed someone recently.

"It's a good job you managed to knock her down and bind her, lad. Maenads have exceptional strength. They've been known to tear their victims to pieces using just their bare hands! Generations of them have lived like that, and as a result they've regressed so that now they're barely human. They are close to being savage animals, but they still have a low cunning."

"But why would she sail all the way here to the County?"

"To kill you, lad—that's plain enough."